I0658850

Love's Command

THE PROMISE OF LOVE

BILLI JEAN

The Promise of Love
ISBN # 978-1-78430-691-5
©Copyright Billi Jean 2015
Cover Art by Posh Gosh ©Copyright July 2015
Interior text design by Claire Siemaszkiewicz
Totally Bound Publishing

Published in 2015 by Totally Bound Publishing, Newland House, The Point, Weaver Road, Lincoln, LN6 3QN, United Kingdom.

Totally Bound Publishing is a subsidiary of Totally Entwined Group Limited.

THE PROMISE OF LOVE

Dedication

To everyone who loves this series —
I hope this one surprises and pleases!

Chapter One

Paris Masters stared over at her best friend and worried she'd not heard her right. They were playing the music loud, but she was certain Sara had just said she was hooking up with this guy for the first time— *ever in real life* — today.

"You've never actually been in the same room with this guy?" A flash of that Craigslist stalker did a quick rewind through her head followed by every warning she'd ever heard about strangers.

"What? Don't look so shocked, Paris. Come on, you mean you've never hooked up with a guy on the first date?"

"No. God, no, I mean, don't you watch *Criminal Minds*?" she demanded then put her eyes back on the road. It was snow covered, and even though it was a highway, it was still dangerous.

"Life is not a television drama, no matter how many episodes you watch," Sara said and lifted her bare foot up on the seat to finish her pedicure. The fact that she could actually paint her nails fire-engine red while

Paris drove was amazing, but that was Sara — always successful.

"I know life isn't like the movies, but the newspapers and such are real, right? I mean, come on, how do you know this guy doesn't have bad breath, or can't put a sentence together?"

"We Skyped and chatted on Yahoo," Sara said, as if that was good enough. "He's hot."

"That's it? You talked to him online and he's hot?"

"You were with Greg too long," Sara grumbled then perked up. "But this place, it might have another guy there, you know? You could see." Sara left that dangling out there like it might entice Paris. "You can take a few days off, come on."

"Uh, no thanks, really, I've had enough of men to last me a *long* time. Besides, I *have* taken a few days off." The drive alone to Wyoming from Canada took a day.

"Sweetie, Greg was an ass. You are such a catch. Any man would be crazy not to keep you. And he just what?" Sara asked. "Had you and cheated on you!"

Paris couldn't argue with that, not really. Sara was right. Greg had turned out to be a slimy cheat. What he'd done, though, was nothing compared to Alexander. Life was much more complicated than Sara would admit but really, Paris didn't want to rehash her mistakes, she just wanted to move on. Again.

"Paris, are you listening to me? You can't —"

"You're right, you are, he was a disgusting pig, but don't you get it? That's why," she muttered and caught her breath. "That's why I need a break. I just didn't get it. Not with him, and I didn't get it with Alexander, either."

At the mention of Alexander, the car turned uncomfortably silent. Any reference to Alex did that, but she'd grown beyond the pain and betrayal, or she thought she had.

Sara brushed her auburn hair off her face and tucked it behind her ear to frown at her. "Alexander was insane, Paris. No one knew he was capable of such a thing. No one. How could we?"

"No, I knew better. You nailed Greg, but I ignored all the warning signs. I stayed with him, even knowing it wasn't good. I got on that ice with Alex knowing, deep down, *knowing* it wasn't safe. I did it anyway. It was like my brain and body went on autopilot. I ignored Greg's excuses and late hours. I ignored the warning tingle that Alex wasn't all right in the head." She stopped to catch her breath and barreled on. "*That's* why I've taken a break from men, Sara. That's why. I had no idea how to stop myself." She was ashamed to admit it to Sara, but it was true. She needed help—something to stop the cycle she fell into with men.

Sara had been her friend since they'd been kids, but she'd gone off to university while Paris had put school on hold for her chance with skating. Now Sara was back and seemed happy dating one guy after another. Sara had to know something that would help.

"I had no idea at all he was cheating, not really. I didn't allow myself to think about it. I just accepted his lies. I never questioned his business trips or late nights. Not once. Two years. He was cheating all that time, from the first," she added, that sick, depressed feeling rising up to swallow her along with her tears. "Alex did the same thing to me, Sara. He stared me in the eye, right in the eye, and told me everything was all right between us. I went on the ice with him sure I shouldn't, but unable to stop. There's something wrong with me. Something I have to fix, you know?"

"Oh, Paris, don't think like that!" Sara cried. "Look, Alex was insane. His suicide after what he did to you is proof. How could you know a person you'd skated with for years would suddenly decide to drop you on purpose! And Greg," she muttered. "Don't even get me started on him. He was a class act, full of dodges and shadows. He talked in circles and wore you down with his complaining. You are beautiful. He is a jerk. You shouldn't take a break—*not for three years*—because of him. You should dive in and have some real, honest-to-goodness orgasmic sex with the first hot guy that draws your eye."

Paris laughed again, but knew she wasn't about to do any such thing. Not with a complete stranger. She wasn't sure how Sara did it. How could she reveal so much to a man she didn't know? Sex was intimate. It left you wide open and vulnerable.

"Just stop thinking about it as some holy grail of intimacy and let your brain turn off. Feel, enjoy, experience life without that big jerk."

"You make it sound like I've been sitting around moping over Greg and I haven't. I just haven't."

"Okay, what have you been doing?"

Paris made a face. "I've been doing a lot of things I want to do, like my own thing," she finally said. "Building my student list and taking care of my uncle without him knowing it."

"All right," Sara said, laughing. "You're right. Both of those are hard, your uncle the trickier of the two, but that's not living." She motioned to the truck stop sign up ahead. "I know you know that, too. You can't hide away from men and relationships because your first real one was horrible. Alex doesn't count. He was your skating partner. He never loved you. And you didn't love him. I bet you didn't love Greg either. So, now you're free. Look deep, figure out what you want, but until you do, why not have some fun along your way to Mr. Right?"

"You make it sound so easy," Paris grumbled.

"It's not," Sara agreed. "But you have to give some lucky guy a chance, sweetie. I get it, I do. You take a break and I'll drive. My toes are dry enough. But think on it. I know you've got a drop-dead gorgeous body, Miss Skating Queen. Until you have sex—*real*, hot sex—you're always going to battle whatever that jerk fed you to keep you with him."

"Sara, it isn't that, I just don't want to have sex— meaningless sex—with some stranger I've never even talked with over coffee," she huffed. "I had that for years, huh?" she added in a whisper.

"Oh, sweetie," Sara laughed. "You have never, *never* had sex the way I'm talking. If Greg had been able to give you that, he'd never have had to play such a number on you. Believe me, when you have your first orgasm, your first earth-shattering, scream out loud enough to wake the neighbors climax, then we'll talk. Until then, trust me, it's not the same."

My first orgasm. By the sound of it, Sara'd had more than her fair share of those. Paris couldn't say the same. But with a stranger? She peeked at Sara's profile and wondered. Sara was willing to travel from Canada to Wyoming to have sex. Maybe Sara *did* know what she was doing. Or the man did. Either way, she'd talked to Sara because she'd wanted help. Could she the advice?

Can I take it?

Sara set her bag down in the back and tugged on Paris' hair. "And who says it has to be one night? Or just one man? I read the hottest story about a woman who had fun with two men. Maybe what you need is a *ménage à trois*. You'd forget about Greg, *and* get a very, *very* hot experience to treasure for the rest of your life."

Paris laughed. "Oh, really? I thought that was every *guy's* dream? Having two women? Not a woman's idea of a great time."

"Whew." Sara fanned herself. "You obviously didn't read *this* book. But, just see, if you find some guy — or *more* than one — and they interest you, see where it goes. Don't put limits on it before you need to, okay?"

Paris frowned, but turned off at the truck stop.

Meet a man and just...let things happen? With a stranger.

Well, she didn't want to do anything with any of the men she *knew*, so maybe a stranger *was* the only logical option.

But two? No freakin' way.

"Well, I'll see," she offered when Sara nudged her with her bare foot.

"That's a start. Oh, man, that's a start." Sara grinned and clapped her hands together like a kid at a candy shop.

"Uh, that's not a start, *or* an agreement," Paris qualified, because Sara seemed way too happy with her. "And one man would be more than enough, thank you."

"Don't knock it until you try it, sweetie."

* * * *

"Tell me again why we're doing this," David Jansen demanded, facing off with one of the toughest women he'd ever met.

Will Bryson had his six, but he considered whether that was actually true when the man whistled through his teeth at him and backed up with his hands in the innocent, surrender position.

Sonya Petrok tilted her head and her long, red braid slid down her back and to the side as she narrowed her green eyes to slits. Not a look he normally liked to get out of her.

"Ballsy, Jansen. Even Will's covering his assets over that, but I'll give you credit for being honest. We're undercover, you knew that, and now that we have Walters in his hole, we lure in bigger fish than Duke."

David didn't like the sound of that. None of it actually was something he wanted to hear. He'd made plans, around warmth, sunshine and sandy beaches. Still, he had a buddy out there, somewhere. "Tazz never showed. What about him? We can't just leave him—"

"Tazz is fine." Petrok smiled. "More than set, I think, actually. We'll see him again before this is through, but by then we need to have the names and numbers of all the players. That means you two have to act like you're one hundred percent behind this."

Will grunted. "This meaning taking some drug worse than what we were already put on by the Sentinels?"

David's stomach nosedived. Chung's drug had been effective—it'd turned him into an unfeeling killing machine who'd barely felt pain, let alone exhaustion. It'd also screwed with his temper and made him anxious all the time. Will had shared that it had given him a hard-on he couldn't tame—and by that David knew Will had tried, more than likely with a few of the women they'd met after the last mission.

"Petrok?" he muttered when she didn't respond quickly enough. There wasn't a chance he was adding more drugs to his system. He never wanted to take an aspirin again, let alone a vitamin C tablet.

"Not a chance, just dupe them. You were a SEAL, act like it," Petrok snapped then did the oddest thing. She grimaced and turned away, rubbing her neck hard while she cursed in what he knew was Russian.

Not a good sign. He shared a worried glance with Will.

"You still high, Petrok? Because we thought you were the first one of us to get smart and drop that shit," David said, maybe with more heat than necessary.

"Jansen—"

"No, it's okay, Will. No." She turned back and sighed heavily as she sat down on a bench. They were in a parking garage just outside the compound where they would spend the next few days. The place was deserted, but must have had twenty black SUVs parked in it. They also had equipment to fix the SUVs, complete with a lift and enough tools to maintain all the vehicles. As far as he could see, there wasn't a mechanic on duty, though.

Both double doors to the snow-packed but plowed yard were open, letting in some of the clear blue sky and a fresh, cold winter breeze. If Duke was worried about security, it didn't show. There was a gate, but no guard. Anyone could walk up the road and right in the back door.

Petrok took a deep breath and shook out her arms as if they were numb or something. They could be. The Chung drug had done a number on him, making him have headaches that wouldn't quit no matter how many things he'd tried. He'd had numb fingers and toes, too, which had freaked the hell out of him. A man needed his limbs working on a mission—and in life.

"This mission is getting longer than I wanted. Walters is scum and I need a shower after dealing with him," Petrok grumbled with feeling.

"Right, he's a scumbag, you should steer clear of him," David muttered.

Walters had taken one look at the hot ex-spy and set his sights on her. To David's knowledge, Petrok never mixed business with pleasure. But Walters could be an ass, more so to women.

Tazz usually reined him in—when he'd been around, which wasn't often. On this mission, Tazz had kept Walters on a short leash. David would bet his last dollar Tazz knew Walters was rotten through and through. Maybe he'd known from the start and that's why he'd kept him close.

Keep your friends close, but your enemies closer.

"Where is Tazz now?" David asked, folding his arms over his chest. It was cold, but he'd rather stand out here and talk than enter Duke's compound. The man's fake soldiers and sick ideas made his stomach roll.

"He's with a woman. He went there instead of meeting you guys and Walters. I can only assume, before you ask," she said, holding up a gloved hand, "that he sensed something wasn't on the up and up with Walters and didn't trust his own reflexes when he wasn't at a hundred percent."

"Why wasn't he at a hundred percent?" Will asked.

"I shot him." Nonchalantly, she shrugged her shoulder. "Not a kill shot, just to get him where he needed to be."

"With a woman?" David guessed, more than a little outraged. His voice went up an octave. "What, are you a matchmaker by gunpoint now?"

Will cracked a laugh and Sonya snorted, stretching her arms over her head like a cat.

"Funny, really," she muttered. "But I do know what I'm doing. I needed to prove I was on board and he was in the way. I didn't *hurt him* hurt him, not with Chung's drug still flooding him."

He'd heard Tazz hadn't gotten off the DNA-altering drug like the rest of them, or he had, but he'd gotten back on when some shit had come up with his little sister. All in all, the Sentinel Program was out of business, but since it was a black ops program, it was also going down quietly, and so far, not easily. Duke was proof of that. But even if Duke hadn't gotten his hands on Chung's formula and altered it for the black market, someone else would have. Nothing was secret in this world, nothing and no one could really, truly be trusted — outside of a very, very few.

A car pulled in and stopped just shy of the garage. As it did, a man exited a side door in the building across from them as if he'd been waiting on the newcomers. As soon as he reached the blue Honda, the driver's door opened and a woman with long, auburn hair and a big smile got out. They hugged but pulled apart as the passenger door opened and a blonde girl emerged, ducking her head as if she was shy but shaking the man's hand when offered it.

David blinked and realized he'd dropped his arms and didn't even recall doing it.

The blonde was small, slender, and hands down the prettiest woman he'd ever seen. Wholesome. When she smiled he felt a punch to his gut. She reminded him of sunshine and long summer days. Sweet, warm days filled with nothing to do but watch her, he imagined.

"Damn," he whispered, then glanced over at Will.

His buddy's attention was on her as well, but focused on the whole scene, not so much on her exclusively. He checked out the blonde's friend for a long time, then glanced away from all of them. For some reason that pleased the hell out of David in a way he couldn't quite explain.

"People can just drive in here, huh?" Will asked.

"Duke thinks he's hidden by being so far out and up a tough road," Petrok muttered. "Looks like it's not that tough."

David agreed. The two girls were driving a Honda, a good car, but he doubted it had any trouble getting up the road and it wasn't even a front-wheel drive vehicle.

The blonde hugged her friend and pulled away to give an obvious shiver at the cold. The sound of her laughter carried over to them. Another odd turn of his gut had him frowning even harder at her. It wasn't as if he knew her, but there was something, maybe the way she waved and got in the driver's seat with a laugh at the chill, that had him out of sorts. It'd been too long since he'd met a nice, normal girl, not some barfly without an agenda for a night's worth of fun in the sack.

The group talked for only a second more before the door shut, ending his view of the pretty blonde. The guy pulled the dark-haired girl away and together they raced back into the building. A second later the car backed up, turned and left. For some insane reason, David's heart went crazy, beating as if he was getting ready to jump from a plane, right into a hotspot.

The sound of the car suddenly went oddly louder, then puttered and died.

A slow grin eased over his face, calming the adrenaline rushing him. If that didn't sound like car trouble, he'd be a monkey's uncle. A car door opening and shutting filled the wintery silence, guaranteeing he wasn't closely related to the primates. His heart did a nosedive to his toes. Whoever the blonde was, she had one hell of a handle on his pulse.

Petrok stood, pulling a second of his attention off his plans for helping a damsel in distress.

"I want you two to stay low, keep yourselves under Walters' radar. Duke will assign him as your direct supervisor, no doubt, but not at first. I want Walters busy with his own thing, with no idea where you two are. This place is big. He'll never know you're here if you lay low. Maybe the blonde will help with that," she added with a laugh.

"But Duke will know," Will clarified.

"Yeah, of course he'll know. He wanted the real deal, so now" — she shrugged — "he has it."

"The real deal?" Will repeated.

"Soldiers, *real* soldiers."

"And he wants what? Security? Because that girl just drove right in the back door." Will gestured to the buildings.

"Sure, he needs it, right? But then, he's not here hiding, remember? He's that bold," she muttered. "Just keep a low profile. I'll be your contact with Duke, unless he calls you in, maybe to meet you before you begin training those Ken dolls, huh?"

Will snorted but David laughed at the reference to Duke's men. It was accurate in his opinion.

"We get this done, find the leads to who knows about the drug then pull them in. That way Walters won't have a clue he's stepped into the trap until it snaps down on him." Petrok brushed her hands on her thighs, giving them a questioning glance.

"Will do," David said, but sounded distracted even to himself. He couldn't seem to stop dancing from foot to foot, either.

Is she outside in this cold working on her car?

"Come on, you want to go save the damsel in distress, huh?" Will slapped him on the back with a grin and headed toward the entrance at a slow jog.

Petrok raised her eyebrow at him as if daring him to deny it. Hell, he not only wanted to go save her, but wanted to do it alone. He couldn't think of a way to stop Will though, so he didn't even try.

"Later, Petrok."

"Right. Later." She laughed.

The coldness of the wintry air added something to the dash through the snow. He wanted to catch up to Will before he could reach the blonde. Something odd, like a sensation that would stay with him for a long time, crept over his shoulder blades, making him slow as he approached. A shiver raced down his skin when she came into view. She had her back to them, but as they approached, she spun and grabbed her throat with one hand as if they'd frightened her.

The first thing that struck him was the unusual color of her eyes. They were blue, but so pale, they might be called gray. She lowered her hand and sighed in relief when he grinned. She was even prettier close up than she'd been from a distance. Dressed in a light blue snow cap with white snowflakes, matching mittens and a light blue fleece, she reminded him of a snow bunny ready for the slopes, only sweet and kind of timid.

"You scared me," she said breathlessly. But she must have thought two guys wearing snow BDUs were safe, which really made him want to grin for some insane reason.

"Sorry," Will murmured next to him. Thank God, because David couldn't get his tongue working.

He'd never been good at being so easy with a woman like this—a pretty, sweet woman. He stopped when he got close enough and waited, but when Will didn't go on, and neither did the girl, he walked over to her car and tried to jump-start his brain.

"What's the problem?" he managed. He played like he was studying the car, when he really knew jack shit about automobiles. He could change oil, fix a flat and a few other things, but he hated working on cars. "Car died?"

"Yes, it just, well, it did this." She gestured to the smoking hood with a blue mitten, giving the car tire a disappointed kick with her boot.

"Damn, that's too bad, but we have a truck—we can take you into town, if you want, or Will knows a thing or two about cars," David offered.

Will stepped forward, and she took a step back, a little wide-eyed, then hurried to say, "It's not my car. It's Sara's. Maybe I should go back and well, tell her."

"Sara's the friend you dropped off?" Will asked quietly.

"Yes, she, oh…" She paused and seemed to think of something more distressing than the car or meeting two strangers out in the middle of nowhere. She bit her bottom lip and winced. "She might be busy," she whispered with a shy smile, blushing pink to her blonde roots. "So, maybe that's not an option, oh, for… A while?"

David coughed hard to cover his laugh at her words. Clearly she knew what her friend was probably already doing.

Will ignored him and focused on her like David maybe should have instead of laughing at what she *wasn't* saying—her friend was having sex with her boyfriend. By the sound of it, she thought they might be going at it like bunnies for a while, too.

"I'm William, Will Bryson and this is my buddy, David Jansen."

"Oh." She appeared even more nervous and took a few steps backward again. Her boots crunched in the fresh powder until she seemed to realize she was retreating. Her gaze bounced from Will to him and back again nervously. "Right, well, um, I'm Paris—"

"Hey, we're safe, promise." David kept his voice low, wanting to ease the nervousness he could feel coming off her. "Really, you can trust us. Besides, it's cold out here. Let's take you to town after Will sees what's wrong. They'll have an auto store in town and we can get what we need to fix it." She seemed uncertain so he grinned and said, "I'll even let you buy us dinner."

"*We'll* buy dinner," Will said sternly, making David's unease settle. Will always knew what to say. "Can you open the hood?" Will asked, indicating the driver's side door. "And I'll fix it while Jansen tries to entertain you. I can see what's up, no problem. It won't take long."

She shifted from foot to foot. The move had his heart doing an odd jump and he felt a laugh building. *How long has it been since I've laughed so easily, not because something was shit and I need to laugh or lose my mind, but really laughed because I felt good?*

"You know there are horror stories that start out this way," she said.

Her comment surprised that laugh right out of him.

"We're not gonna hurt you, promise," he offered. They were out here alone, and there were two of them. He knew they looked like the badasses they were, it was hard not to, besides, she was alone. It had to freak her out to face them, but she was, and she was able to joke around, too.

"Those horror stories are all at summer camps, right?" he reasoned. "Not in some mountain in Wyoming in the snow. And I swear to God I don't own a ski mask, or what was that? An old hockey mask maybe?"

Will snorted. "Hockey mask. There was that crazy Red Rum one, right? Jack Nicolson movie. Classic. It was in the snow."

"Oh." Her eyes widened. "I've seen that! *The Shining*. What a horrible movie, really, that scared me for weeks." She examined them, relaxing a little as she did.

His face warmed under her scrutiny before she switched her clear gaze to Will. A smile tugged at her lips probably because of Will's not so patient posture. He'd been waiting for her to pop the hood for a while now. She finally stopped shifting her feet, so David thought the wait worth it when she gave them another sweet smile.

"Okay, but if you can't fix it, that's totally okay," she said, giving them both a hopeful smile that made it clear she was going to be much happier if they *did* fix it. Hell, maybe he needed to learn a bit more about the mechanics of a car, instead of a gun.

"I'm sure someone in the town" — she waved off behind her — "can fix it. Really."

He grunted at that. No way would they let some town mechanic win a smile from her. He speared Will with an impatient frown that got his buddy grinning but at least moving toward the smoking car.

"Can you release the hood? Let's see what's wrong, first," Will said.

"Oh, yeah, sorry, forgot." She blushed again, a cute pink. She opened the car door and bent to find the release.

Will caught his eye and David knew his buddy was interested in her. They'd shared women before, but Paris—she was going to be different. For one, he wasn't so on board with sharing—a first for him. In his life, sharing a woman notched the sex up to sky rockets going off. *Paris is obviously nervous, shy and beautiful, but is she into us?*

"All right, sorry, but I can't find the hood thingie." Paris gave them a frustrated frown.

David tried to pick out something about the woman he didn't like, and not a thing surfaced. He felt awkward around her, as if he'd suddenly been shifted back in time to when he'd been a teenager with his first girl. Shoving the anxiety aside, he grinned his normal smile, one usually reserved to hide his unease, and walked over.

"Here, they're tricky to find, let me help out, okay?"

She nodded and moved back to let him in. This close he could smell something citrus and warm woman on her—soft and sweet. He imagined she tasted just like that. The thought had him twitching below the belt. He ignored the response and ducked in to find the latch, pulled it and winked at her. "See, always hidden, these things," he assured her.

"Why do they do that?" she asked, but she seemed grateful he'd had some trouble finding the latch, too.

"Messing with you is my guess," he teased and stood.

She grew nervous again and headed over to where Will was. Will stopped her with a hand out on her arm, freezing her in place. "Not too close. If it overheated it might release hot air when I raise the hood. You could get third-degree burns."

"Oh," she whispered. "And you won't?"

For some reason that tiny response made David grin. "Hey now, he knows what he's doing. Come over here and we'll see what Will finds out."

She nodded and backed over next to him then did the oddest thing. She gave him a head to toe glance, shaking her head. "You two are really tall, aren't you?"

Will snorted but shot her a smile—something his buddy hadn't done much in the past few years. "It helps being guys, you know?"

She nodded seriously, as if that made sense to her.

David had the irresistible urge to hug her. He shoved his hands into his parka to keep them off her. For some insane reason when she did that he wanted to haul her in close. Maybe because she was so damn cute taking Will seriously.

"You're in the service?" she asked. "American military?"

"We were," he told her, because Will was already tinkering with the engine, clearly only half listening. If David had to guess, Will would not only fix the car, he'd make it run like new—all to impress one little blonde they'd just met. Or maybe her friend—David considered recalling how intense Will had checked out the other girl.

"Yes, that would help, wouldn't it? Being so…" She tilted her head to examine them again. "Big."

"Not always. Some of the other guys are bigger. I'm only six-three. Will's what? Six-one?"

Will nodded.

"Well, compared to five-two that's pretty tall," Paris offered.

"Yeah, well, size doesn't always matter." The comment went completely over her head.

Will shot him a cool-it frown. Since neither of them were lacking in that department, he couldn't offer to see if the saying was true or not.

"Besides, I know a woman that can hold her own in anything and she's about the same size as you," he admitted.

"Really?" she asked, sounding interested.

"Absolutely." Will stood. "It's a belt. We can get one in town. I should have you back on the road tomorrow. Do you want us to take you somewhere? Home?"

"Oh," Paris murmured, shifting her feet again. "I don't live here, but yes, if you don't mind, I rented a hotel room in town. I could use a ride, and I guess you two are safe enough," she teased.

David ducked his head to hide the rush of anticipation he experienced. Would he be able to interest her in more? He wanted more. He wanted *a lot* more and he knew, without asking him, his buddy would be on board as well. Again, David felt a rush of anxiety at the thought of sharing her, but more, his brain seemed to spin on the possibility of there not being a chance at more after the heat settled. *What if I go for sex and that is all I get from her? Sex.*

Why does that bother me? Isn't sex the goal?

It was *always* the goal when it had been this long without it. He rubbed the bridge of his nose with his jacket sleeve and thought about that. Hell, that made him sound like some guy only after a girl for one thing, like Walters. He wasn't that kind of man, but when he met someone he was interested in, he pursued. It might not be for more than a brief time, a few weeks, maybe longer, but sometimes he was too engaged in a mission to offer more.

Suddenly that didn't sit well. And it wouldn't work with her — Paris.

What the hell is wrong with me? Now, out in the middle of the freezing wilderness, I'm getting a conscience about sleeping with women — women who only want to sleep with me?

"We can take you into town, no problem," he offered, trying to dislodge the misgivings.

"That's right," Will said, shutting the hood. "You're never gonna be safer, right, Jansen?"

David swallowed and got his head back on straight. She would be safe. He'd never pushed a woman into anything, no matter that he suddenly felt wrong about never having had a real relationship with one. Paris wouldn't be safer, and for some reason he wanted to be the man who made sure of that.

The thought had him staring at her, trying to figure out what it was about Paris that made his head spin faster than any jump from a plane into enemy territory he'd ever made.

Chapter Two

"There are ten things in this world I can't live without," Savage said and tapped his cigar on the crystal ashtray. "Duke is messing with the top two. Money and Sex. Tell me you have some answers for me, Martinez."

Juan Martinez blew smoke out on a big exhale and shifted the bleach-blonde with jugs the size of cantaloupes he had on his lap to reach his drink. His enormous belly interfered with the move, but he managed to keep the woman in place while he sipped his vodka. No one would have guessed Martinez had once gone through the toughest Special Forces training on the planet—the Russian *Spetsnaz*. They'd been hand-picked then given training that wouldn't be allowed in the U.S. where everything was ruled by law and order. *Human rights and blah, blah, blah.*

They'd both survived and look at them now. *Living the American dream.*

"I have more than that. I've set up a team outside of Duke's location. He shuts us out of his deal, and we simply take what we want."

Savage narrowed his eyes to see Martinez through the dim interior of their private club. The strobe lights out on the dance floor lent a soothing background for him, but made it difficult to gage his long-time partner's expression.

"You've set up camp in Wyoming?"

Martinez grimaced. "I didn't set it up. My men are camping out with a group of gun crazy lunatics, but"—he laughed—"they are a perfect cover. If anyone finds our location, we simply blend in with them."

"America. Only here can such men exist," Savage muttered in Russian.

"True. They have a few AK-74M rifles."

"Really?" Savage murmured, impressed. Weapons like that were highly sought after and highly illegal. He stroked the back of his own woman at the memory of the power in such a weapon.

"When do you meet with Duke?"

"A few days," Savage replied, not happy with the time it was taking to get a meeting with the elusive billionaire. "He will send someone to DC in a few days. Then he will meet with me personally."

"If Duke pulls out, then we simply take it." Martinez lifted his glass and Savage joined him. "Then we even a few scores, brother. I have word from sources that the men we want are in the area. They're undercover, hovering over Duke, ready to take him out."

Savage clenched his fists. "We can't let that happen before my scientist gets his hands on the formula."

"Oh, we won't. Your scientist is also there, waiting for his chance to get a sample." Martinez made a face and tapped his cigar on the floor. "He is an odd one, no?"

Savage agreed. The young MIT graduate wasn't normally the kind of man he would ever associate with. But money talked and oddities could be forgiven — to a point.

"He can make us richer than our wildest dreams, brother. Remember, money first, then we settle some scores," Savage cautioned. "Duke will come here. He's too greedy and too much of a show man not to parade his genius for us to see. If he does not" — Savage shrugged — "then we will still gain what we want with your men. But first we wait. Remember, always the money first, then the scores."

* * * *

Paris laughed and shook her head at David's joke. He was a surprisingly fun guy, and way more honest than anyone she'd ever met. His friend, William — Will — was nice too, but David had a way of saying things most people just didn't. She liked that about him. And, she just *liked* him.

They surprised her. Not half a day ago she'd been lecturing her friend and telling her she never wanted to be near men again, and now she was in a restaurant downstairs from her hotel room with two of them and didn't want dinner to be over.

Or the night. Specifically the night.

It was as if all the time she'd been alone had suddenly become unbearable, and she wanted to make up for it now — immediately with them or, if she were honest, with David Jansen and his quiet sarcasm and rugged smile.

But, worse, every time she nervously sipped her drink, she'd recall what Sara had said about two men. '*Does that really, truly happen in real life?*' For the first time ever, she regretted not owning a cell phone. Sara had one. She could have called her and asked what it meant when two men sat over dinner with her, and seemed to want the night to go on and on...

"Yeah, well, that didn't go over so well in the long run," Will commented after taking a drink of beer. He reminded her of the actor who played Hawkeye in *The Avengers*, but much, much bigger and way tougher, simply because he was sitting inches across from her. Will was a warrior, through and through. They both were, but she'd never met a man as intense as Will.

Except for maybe David.

With his sleepy blue eyes and narrow face, he reminded her of Ryan Gosling. He had more of a warrior build instead of a bodybuilder thing like Gosling, but he had the eyes and the smirk hidden just below the surface. Maybe it was the rough shadow of darker blond hair on his jaw — it made it seem like he hadn't shaved for a few days, which added to the Gosling image.

Or maybe I watch too many movies.

He also watched her — all the time, it felt like. She'd almost dropped her drink twice just because he made her so nervous she couldn't think straight. Worse, she seemed unable to take her eyes off him either. She'd never been so attracted to a person so quickly. *Why now? Why two of them?* Will was...interesting, but David...

Does he even live here?

"If I remember right, we were stuck wading through swamp because of that dumb move, and I still have snakebites that bother me," David said, his voice going higher in indignation.

It was obvious they were good friends. She found herself becoming relaxed around them, enough to stop stuttering over what to say. But both were men—real men in ways that made Greg and every other guy she knew seem sheltered and well, kind of pale in comparison.

She knew she was small, but next to David, she felt delicate and fragile. She really wasn't. Not after years of figure skating. She liked that next to him she felt that way though.

"There were only a few snakes, and if they bit you, you probably antagonized them." Will's quietly spoken comment drew her out of her mooning over his friend.

"Did they really bite you?" she asked, then gasped when David nodded over his beer. "Oh, that's horrible," she managed. "I wouldn't be able to go near water where I knew there were snakes. I don't even like the garden ones."

They didn't laugh at her. They listened and nodded, seeming as if what she said really interested them. David's grin grew around the toothpick he was playing with, but they didn't act as though what she said was silly.

"Will's got a thing for snakes, so they like him," David muttered, bumping his shoulder against hers, which nearly toppled her, since she hadn't been anticipating he'd do any such thing. "Careful, pay attention."

She smothered a laugh behind her hand then bumped him right back. "Wait, what do you mean, a thing?" she asked, not sure what that meant. "You have a thing for snakes?" she asked his friend.

Will shrugged. "They don't bother me. Most are just trying to survive. Only a few want you dead, and those warn you." He sounded as if he was serious—

like a professor or something. "What? You don't believe me?" he asked around a mouthful of burger.

She reached across the table and, without thinking, brushed away some of the hamburger bun that had stuck to the whiskers on his chin. Immediately it dawned on her what she was doing, and she dropped her hand hastily. "Sorry, I'm sorry, you just have—"

He reached for her hand and squeezed it gently. "No problem, I don't bite."

"Only if you ask." David bumped her shoulder again. "And then it won't hurt."

With that surprising comment he gave her a crooked smile that sent all kinds of shivers down her spine. And to some inappropriate places. *What am I thinking? These are men, not young guys who think they can get something from me if they lay it on real thick. These are men who not only* know *they can, but probably do it so well I'll wake the neighbors!*

"What? That sounds good, or is that a look of complete horror?" David asked in that teasing but straightforward way she liked, but hadn't gotten used to. He tugged her hair, reminding her of Sara, and winked at her. He was so close she could feel the heat of his body all along her side.

"Oh, I don't know, I mean..." She pushed her hair back behind her ear to break eye contact and tried to calm the flutters in her stomach.

"Jansen," Will muttered.

"What? She is sweet. I bet she's never let anyone find out how sweet."

That sexy comment had her breath stalling in her throat, especially when David leaned over, slowly watching her face until he was close enough to kiss her, then rubbed his warm, bristly jaw against her cheek and whispered, "I'd like to find out, in case you haven't noticed."

With that shocking statement he gave her a cocky grin and got up to head to the back of the restaurant where the bathrooms must be. *Oh my God....*

"He's a smartass," Will said.

Find out. Find out how sweet she was—he meant oral sex. *Oh my God.*

By the heat of a blush on her cheeks, she knew she had to be pink all over. Of the two men, David made her much, much more nervous. He made her feel as if she'd sipped her way through seven cups of high-octane coffee from the local diner. In all her life, she'd never met someone she'd been so attracted to. Not even Jimmy Logan in middle school, and he'd been her crush for years and years.

"He's funny," she said when she realized Will was watching her.

Will had a way of being silent that made her worry he could blend into a space and she'd lose sight of him. David made her think the same thing, with the way he casually sat, not moving for so long. She fidgeted. She always had. It was apparent right away neither of these men did. She'd bet they never even bit their nails. "I don't mind," she added.

"That's good." Will eased back from his plate and sighed. "Wyoming might have the best burgers on the planet."

Both men had devoured their food like they hadn't eaten in weeks. On the way over, she'd thought Will might be the strong, silent type, but he'd eased her with interesting conversation all through the drive, then the meal while David had added silliness and his own two cents here and there. Not sarcastically, like her ex, but usually with a hit aimed at himself.

"How many places have you been? You know, in the military?" she asked, playing with her straw to avoid looking at Will fully. They were both handsome men — either of them would make any girl nervous, let alone both.

'I don't bite. Only if you ask. And then it won't hurt.'

Does that mean they are both interested in me? A shiver of excitement ventured down very inappropriate places at the thought of both of them being interested in her — together.

Sara's words were still fresh enough for them to come back startlingly clear.

'Maybe what you need is a ménage à trois.'

But that was Sara, and those things didn't really happen. Did they? She had to wonder because more and more it felt as if they were both coming on to her. *Both. At one time.* The thought should have freaked her out. She should have made up some excuse and run from the room. Her butt stayed glued to the booth. *If I want to break this cycle, I have to listen to my instincts. My instincts say it's okay. David's okay. Will...is a good guy as well. But David and Will?*

Is David into such wild things? What does it say about me if I am?

"Oh, we've been to some very far places, some of them not worth mentioning, but others, like *Paris*," Will said with a soft smile, "were incredible. How did you get that name?"

Paris smiled shyly and swallowed her mouthful of rum and Coke. "My mom. She always wanted to go there. She thought if she said it all the time, eventually she'd have to go."

Will tilted his head at that and she laughed, agreeing with his doubtful expression.

"Yeah, never made sense to me either."

"Did she?" he asked. "Go, I mean?"

"Yeah," Paris said, feeling the old pain surface at his question. "She did. Did you go to the Eiffel Tower?" she asked quickly to stop any more questions. Taking a sip, she watched him slowly grin.

"Yep, all the way to the top."

"Oh, I bet that was romantic," she murmured, jealous of whoever the lucky girl had been. She wanted to ask if David had gone, too, with some beautiful French girl, but held off by taking another sip.

Will laughed a low, rough sounding laugh and sat back more in the booth.

"Hardly. It was with Jansen, and he complained the entire time about the stairs until we crammed in the elevator with all the other tourists."

Her heart did a funny little backflip. So, David hadn't been with some glamorous European she couldn't compare to.

David. He's the one that makes me feel like those butterflies were set loose in my stomach. I like him. She scanned the restaurant for him, realizing when she did that she'd already done the same at least ten other times.

"Seriously, the smell in there was pretty bad," Will added, getting her attention back on him.

"Ew... That doesn't sound so fun."

"No, some of those foreigners don't believe in regular bathing or deodorant."

Shocked, she laughed, not believing a word until he nodded and said, "Absolute truth."

"Oh wow, that just blew my dream of a romantic kiss at the top, thanks!"

"Romantic kiss, huh?" David sat down next to her and handed her another drink, then passed one to Will. The butterflies returned and moved on to whirl around her stomach as David's warm body settled next to her. He slung an arm up on the booth behind her and leaned closer. He smelled good. Like pine and clean soap, but something else, something she assumed was David-smell, which she liked more than she should.

"That sounds like fun, is that on the menu?" he murmured.

She blushed harder at the clearly interested tone.

"Yeah, and it wasn't with me," Will supplied, adding another layer of sexual tension to the table. "Although a man can dream."

She'd had just enough to drink to give her that bold feeling only alcohol could provide. "You two are teasing me."

"Not for a minute," David said, suddenly serious. His eyes had turned a clear, intense blue and were pinned right on her.

"We're here, and believe me, we're not teasing," Will added.

"Any teasing we do, I promise, you won't complain about," David whispered.

She was in the process of swallowing another boost of courage and ended up choking. David tried to pat her back and force water on her at the same time. Breathless, she wiped her eyes.

"I can't believe you said that," she wheezed.

"I hope that means you finally realize I was hoping for a bit more than dinner, princess."

"Only if you want," Will added.

"Absolutely only if you want." If she had to guess by David's expression, he didn't think she was brave enough to take them up on that offer.

Both of them. At one time. Maybe he's right.

Just the thought of David kissing her made her feel lightheaded. Her mind stalled over imagining more from him, let alone both of them.

"Oh," she managed, staring at one serious, handsome face then the other. "I don't know, I mean, who, I mean, how, I..." She stopped embarrassing herself and covered her face with her hands, knowing she was blushing to her roots, but still interested, more than interested, she admitted. She was so turned on she knew with complete clarity that Greg had never been the man for her. He'd never turned her on. Not once—not like this. Just imagining David's naked body against hers made her feel high on more than the alcohol.

"Breathe, princess, it's going to be okay. We're not going anywhere and really, we aren't in a rush here," David coaxed. "Well, honestly, I am a bit, but I can hold off." He tugged at her hand until she let him pull it up to his lips. He kissed her fingers, but his expression was both concerned and amused. "You're okay, we promised, remember? Believe me," he added, breathing against her fingers as he spoke. "You'll love every second."

She swallowed. The sexy quality of David's voice, let alone the hot feel of his breath on her fingers, made her shiver all over. *Can I do this? Insane. It would be insane.*

David massaged her fingers and winked. "You're thinking too hard on this."

She glanced at Will, suddenly remembering there was more to this than David Jansen. Will's color was high and his hazel eyes were much darker than earlier.

"It's hot," Will said in his low voice. "Very hot, Paris. Once you say yes, Jansen's right. You're gonna love every second or we aren't doing something right."

Their sexy confidence made a shiver tingle in circles over her nipples all the way down a teasing pathway to her toes. She felt as if she couldn't breathe properly. At the same time, she was more alive, more aware of what she was doing than she ever had been in her life. It wasn't from fear—it was from excitement.

"You've—" She swallowed again, not sure she wanted to ask, but wanting to know all the same. "You've done—"

"Yep, we've done this before, but not often," David said. "And we've never met a woman like you, and believe me, I know that sounds like a line, but I can swear, it's not."

Will shrugged a big shoulder and licked his lips, making her squeeze her thighs together just thinking of him doing that to her. *Anywhere.*

"It has happened before, but not often. And, yeah, you—" He sighed heavily and arched a dark eyebrow at her. He was so sexy she couldn't believe they'd gone from talking about aimless things, to this. "You're not someone we want to hurt, Paris."

Hurt? He meant emotionally, she could tell, and the forethought made her feel even more out of her depth. They meant that—about her.

"Not a chance of that," David added, brushing his hand along hers, then squeezing lightly. "It's a good way to start," he murmured, again for her ears alone. "Then when I suggest kinky stuff later, you can't balk."

She choked on a laugh at his teasing. The fear she'd started to feel melted away. He was just so...so full of himself.

He winked and curled his arms around her shoulders. "Just breathe." He jostled her with a half hug, then seemed to want to give her room and parked his arm back on the booth. It didn't matter. She could still feel the warmth of his body and Will's stare.

They wanted her, together.

"What, exactly...? I mean, what...? Oh!" She laughed, frustrated with herself. "I don't even know where to start. Or what to ask."

"Then don't," David said, scooting off the booth and pulling her after him. She should have resisted, she knew it, but she let him guide her to her feet. "Will's got the bill. Let's go," he said.

"Wait, no, I can pay for—"

"With what? Didn't you say you lost your wallet?" David asked.

She rolled her eyes. She never should have told him that she couldn't find her wallet when they'd waited for her at the car to gather her stuff. "I couldn't find my wallet, but I have plenty of cash and my cards."

"Well that's a relief, but we pay for dinner, or he does." David pulled, and she bit her lip, but let him. She amazed herself even as she walked through the deserted restaurant and through the hotel dining room. This wasn't for them, it wasn't even because it'd been two years of sleeping alone and two years before that sleeping next to someone she didn't love. This was because it felt good, right in a way nothing else ever had. David. David felt right. Will simply made it so hot she was afraid she really would scream loud enough to wake the neighbors.

"You're doing good," David murmured. "But you know, you shouldn't drive without an ID."

"I have an ID!" She winced. "You're teasing me."

"I am," he admitted. "Just calm down and enjoy."

"I'm scared, but not *that* scared. Does that make sense?"

David immediately stopped and with a warm half smile said, "It really will be all right. No way do I want you scared. Trust me, Paris, this is going to be okay, more than okay."

She bit her lip then finally blurted out her biggest worry, or one of them. "We just met and I just don't—"

He shrugged. "I know, so if you're chickening out—"

"I'm not chickening out," she said, even though a niggling worry about what he might think of her for not chickening out began to weasel its way into her resolve.

David's grin grew and he winked again. He stepped closer and all she could see was him, his handsome face and sleepy blue eyes, which weren't all that sleepy right now. This wasn't a man who was going to think less of her for being wild. This was a man who'd demand it, and more.

"I enjoyed every second of dinner with you, Paris. If you want, I'll just walk you to your room and hope that you give me your number so tomorrow I can take you out for lunch, maybe breakfast."

His softly spoken words were so different than all his teasing she had to swallow and hope to think of something to say. "I just don't want you to think I'm like this. What if I disappoint...uh, you know? I just met you—"

He squeezed her upper arms and soothed them with a stroke of his strong hands while keeping his eyes glued on her face. "We know you're not. Believe me, that's pretty crystal clear, but if ever a woman needed to feel what it was like to have two men treasure every inch of her, I think you're that woman, Paris. But we can walk you to your room, make sure you're safe and hold off on all this. We're not going to be upset with you. Does that about cover it?" David asked, rubbing his hands down her arms then back to her shoulders. He'd gotten her jacket and had her bag tucked under his arm, she noticed. She'd completely forgotten them in the thrill of having him take her upstairs. He lifted his hand and brushed her hair off her shoulder. "Well? Holding your breath again?"

"You are a smartass, aren't you?" she whispered.

"I've heard that before, once maybe."

Taking her courage in both hands, she turned away and started toward the double elevators. Once there she hit the button and anxiously let go the breath she'd been holding.

"Oh, ho, I think we better hit the stairs with her, or she's going to lose her nerve," David said to Will when he arrived.

"Are you? We're not trying to push you here, Paris," Will assured her.

"Not at all," David said, turning serious.

The out was there. All she had to do was take it, but so was this chance — a once in a life time chance, maybe. She met David's eyes and saw the sincerity there, as well as the attraction she felt reflected back at her.

"I'm not chickening out. Are you?"

The bold words were worth it because David's smile grew and he laughed. "You heard her," he muttered to Will. "Let's give her a hand." The next thing she knew, they were each taking her by an arm and guiding her up the stairs.

Laughing, she let them. As soon as they hit the right floor, David suddenly turned her and breathlessly leaned down and, before she knew it, brushed a kiss to her lips. It was so quick, she couldn't understand the impact he left behind. She felt as if he'd dropped a stone in a still pond and the ripples from it overflowed the banks. With the same gentleness he caressed his lips along her neck, breathing deeply.

"You're so beautiful, Paris, so damn pretty," he whispered. "It should be illegal, you realize that, right? What you're doing to me."

"Come on," Will said. She shivered. His voice had dropped down to a deeper level—one she instinctively knew was because of her. The realization was as devastating as David's kiss—*she* did this. To both of them. More to David, she thought, but both of them were clearly on board for something she might not ever experience again.

The walk to their room was the longest of her life, but the most exciting. Both of them were touching her, waking her up to such a level of excitement she ached and they'd only just started. But she wasn't complaining, not in the slightest, especially since she couldn't stop touching them, either. Not once she started.

Will went for the key card and, daring more than she ever had in her life, she took hold of David's T-shirt and dragged him down to kiss his firm lips. His taste exploded on her tongue, sweet cinnamon mixed with sugary cola and rum. Not letting her have her way too much, he hauled her in close to his hotter body and deepened the kiss with a hungry growl. The sound was so thrilling she rubbed along him until, with a shock, she felt the unmistakable impression of his erection jutting up along her stomach.

He stroked down her back to cup her butt and brought her much, much more firmly against his penis. A rush of heat flooded her. She'd never slept with anyone other than Greg and he'd been small, and more often than not, done before they'd even started. The size and hardness of David's erection had her heart racing in anticipation.

Before she knew what was happening she was in their room, Will brushing kisses to her shoulder and David kissing her like he couldn't get enough. She broke away to meet his blue eyes, so overwhelmed she cupped his face in both hands. "I've never had an orgasm before," she said breathlessly, then bit her lip.

David's sleepy eyes widened then narrowed to slits of such intensity her legs grew weak. "You're not going to say that again. In fact, princess, we'll take care of that in less than five minutes."

"Three," Will corrected from her shoulder. "Don't be scared, Paris, trust us."

"I do," she blurted, then went all-in with the most shameful thing. "But, I don't know how to please you, so I want you both to tell me. Everything, okay? Even if it's, well—" She winced, stroking David's face, and whispered in his ear, "Dirty."

His hands clenched on her butt. He breathed out deeply, and she thought his penis grew larger against her.

"Baby, this is going to be something, but it's going to be about you and making love to you." He was as breathless as she felt. "What we do is going to please us, believe me. I'm close to coming just from that kiss."

"Oh my God," she whispered as he ducked his head and bit down lightly on her jaw. Sensations flooded her, making her pussy swell with needs she'd never experienced before. No one had ever said such things to her. She liked it. More, she wanted more, too.

"That sound good?" he asked.

She nodded so anxious she couldn't do more.

"Good, damn good," Will murmured, a silent until then presence at her back.

She'd almost forgotten he was here, and that was okay, too. This was about David, and yes, Will, but it was more about her and David. Everywhere David touched her, kissed her, breathed on her, she felt alive. She thought perhaps David felt the same way. Or at least it seemed that way to her. Their eyes met and she wanted to grab his face and kiss him but he threw her things down then was back, reaching for her and not leaving room for Will, which was fine by her. She opened her mouth and David plunged inside to lick along her tongue, beginning a stroke that had her aching for much, much more. But when he tugged at the bottom of her shirt, she panicked.

"You first."

"Not a chance, I'm dying to see you," he said, then paused and, watching her face, he slowly nodded. "Shirts, we'll take off our shirts, but, princess, we get our pants off and this" — he brought her hand down to his penis — "is going to want in, and we want you ready for that."

In?

Oh. In.

"Only where you want it," he added with a wicked chuckle against her throat.

She shivered and clung to his hard shoulders.

"We might build up to some back door, but not now, not this time or the next, so relax, and — " He breathed out through his nose, tickling her neck.

She wanted to seep inside him.

"Just let us see you. Man, I want to see you naked." His whisper was so funny, and so hot she laughed and tugged at his hair, kissing *his* throat just like he'd done to her.

It was crazy, but his words helped. She relaxed, and with an effort shoved everything, every doubt, ever insecurity and every bad experience, away from this and concentrated on them. *Here. Now, just enjoy. Feel.*

She eased away from the security of David's arms and nodded. He winked and his grin made her smile grow.

"That's it, baby, that's it," Will coaxed and tugged his T-shirt off, revealing a broad, tanned and well-defined chest. He had so many muscles she felt as if the breath left her and she didn't know how to get it back because her heart was racing too fast.

David did the same and she lost everything but the ability to stare. She knew she was wide-eyed. Part of her got that she was stunned, but she couldn't glance away from David, from the solidness of his chest or the definition of muscle lining his shoulders and arms. Even his stomach was hard, and she knew lower he was much, *much* harder.

"Breathe, Paris," David murmured, stroking her sides and hips. "Just breathe for me."

"How can I do that when you look like this?" she whispered.

David sounded like he choked on a laugh, but she was too busy to see for herself. She touched the rough patch of golden brown hair in the center of his chest and smoothed her hands on his warm skin. His nipples drew her attention because they were so different from Greg's.

Everything about him is different. Greg had been…well, scrawny, but he'd also been pale. David wasn't. His chest was so muscled it would have been intimidating if she weren't so turned on. His nipples were brown, round discs she really needed to kiss.

Would he like it?

Not daring to meet his eyes or even to breathe, she caressed back down his chest, marveling at the firm smoothness of his muscles.

David simply let her touch him. Will was behind her, stroking her sides and kissing a path down her neck to her shoulder, but it was David who dared her. David's sleepy blue eyes she latched on to and let guide her.

She leaned in and licked his nipple. The sound of his heavy groan was answer. If that wasn't thrilling enough, he said, "That's it, hell, that feels so damn good, princess."

Behind her, Will gently pull at her shirt again. This time, she gave in. She also let David tip her head. He kissed her with enough heat to make her anxious when Will made her stop for a few vital seconds to get her shirt over her head. After more drugging kisses, David released her lips but not her.

"Holy hell in a handbasket, princess," David breathed. He cupped her breasts, staring at them with an intense expression, then ducked down to kiss and suck the tender flesh.

Will tipped her head and suddenly kissed her for the first time. His kiss was different, not as passionate as David's. He eased in slowly, like he had all the time in the world, where David had devoured her as if he'd been starved. Much like he was doing to her breasts. She gasped and pulled free from Will at the first feel of David's mouth on her bare stomach.

David was there, immediately taking her lips back as if he'd simply let Will have a taste. She latched onto him even as Will returned to stroking her body with his hands and mouth. The passion burst along her, more so when David took over. She surrendered, letting him show her every single delicious thing he could do with his mouth. He groaned and drove in deeper. He controlled every aspect of the kiss until she matched him stroke for stroke. She loved it, didn't even care when her boots were taken off and her jeans unbuttoned and smoothly tugged down her legs and off. David made a low, appreciative sound and slid his hands along the top of her butt.

Will kissed her there, surprising a gasp out of her. She shivered and turned her head to see him squatted down, both big hands cupping her flesh as he pressed kisses along her skin.

David hugged her in closer to his chest and unlatched the fastening of her bra so he could ease it forward over her shoulders. He licked along her neck and down every inch of her he revealed. Any doubts she had disappeared at the admiration in his eyes. There wasn't room for thought, not with the heated kisses and low, intense sounds of pleasure both men made at her body.

Will suddenly stood, cursing under his breath, and turned her sideways, kissing a path to her lips even as David murmured how beautiful she was in her ear.

She held her breath when David suddenly bent and sucked her nipple. He groaned around it, then started rubbing it roughly inside his mouth as he stroked his hand down her ribs and around behind her back to cup her ass. She felt dizzy and hot, then chilly. Her breasts grew heavy and she absolutely knew this was what they'd been made for — David's amazing mouth.

He lifted up and took her mouth again. She wrapped her arms around his neck and meshed her body to his. A thrill raced downward at the rough tickle of his chest hair on her freshly devoured nipples. Everywhere they touched thrilled her.

But it wasn't just them touching her—it was their bodies brushing along hers, their warm skin and the scents of them—cleanly masculine—that, combined, were perfect. She couldn't keep her hands off them. There wasn't hesitation or doubt on whether she should touch or how, all that had gone with the ability to stop this.

Between them every inch of her seemed to earn their notice, until she knew if they didn't do something— anything—she might just collapse.

How can this be so good? I should feel bad, dirty, but I feel—free.

She knew David was easing her panties down, but he was also leaving hot kisses along her outer leg as he pulled them from her. At the same time, Will stroked his hands up and down her body from her hips to her breasts, then down again, each time growing closer to her bare mound.

Do they like that I'm bare?

The thought echoed through her head, but she was beyond worry. She leaned in and meshed her body to David's, kissing him deeper than ever. He gathered her hair in his hand, and built the kiss higher by angling her head just so for his mouth. It was perfect, so hot she had to touch him, had to feel the thick erection she knew he sported. She did, stroking over his pants where the bold outline warmed her palm.

"Paris, baby, damn." David's murmur against her skin had her shivering.

"So beautiful. Get hot, Paris. Show him what you want," Will said huskily.

Will's hot breath shivered along the back of her thigh even as David brushed his fingers along her pussy. Before she could gather her thoughts, he caressed her intimately until he circled her clit. She moaned at the pleasure.

"So beautiful and soft. You like that, princess?" he whispered for her alone.

She turned her head and nodded into the hot, solid muscle of his shoulder. His warmth calmed her fears, but at the same time, excited her.

"Good, good, let me show you more," David coaxed.

Will laid his hand along her hip then caressed slowly to her leg and lifted it up against his thigh. David kissed a hot path along her throat.

"Hold on to Will," David whispered so that his warm breath tickled her stomach as he headed lower.

She shuddered and Will caught her, kissing her behind the ear. David kept moving, showing her entirely new erotic zones along the way. Will brushed kisses over her neck, then traced more in a path down her collarbone, and onto her breasts. He cupped one in his hand and gently twisted her left nipple.

"Oh God." She dragged her hand through David's hair, using her other to draw Will even closer. Will groaned and lifted his head to rediscover her mouth.

"Steady, baby, steady," David whispered and caressed his lips closer to her exposed sex. Before she could grow embarrassed, he trailed hungry kisses along her inner thigh all the way to her pussy. At the same time, he gently pressed above her clit. The double impact trembled up her thighs to deep inside as the delicate brush of his breath heightened her experience to a degree that drew a moan from her as she broke Will's kiss.

Will's eyes were darker in the dimness of the hotel room, his face flushed and his lips still wet from their kisses. Swollen, too, she noticed, and went back in to suck along his fuller bottom lip.

He groaned and cupped both her breasts in his hands and brushed his fingers gently over her nipples then pinched them again. Another moan of pleasure rushed from her. The two of them would surely kill her with this. It was so good, so very good.

"There, there, baby," David said, sounding so sexy she couldn't take the overload to her senses. "Come for me." He pressed his palm on her a little harder, and stroked his fingers over her clit at the same time as he began licking her opening and flicking his tongue inside.

Her climax exploded from deep inside, to rush through her body like hot flames. She clenched down on nothing until, with a groan, one of them, David, she assumed, slipped his finger deep, giving her climax that full feeling she had to have. He also groaned heavily and stroked her butt and up the curve of her spine. Will pinched her nipples again, twisting a little at the end, too. The combination made her feel as if she were being tossed into a sea of pleasure.

The room spun and her legs trembled uncontrollably for such an intense time she distantly feared she'd fall down. Will held her firmly, but she gasped into his neck, too lost to worry over collapsing. He took her mouth again at the same time that David heated her back with his naked body. With a thrill, she clenched her fists in his short hair, wanting to beg David for more. As if reading her mind, he stroked his bare penis along her, thrilling her to the tips of her toes.

"David," she cried, breaking from Will's hot mouth to turn her head, searching for David. He didn't make her wait, but kissed her cheek until he had her lips meshed with his. His kiss was heated, so passionate, she knew he was ready, but waiting for her. The excitement built at the thought of his hot hardness filling her very, very soon. The heaviness of his erection resting along her lower back shocked a shiver out of her and she broke their kiss to turn slightly and get her first view of him.

Her heart raced. He was big. Every inch of his body was big, so his erection shouldn't have surprised her. But it did. He was long, thick and heavy.

"Ready?" he asked, tipping her head to meet her eyes. He'd done that several times, as if checking on her.

She nodded, unsure if she had the power to speak, but not about to stop him. "You're so big." The words burst from her before she'd had a chance to hold them in.

David winked, even though she could tell he was breathless and clearly, by the size of him ready.

Will's chuckle tickled her neck for a second before he kissed her behind the ear and murmured, "Complimenting him only makes him bigger."

David kissed her shoulder, then her chin, then her lips. "We'll fit, princess," he whispered, and coaxed her around so he could hug her from behind. His hot skin filled her with such excitement she clenched her fingers on his hands. He held her hips gently yet firmly. When she rubbed back into him he growled like a wild animal and bit down on her shoulder. She laughed, just like she knew he wanted.

How does doing this feel so...okay?

"Gentle, Jansen," Will warned, reminding her that he was the warm, solid flesh she felt against her front. David just filled her with sensations so much, it was as if Will was there, but wasn't. David made it all okay, she thought with another shiver of anticipation.

"Always," David whispered, kissing his bite mark. He also positioned her so she leaned into Will but her upper body was turned a little. At first she couldn't figure out why, then she realized it was so she could watch his face as he fit himself to her from behind. "Hold her there," he instructed, and with a start, she once again remembered they weren't alone. Will was there. He kept himself back, though, maybe because he too felt the connection she did between her and David.

With a caress up her side, Will steadied her and took more of her weight so she was sandwiched between them, but with most of her weight rested on him. If he minded, he didn't show it by the way he sucked and licked along her shoulder.

Their thoughtfulness seeped in under the excitement, adding warmth to her chest.

"There, that's good, now, just hold onto Will while I make you scream this time," he teased—or she hoped he teased. David pressed a gentle kiss to her lips after he said it and winked, so she bit her lip and nodded. It seemed to be enough.

He gripped his shaft, clearly ready for more, but being gentle, eased the tip to her waiting entrance. It should have been awkward like this, especially her first time having sex standing up, but it wasn't. He lifted his head from watching what he was doing and gave her a crooked grin.

"I'm gonna go slow, Paris." He watched her face intently until she nodded again.

As soon as she did, he eased himself forward. His cock was hot and so hard she knew Greg must have never been as turned on by her as this man clearly was. She shut those thoughts down and just watched, wide-eyed, as David's handsome face creased with sexy intensity. His broad shoulders tightened and the hand guiding his erection caused his biceps to clench. It was clear he was taking his time for her benefit, but he was large.

"Jesus," he swore and broke the intensity of their eye contact to lean his head against her temple. He was panting, but after a second he tightened his hands on her hips and thrust forward, feeding her just a bit, then backed out, then a bit more on his next push. Each time she was sure he wasn't going to make it past the resistance he met, but wanted him to.

"Don't stop," she whispered in his ear.

He pressed a hot kiss to her shoulder. "Not a chance." He sounded as if he was amused by the thought, but it was a rough, passion-filled amusement.

"So damn pretty," Will murmured, caressing her breasts and kissing along the side of her forehead. "Let him in and that first climax is going to seem pale in comparison."

She didn't have the breath to tell them she was relaxed, or that she wanted him inside, because David shifted his hips and suddenly the smooth, long length of his penis was spreading her as he went deeper than before.

"So tight," David groaned, kneading her hips with his big hands. "So damn small. Relax, Paris."

"Let him in, angel."

Let him in? He was in. She was in. So far in she couldn't catch her breath.

David pulled back and his erection stroked her pussy. Excitement built inside her until she swore she couldn't breathe. It felt so good she could feel herself growing wetter. Suddenly David thrust with a heavy grunt and there he was. Filling her so completely she dug her nails into Will's shoulders before she could stop herself.

"Ah, angel, that's it," Will said.

"Almost there, princess," David whispered against the nape of her neck.

"Almost? I thought..." She broke off with a gasp when David thrust forward again. This time she knew she'd taken him—all of him. There was some discomfort, but the pleasure, *oh God*, she never wanted it to end.

"Paris, relax, princess. You're so tight, hell, gotta take a second here," he said, saying more, but she couldn't make it out. The sensation of his erection inside her was more than she could handle. It was heavy, thick, and standing up like this, she could feel him—every inch of him. Maybe she would no matter the position.

He pulled his hips back, dragging his flesh outward until he pulled free, but before she could protest he thrust again. Instead of moving after, he jutted his hips upward and just held himself in place.

It was amazing. She squeezed down on his erection. Her climax hovered just out of reach.

"Paris." Will pressed his erection into her hand.

"Oh my God," she whispered and started trembling.

David was big and long. Will was thick, not as long, she thought, but wide and velvety smooth. She could even feel the grooves along his cock under the super-soft foreskin. Will covered her hand with his and guided her. As soon as they'd built up a hard, fast rhythm, he made rough sounds in his throat she knew had to be pleasure. It was her first time ever doing such a thing, and now she could tell she was going to stroke Will off. The thought sent a sharp spike zipping right down to where David penetrated her.

As Will's breathing grew deeper, David shuddered behind her like she'd begun stroking him instead of Will. Before she knew what David was doing, he pressed her forward into Will just a little harder. The new position tipped her, apparently exactly where he wanted. He took her lips and kissed her — or devoured her — and started a slow in and out pace that made her toes curl.

"Fuck!" Will grunted, squeezing his hand hard over hers and stopping her. "No condom, Jansen, you forgot to put on a condom."

David lifted from her mouth with a curse.

"No, don't stop, I'm safe," she whispered, so close to coming she could barely speak.

At her words, David made a strangled sound in his throat and lost the slow, steady pace. "So are we, Paris, but hell —"

"Don't stop, David. Please, don't stop," she said in a rush.

David tensed to one huge, muscled mass of man behind her and inside her. She worried he'd stop, but with a low groan he bent and, whispering her name, tightened his hold.

"Never."

The first rough, deep thrust he delivered wiped everything else from her head. Just like that — *zip* — every thought disappeared, leaving her unable to do more than hang on as he began to fuck her for what she realized was the first time in her life. The press and pull on her pussy as he built up speed thrilled every inch of her.

A soft sound, not words, not moans, but the unmistakable melody of a woman lost to pleasure erupted from her lips, unfettered by fear and uttered in the sheer bliss of the experience.

David was so out of control he said her name in time with his frantic strokes until, with a long low groan, he gasped.

"Paris, hell, baby. Can't hold back." He leaned forward, biting down on the nape of her neck lightly, and curled his hands around her breasts and squeezed.

She cried out his name then, or tried to, but she was too lost to her orgasm. He filled her in ways she never knew a man could. He tensed, and gently turned her head to breathlessly kiss her as he shuddered. Hot pulses warmed her deep inside making her climax grow.

In her hands, Will's cock grew impossibly hard and with a low grunt he began spilling his cum over her hands.

"Yeah, yeah," David murmured, still thrusting into her steadily. Will didn't stop either, but continued to heat her flesh with his kisses and the hot, slick flesh he pressed through their hands.

"Angel," Will whispered along her jaw, tightening his hand around hers so she could feel how hard he still was.

Another tremble seized her when she realized both men were still ready for much, much more.

She cried out in surprise as another orgasm erupted at the thought.

For the first time in her life, something good, something beyond good, had found her. Or she'd found it.

David tipped her head to the side, and captured her cry with a kiss as the pleasure continued to grow, but he also swallowed her desperate wish that this—this man she'd just met—would promise to hold her close forever.

Chapter Three

David breathed in the scent of Paris, not completely sure why it soothed him. Will had left for the compound, already on the task of nailing Walters and Duke. David was staying right here until something or someone forced him to leave. Hopefully that someone wasn't the exhausted woman in his arms.

Her pretty blonde hair was a tangled mess but he'd brushed most of it off her face so he could figure out what she was all about and why leaving her side made his heart feel as if he was nearing an anxiety attack.

Her face was the clear, beautiful face of a woman who lived a healthy life. He doubted she'd even had a pimple as a kid. Now none would dare blemish the smoothness of her skin. She hardly wore makeup—he'd snooped in the hotel bathroom and only found a tiny bag with a few things. Her clothes were comfortable, not flashy, but he was certain they would drive him insane. *What wouldn't?*

The body she rocked was stunning. She might even be fitter than he was, he thought with a smile, remembering the awed expression on her face when he'd stripped off his shirt. He could get used to making her speechless. Not that she talked too much.

There wasn't a thing about her he found wrong — which was worrisome. Usually he could nail something on a woman that would drive him nuts after less than an hour in their company.

He'd spent the afternoon and a big chunk of the evening seducing her into letting them into this room, and not one thing about her had his radar predicting the end.

The way she'd been shy, the blushes, with the heat in her blue-gray eyes, made him hard from just thinking about having her again. He shot that option down firmly. He hadn't been exaggerating. She had a small pussy, thin inner lips even, that had thrilled him, but worried the hell out of him, too. After the first round, he'd stayed put like the selfish guy he was — and had kept Will on the periphery. Not that Will seemed to have minded. He'd deal with it if his buddy had, but Paris had been too...

God damn. He rubbed a hand over his jaw at the memory. *Pretty.* A woman's body amazed him, always had, but his first glimpse of Paris had frozen him in place. Slim, but rounded in all the right places, with cute, natural breasts, she knocked him for a loop. She was all the way bare, too. Not shaved, but soft as a peach, bare. Her knock-down gorgeous butt was just topping on an already incredible package. Her body was naturally creamy, not tan, but not pale white either. He'd never felt such a sharp, deep, thrill over a woman's body before. He'd worried even then, in the height of passion, on the possessive rush he'd experienced at seeing her intimately for the first time.

The feeling was still there, too. He knew all he'd have to do was lift that sexy thigh she had over one of his and slide down the bed to get more of her soft little cries. His mouth watered just at him remembering the clean, fresh scent of her arousal.

He held off and considered the odd idea that holding her was possibly better than waking her up for more sex.

She would be tender for certain. Maybe that explained it, but he knew even while he thought it that he'd make sure she loved every minute.

She'd given so damn much, much more than he'd ever experienced. It wasn't just the hot feel of her pussy clenching around his eager cock either. She'd touched him as if she'd never wanted it to end, as if every single moment was going to be memorized. She'd whispered in his ear, asking for more and making him feel like he could lift mountains.

It wasn't the norm. Not at all. He'd pushed for the threesome, but even that had been a new experience. Usually when he and Will shared a woman, she was already coming on to them both so strongly that they knew exactly what she had in mind. Not the case with Paris. He had a feeling if Will had paid the bill and left, she wouldn't have noticed. That kind of thing rocked his world, but it also felt damn right.

He swallowed at the memory of that first kiss, and had a sinking sensation in his stomach that he wasn't growing tired of this little bundle of cuteness anytime soon. Reaching out, he carefully adjusted the blanket so it lay higher on her slim shoulder. A rush of tenderness warmed his chest, adding to the worry already building.

Careful not to disturb her, he pulled away and untangled himself from the bedding. The room was freezing. He'd turned the air on high partly because they'd both worked up a sweat, but mostly because he'd wanted her to cuddle up in his arms for warmth.

She murmured his name sleepily and he froze halfway off the bed. When she didn't wake completely he eased off the mattress.

Why my name? Why not Will's?

Because it was me the entire time. I didn't even let Will fuck her.

Damn right.

He rubbed the whiskers on his jaw and winced at the thought. She settled on the bed again, but a frown pulled at her smooth brow. She reminded him of a poster he'd once seen for some cola with a country girl in a field of wheat or something. Wholesome and sexy. That was Paris to a T.

Can such a woman exist?

Paris shifted her legs under the thin blankets, outlining her sexy butt perfectly.

Yeah, she does, and she's sleeping while I stand here like an idiot.

Not sure what else to do, he quietly walked to the bathroom before he climbed back on her and urged her to let him work out the morning wood he sported. Rubbing a hand over his hair then his face, David examined his reflection, trying to figure out why he felt so off center. He was jealous. Jealous of Will even kissing her. Last night, he'd been wild for her, and as long as Will stayed in the background, he'd been fine, but as soon as Will had kissed her, David had experienced a need to make sure she knew he was the one, not Will, who would send her into climax. He might have taken too much from her trying to prove that, too.

The thought made his worry grow, until he took a good look at his chest. She'd left little red strawberries on his pectorals, and a few farther down his ribs. She'd been fascinated with his body, something that soothed the jealousy down to a manageable level. He brushed his hand over one red mark near his collarbone. If he remembered correctly, he'd left one along her throat right where everyone who saw them would know exactly who she belonged to.

Jesus.

Belonged to?

He leaned on the bathroom counter and hung his head, shaking it at his insane thoughts.

Enough, just wash up. Deal with this as it happens.

The thought made him laugh quietly, but he went through the motions and washed his hands and face, then brushed his teeth with her toothbrush. He got a bit of a thrill at using her toothbrush because of all the intimate things a couple did together, in his mind, sharing a toothbrush was up at the top of the list.

Once done, he hung his head again and worried his way through what he was doing with a woman like Paris. A sweet innocent he could spend every day with if he were allowed. But instead of romancing her right, he'd coaxed her into bed with not only him, but his buddy. *The first night I met her, too. What will she think of that when she wakes up?*

"David?"

"Jesus on a cross!"

He jumped about a foot and turned to find the woman confusing the hell out of him wrapped in a sheet, sleepily rubbing her eyes and peeking at him around the partly open door.

"Damn, you snuck up on me, girl." Not only that, she'd gotten the door wider without him knowing. He pushed it all the way and she blinked, at the light, he guessed, but smiled at him. There was shyness in her expression, but at his teasing words, she lost a bit of it.

"Sorry, I have to, you know." She gestured to the bathroom then fixed her gaze on his face firmly.

Suddenly he realized he was naked, sporting an erection—of course—and she was embarrassed. A sense of such happiness flushed him that he couldn't stop himself from grabbing her and kissing her quickly. She made a surprised sound but relaxed in his arms after a few seconds of deep strokes of his tongue. To hell with what she might think, he'd set her straight. The way they started would just be the way this continued—hot, fun and one hell of a thrill until he figured out what he was going on between them.

He snuck his hands up her sheet and stroked her butt but broke the kiss and grinned at her surprised face. Just seeing her blush made his chest feel lighter, and that warm tenderness returned. *Shit's crazy, but hell, she's fun to catch by surprise.*

"Oh? You have to pee?" he asked.

"David." Her blush deepened to a rosy pink but her lips twitched in a cute smile.

"Aw, come on, you can say it, but maybe we can work up to that. You know, once you get to know me for a few weeks." *Or longer,* he thought.

She bit her lip and pushed against his chest, making the sheet slip down over the curves of her breasts. She had beautiful breasts. Smooth, round and the kind that were close together because her tiny chest was so narrow. When she held her small arms up like that, the two mounds pressed into a mouthwatering valley he wanted to coax her into letting him slide his cock between. Later, when he wouldn't shock the hell out of her, he'd suggest it. He hadn't spent enough time on them, he remembered, but stopped himself from doing anything about that now. Soon, he assured himself, when she had some time to build up an ache only he could tame.

"All right, stop teasing me with those beauties, okay? How about we go get some breakfast?" he asked, leaving off the 'if you want' because he wasn't taking a brush-off. Not after last night.

"Oh, breakfast sounds wonderful," she whispered. "I was too nervous to eat last night," she admitted, tugging the sheet up with a giggle.

"You were?" he demanded, thinking back on it. She hadn't eaten, not much at all, he remembered. She had to be starving. "Well, come on, let's shower—"

"First, I have to…pee."

He laughed and kissed her shoulder. "Good, real good, now get in there and give me the signal when it's safe." He smacked her butt when she walked past and laughed when she sucked in a shocked breath.

"David Jansen, you are too full of yourself!"

He was full, but not the way she meant. In fact, he'd never been so full of a sense of happiness, and maybe something damn close to contentment.

"That's right, now march."

She blew her hair off her face and with a sexy glower went into the bathroom and shut the door in his face. He heard her giggling behind the door then she said, "Go away and let me wake up, then you can shower with me."

"Fine," he called, already knowing that was code for privacy. She was shy still, but that was fine by him. He busied himself making coffee and trying to locate his clothes. He stumbled over a bag and stubbed his toe on something hard in it. "What the hell is in your bag, girl?"

"Oh, my skates," she said, once again sneaking up on him. "Are you going to walk around naked all morning?"

"Well, I'd considered that, but thought I might tempt you too much and after last night..." He sighed as if he'd been abused and grabbed her again to hug her close. "You might be too tender."

Her blush was all the answer he needed, and for some damn reason his heart got all crazy. He should want more sex, not be thrilled they had to wait. But the gentleness he'd experienced from earlier once again heated his chest. "I'm thinking a day of fun— maybe outside of the bed, huh? Then maybe later I'll let you ravish me again."

"David," she cried, but drew his face down and kissed him quick-like before he could stop her. Not that he would have. He got the sense she'd done it before she lost her nerve, and that got to him even more. "Do you know how to ice skate?"

He frowned at that. "Sure, I did a bit in high school."

"Hockey?" she guessed, with a grin when he nodded. "I bet you were mean."

"Mean?" he asked indignantly, getting another handful of warm, lush ass in both his hands. "I was good."

"No doubt," she murmured, her expression thoughtful. He hoped that meant she was reconsidering the sex. Her nipples had turned pearly hard against his chest and the sheet did nothing to hide how the firm points begged for attention. He wasn't very strong, he realized, when he bent his head and caught one erect point in his mouth.

"Oh God," she whispered, grabbing his hair and rubbing her fantastic body against him. "David, oh my God."

He pulled back from the edge, certain of one thing. He was making her come again in the shower.

"Come on. Get your pretty butt in the shower before you make me come all over your sexy body. I'll do your back and you can do mine." He tugged her sheet and she reluctantly let it go. "Damn, this is gonna be harder than I thought," he admitted, soaking up every inch of her dynamite body. Her cute checkerboard nail-polished toes, to her matching fingernails, and every spot in between, was stunning. Her slender legs made his hands twitch along with his cock. He wanted to press her back and go down between those thighs and feel her tremble against his face from her orgasm.

"I like every inch of you, baby," he managed.

She shyly smoothed her hand down his chest to where his heavy cock was getting heavier. Just the light caress stroked down the length had him primed for her.

"I like every inch of you, too. Too much, I think," she said in a whisper. "Because you are *very* big." The way she said that indicated a great deal of pleasure and a bit of worry. He had a feeling Paris hadn't had sex much in her life. If that was true, having to handle what he had must have left her pussy a bit bruised at the least. He hoped not, but he'd be finding out soon enough.

"Not too big, we'll just take it nice and slow. And I'm never going to be too much, hell no, never too much." He ducked down and picked her up. She squealed out a laugh and hugged his neck. "Just hold on, let's get in the shower and see about taking care of business."

"Business?" she asked when he set her down.

"Yeah, you," he promised, stroking down her curvy hip to brush lightly over her bare mound. She was already breathing unsteadily, and when he gently slipped along her pussy she was wet to the touch. "You, princess, you. I promise we'll get your business settled first before you have to tackle this again." He squeezed her hand down his shaft to the thicker base and watched her color deepen but her eyes glow a lighter blue-gray.

"Oh, I like that," she whispered, and used both her hands to explore him with a soft hum. She'd not had time to learn his cock by feel last night—he'd stayed inside her pussy and not backed down from the ground he'd gained. But this was just as amazing. Every hesitant touch thrilled him.

Not about to stop her, he reached back and turned on the water, adjusting it to just the perfect temperature, but then had to tease her. He thrust his hips through her warm hands and pulled her blonde hair back in a ponytail as he did. She gasped. He gently tugged until she tipped her head back then he stroked his tongue along the fullness of her bottom lip. Her warm, sweet breath teased him into diving in for a full kiss. He grinned into the kiss as mint exploded in his mouth. She'd brushed her teeth for him. She reached up and pulled his hair, making him laugh harder.

She seemed to know exactly why he was laughing, too.

"You used my toothbrush," she accused, in a voice he recognized from last night. She was turned on.

He lifted her up and set her inside the shower, then joined her. "I did."

Her laugh filled the shower and his heart.

"Mmmm, I wondered why it tasted so good." She thrilled him even more by sliding against him. Her silky soft breasts brushed his chest, reminding him he'd still not gotten enough time with them.

"*You* taste good," he assured her, sampling the top of her slightly bigger left breast.

"I hope you have something planned for this." She slipped her hands along his erection, which made her jiggle in all the right places.

"I have millions of things planned," he assured her, cupping both breasts in his hands for the thrill of seeing the mounds pressed into two lush curves. "Damn, I could use these as a pillow," he added and slowly kissed his way down to her nipples.

"David." The passion in that one word was permission enough. He took his time, though, licking and kissing every inch of her breasts. The water spilled over her and he sucked it off, adding tiny bites here and there along the soft flesh until she was squirming. She also managed to work him up into a harder erection than he'd ever had in his life. Only when she moaned did he press her back against the shower. She reluctantly let go of his cock, making him laugh.

"Don't worry, you're going to get every inch of that soon enough, but first we need to make sure you're ready."

"I think I'm ready. What—" She gasped, then grabbed for his head when he lifted her until she was high enough against the shower wall for him to settle between her silky thighs. Quickly, he positioned one slim leg over his shoulder. "Oh, God, what are you doing?"

"Don't fall down, princess," he warned and lifted the other leg and gripped her sweet ass in his hands to raise her up just a bit higher. Her pussy was spread and ready for him this way, and so damn pretty he wondered if he was going to climax just from tasting her orgasm. "I want to hear you scream this time."

"Oh, David," she whispered, already flushed with passion—for him. She gripped his head and tugged until he met her eyes. Her heavy breasts were a distraction like this, but he managed to focus on her face. She was a bit panicked.

"I'm not going to drop you," he assured her. "I promise."

At his words, she blinked and seemed to catch her breath. The quiver of her chest was fucking unreal, but he kept his attention mostly on her face.

"I, oh, God, you are so strong! Are you sure? I don't think I can…uh, I can't climax like this, I don't think."

Laughing, he lifted her higher and gently pressed a kiss to either slender thigh, knowing she was embarrassed but she was also getting hot all over again. He turned his head slightly and boldly pressed a kiss to the lips of her pussy.

"I am. I want this." He kissed her again and held in a groan at the sweet flavor of her skin. "I want this as often as you'll let me, Paris."

Her eyes darkened and her breathing had her breasts rising and falling rapidly above his head, giving him one hell of a hard-on.

"Now, hold on and let's see about that screaming, okay?"

She swallowed nervously, but when he kept pressing warm kisses to her mound and tiny clit, she nodded.

"Okay, but then I want to…you know…" She nodded, and he knew she meant get him off—possibly with her mouth, but more likely with her hands, or hell, from behind again, since she'd loved that last night.

Grinning, he settled her more comfortably and turned his focus on her pleasure.

"Paris, you can *you know* me anyway, anywhere, anytime you want."

Chapter Four

Paris felt as if she was walking on air. David amazed her. Everything he did, he seemed to do so well. All her life she'd done one thing well—skating—while most everything else she got through by bumbling around. Maybe gardening, she admitted to herself, she was good at that. But being with David was exciting, but also comfortable.

Even though you slept with him and his friend. Not slept, either.

She should've felt horrible about that, embarrassed at the least. David didn't allow that. He was just too consuming.

"You sure you want to ice skate? It's cold outside, now we're going in to be cold *inside*."

She laughed at the dismay in his tone, knowing he was teasing her. They'd only known each other a day, but it seemed like longer. Maybe because she'd barely had one second to herself since she'd met him yesterday. She'd woken, missing his warmth in the hotel bed, and gotten up to find him.

"Well, if you aren't sure you remember how—"

"Oh, ho! I remember how, I thought I'd pretty well covered how much I know, but if you need another lesson..." He edged his hand up her thigh.

She caught him and giggled when he sighed as if she was being mean. He'd let her stroke him off in the shower, amazing her with how quickly he'd turned frantic under her hands. He'd groaned loud enough that she'd gotten hot all over again thinking of the people in the neighboring rooms hearing him.

"No thank you, mister. I've had enough lessons to last until, oh"—she considered his handsome profile and couldn't suppress her smile—"later today, maybe after lunch?"

"Yeah, that's what I was thinking." He nodded eagerly and pulled her close by his grip on her hand and kissed her at the red light. He tasted like McDonald's coffee and the six hash browns he'd consumed in less than ten minutes, but she loved it instantly. "How long is that?"

"David," she whispered. "Green light."

He turned his attention back to the road. His grin meant he was going to tease her again. "You know they have this red-light district? All the girls are behind glass, kinda hot, you know. Ever consider that?"

"What? Being a prostitute?"

"No, hell no, where'd that come from?" he demanded, sounding outraged and a bit jealous, she thought. "Sex, you know, where someone can see if they chanced by."

Chanced by. Considering she'd had an orgasm in the shower when she'd thought about the rooms near them knowing they were having sex, she had to think for a moment before she responded. "Are you suggesting we park?"

His grin grew and he settled his hand back on her leg and squeezed. "Maybe a bit more public than that."

For some insane reason, her nipples ached at the thought. Her heart rate sped up and she just knew she was never going to be safe with this man—and didn't want to be. As insane as it was, especially after only meeting him yesterday then falling into bed with not only him, but his friend, she liked David Jansen. *Like him way more than maybe is good for me, even.*

Much more than I should. Where can this go? No one starts a relationship with a ménage à trois.

"Just an idea," he murmured, giving her an arrogant, knowing smile.

The heat already simmering under her skin made her goosebump. No doubt about it, his suggestion turned her on. He'd been in the shower with her, after all, and she'd joined him when he'd come. The 'oh yeah, princess' he'd shouted had made that clear, so had his possessive hand on her pussy and the fingers he'd filled her with. The man was deadly, and so able to bring her to climax, she wondered why she'd never had one before, then she remembered she'd never had *him* before.

David was just…David.

His hard body, wicked smile and ten inch erection combined in the man to create a truly heady impact. When he directed all that maleness at her she was helpless, and absolutely loved it.

She smiled at her thoughts, wondering if his erection really was that long. It felt like it.

"You're giving it some thought, huh?"

"God, you should be illegal," she whispered, feeling hot and achy along her pussy.

He laughed lightly and kissed her again at the next red light. Her lips were tender, but she didn't mind, not a bit, especially when he seemed to know and gently coaxed her tongue into his mouth for the briefest second.

A horn behind them had him pulling up and paying attention to the road again. She did, too, so turned on she had to breathe deeply just to get her silly heart rate under control. He really was lethal—and fun.

"There!" she cried, suddenly seeing the ice rink.

"Damn," he grumbled, and she guessed she had surprised him because he quickly turned into the parking lot and gave her a raised eyebrow. "You really like skating, huh?"

"Love it," she whispered, and dragged his blond head down to kiss him once more. Screw the tender lips, she wanted more of him and wondered why she'd been insane enough to take him out of the bedroom. He didn't let her run the show for long, but when he took over and dragged her closer and smoothed a hand down to cup her breast, she broke away with a laugh.

"Oh no, skating, lunch, then…maybe."

"I like maybe," he said, sounding hoarse.

She couldn't help but glance at his lap, and bit her lip at the size of his bulge.

"But let me have a second here since you just shoved my soldier into full attention," he added with a wink when she met his eyes.

Oh, God, that was sexy. She'd never met a man who named his…well, penis.

"Like that, do you?" he asked, brushing his knuckles along her cheek. "You don't have to salute, just remember to give him the same attention you've been and he'll be fine."

"David!" she whispered, and covered her face with her hands, laughing at his teasing.

He tugged her braid and pressed a kiss to her fingers. "Come on, show me how hot you are ice skating and we'll try to keep your mind off sex, okay?" he said, tugging the truck door open and getting out to turn and pull her with him.

She grabbed their McDonald's sack full of empty wrappers and hugged him around the neck when he picked her up.

"My mind, huh?" she asked.

"Well, hell yeah, you give me that kinda kiss and hot look and I know for sure what you need, baby. I'm the man to give it to you anytime, too. Here, back at the hotel, Applebee's, you name the place."

"Are you…? Do you like…? I mean, do you usually have sex with women in public?"

"What? No, I just thought of it," he said, guiding her to the rink. "It just kinda popped into my head, thinking of you getting all wild in the shower when I was waking the neighbors."

She stumbled and he caught her.

"David!" she whispered, checking that no one was near enough to hear. She wasn't a fool. She knew a man who could make love like David was sexually active, probably a lot. He wasn't dating anyone, she hoped, then immediately knew he wasn't. David had an honorable side to him, she thought, that wouldn't allow that. Oh, he might leave her broken-hearted and move on to the next, but he was here, with her, and that meant there wasn't anyone else.

"You're not buying that, huh?"

"Well," she stalled and let him open the door for her. "I know you're very good at what you do," she said, then whispered, "in bed. So I think you've done a ton of things that probably include public sex."

"Man," he sighed. "You have me pegged, huh?"

She blushed and felt bad immediately. "I didn't mean, I mean, that's *okay*, I know most people, I mean everyone has tried things—"

"Slow down," he said gently and turned her to face him. "I'm here, now, and not going anywhere soon. I know we pushed you, I know I did, and yeah"—he leaned in to brush a kiss to her lips—"I might have been wild in my younger days, but relax, I'm not about to toss you down right here and do the dirty."

She thumped his chest, but he laughed and caught her hand, kissing her knuckles.

"Come on," he said again, tugging her along to the skates. "I need to rent some skates."

She tucked her hand into the back of his jeans pocket as he settled his arm over her shoulders, feeling a thrill at how easily he fit her. Even as tall as he was, he simply *felt* right. His grin grew and he squeezed her shoulder.

* * * *

Twenty minutes later they were on the ice and she was laughing as he got his skating feet under him. He was good. He'd done more than play a little in high school. She'd bet he was a center or a wingman. Clearly he liked to score. She giggled at the thought and earned herself his complete attention. He skated over and easily caught her in his arms.

"What's so funny?"

"You. I think you skated a bit more than a little."

"Ah, busted. I did," he said with a grin, turning her to circle the rink with the others. There were only a few people out today, maybe because it was a weekday, or maybe because it was still so early, but she liked having the rink to herself and David. "I sold stuff to afford my skates. I worked three jobs to get the gear for hockey. It was worth it. Football was great, but hockey... Nothing beats it."

She nodded, understanding completely. "It's the ice, the chill and how fast you can go."

"Exactly. You get one hell of a workout, too," he added. "But even sweating buckets you're chilling."

"You were a center?" she asked after a few minutes of matching his speed. She broke away and circled him, tugging on his arm to get him to follow.

"Yeah, how'd you guess that?"

"Oh," she murmured, going backward to face him, and slowed so he bumped into her and guided her backward with his bigger body. "You like to score?"

He laughed hard and she broke away so he'd chase her. They played around for a while until the music changed and she slowed to spin with the melody of John Legend's *All of Me*. She loved the song and let it flow over her and guide her through a few spins. When it was over she was breathless and smiling, only to spot David leaning on the side of the rink, watching her so intently she felt her stomach drop.

She skated over to him and watched his gaze skim up and down her body in a way that drove every insecurity she'd ever had out of her mind. He made her feel sexy, like a woman who had his attention and was keeping it.

"Damn, princess, you're full of surprises," he murmured and wrapped his arms around her so she leaned fully against his hard body. He brushed a kiss to her lips, but she could tell he was bursting with questions.

She kissed him and tangled her fingers in his short hair. "So are you," she whispered. She was just about to kiss him again when between them something vibrated. His immediate scowl registered at the same time as what was trembling between them. "Your phone?"

"Yeah," he said with a deep exhale. "Gotta get it," he added, relaxing his arms, but keeping her close when she moved back. "Stay, it'll be quick."

"Okay," she agreed and settled against his side, watching the way the little girls in the center of the rink were trying to do a few of the spins she'd done.

"Hey, Will," David said, immediately reminding her that she'd not once thought about Will. She frowned. It was true, though. But of the two, she knew David drew her in ways that spelled disaster. Especially, she reminded herself, when or if he left. *Why wouldn't he? If he doesn't you have to.*

David hugged her closer and listened to whatever Will was saying as he played with her hair. The braid seemed to amuse him, and she liked the way he liked to touch it. Her hair was just a bit darker than his — lighter, maybe, at the tips.

"Fine, give me a few, I'll drop Paris off and be up there after."

Her heart sank. She tried to hide it, but as soon as David hung up, he gave her a half smile and tugged her braid. "I'll be gone for a bit, but not long, so don't look so sad."

She snorted and thumped his chest again.

"Aw, come on, admit it, you'll miss me," he teased, kissing her knuckles. When that got him nothing, he kissed along her neck up to behind her ear and tightened his arms until she could feel his biceps and pectoral muscles flexing. "I sure the hell will miss you, princess."

The press of his body, especially the long, thick evidence of exactly what he meant, thrilled her, but at the same time, her heart clenched. She swallowed past a sudden painfulness in her throat and pasted on a smile for the first time since he'd run to her rescue.

Is it all about the sex? Why does that matter so much? Focus, here, now, with him.

But it *did* matter, and she couldn't stop the worry, or the realization that she wanted more, much more of David Jansen, than a sexy weekend getaway.

Chapter Five

"All right, here I am. What's the deal?" David snapped. Paris had been too quiet on the drive back to her hotel, and the brief peck on the lips had been so different than her other kisses he'd wanted to pull her back and ask what was wrong, but hadn't had the time.

"We have to go to meet with Duke," Will said.

"I heard that, why?"

"Because he wants to meet you, why else?" Petrok said. "Hey, I don't want to bust up your little vacation, Jay-Jay, but this is work. Get your head on straight."

"My head is always on straight, Red."

She snorted and flipped him the bird.

He took that and strapped on his firearm, adjusting his shoulder holster with a flat stare in her direction. She was amused, no doubt, but he really didn't care. In fact, he wanted this over with so he could get back to Paris and find out what was up with the tension he'd felt building between them.

"He wants to meet us so he can do what? Be sure of us?" Will asked, standing from where he'd been seated at one of the cafeteria tables.

"Something like that. He wants you to train his men, remember? So he wants to see how you are, and probably give you some drugs," she murmured. "Just remember to fake it. Under no circumstances would I recommend taking what he dishes out."

"Not a chance. I just beat that other shit," David grumbled. Besides, no way would he chance harming Paris if Duke's messed-up drug was as bad as it sounded.

"Ditto," Will said. He was relaxed, not at all as if he was anxious to get back to Paris or pissed he'd only had hand jobs and not the super soft, silky wet slide of Paris' body around his cock. For some reason that eased the lockdown David had on his muscles. But it also gave him a dose of 'damn right' he needed time to analyze, but wasn't getting. As soon as he was done here, he was going back to her. All he could make out was that he didn't want Will too close to her. Maybe they'd share again, but he had to let Will know that things weren't going the full share.

As soon as Petrok stood she started walking. They got up as well, but not as fast. A few of the men casually eating watched her, but if the redhead knew, she ignored every single one of them. He'd never seen her take up the offers she got, so it wasn't a surprise she didn't show any interest.

"Hey, about Paris," Will said next to him. "I kinda think you're on board there more than usual."

David focused on following Petrok, not sure what Will meant by that. "I'm on board, yeah."

"Yeah?" Will muttered. "Did you tell her you'd be back?"

David scowled at him. "Of course, what kind of guy do you think I am, man?"

Will raised his eyebrows at that then rubbed his hand over his hair. "Right, so she's expecting you, or…?"

"Me."

"All right."

"Here we are, just remember, look big, bad and in charge." Petrok frowned at them both. "That shouldn't be a problem with those sorry expressions."

Without waiting, she opened the door and waltzed in ahead of them. He followed, not glancing over to see if Will was upset by his setback or not. Just the thought of Will alone with Paris had his heart racing and some damn jealous thoughts going through his head.

"Ms. Petrok, ah, this must be Mr. Jansen and Mr. Bryson. Welcome, welcome, it's good to have you on board. Ms. Petrok speaks highly of you." Duke shook David's hand with both of his. David assessed the guy in less than ten seconds as a rich, spoiled motherfucker with more time to waste than was good for him. David doubted the guy had ever worked up a sweat on a hard day's work in his life, let alone ruined his manicure.

"Sir," he said respectfully. "You've got quite a set-up here."

"Thank you," Duke said, clearly thinking the same. "You didn't stay here last evening, though. I had hoped you would sample some of what we have to offer."

"We had to help a friend," Will said smoothly.

"Ah, a friend, yes, that's good. Well, bring her up here, then. The more the merrier." He laughed and shook Will's hand. "But come, come, let's discuss what I have in mind for you both."

Hell, he didn't like the sound of that. He caught Petrok's eye but she narrowed hers and nodded slightly. He swallowed past the unease and followed Duke farther into the luxurious room. The place seemed like an apartment, but was obviously the man's office. David settled into one of the four chairs positioned around a low coffee table. There were magazines organized in rows with a large floral arrangement in the center. The chair and bouquet alone probably cost more than he made in a year. Hell, probably keeping the flowers fresh cost more.

"Well, it's a pleasure, truly, to have such talent interested in what I'm working on," Duke said, clearly thrilled to have them there. "I am hoping you will take my offer further, and with your skills, build me a working force I can shop out, if you know what I mean? I have men in certain places interested in such."

The vague statement was so suave even the ex-spy Petrok seemed impressed. With that kind of force, the man meant, he could sell soldiers—or the drug that would make them perfect killing machines.

"We're interested, sir, that's why we're here," Will offered. "What do you have in mind?"

"With your combat experience, I think training some of my other branches, first here, with Walters as your head, then each of you with your own division in different locations. I think within the year we should have a solid operation, especially if the tests go as planned."

"Tests, sir?" David asked, leaning back to cross his foot over his knee, trying his best to appear casual and damn happy to be sitting in a room with such a scumbag.

"Yes, Ms. Petrok can fill you in more on that, but the essential job for you two is to help me market the new, improved drug and for that I need highly trained men able to protect my interests."

"And Walters? What of him?" Petrok asked.

"He's to secure the formula so that no one else beats us to market with what I've created. We don't want competition before we even begin, now do we?"

The guy was slick, David would give him that. With his dark hair, handsome features and a bodybuilder physique, he probably could walk into any top executive position and do well. He was rich, filthy rich, and because of that, he didn't have to work. Instead he played at being a scientist with a stolen formula to build the perfect soldier. Only the drug didn't simply enhance physical attributes necessary in battle—for some subjects it screwed with a person's sex drive and *that* was what he bet Duke was after. He might also dabble in creating super soldiers, but David's money was on Duke wanting to market his take on the Sentinel drug as a sex cocktail that would make Ecstasy a thing of the past.

"And we're to train men, sir? Do they have any prior military training?" he asked.

"No, I'm afraid not, but that's where you two are essential." Duke had been told they were both black ops from a private firm, CRCT—Combat Ready Combat Trained—one of the mercenary groups that ran under the radar. "Your training is perfected by years of combat, something my men lack. I've picked only the most handsome, most physically fit men. With my enhancements, I dare say they will be ready for anything you throw at them."

David doubted that. It took more than looking good and taking drugs to make a soldier. But he nodded as if that made sense. "Sounds solid, sir. When do we start?"

"Ah, now, no need to rush. I'm still pulling in men, but if you would like to sample what I'm offering to the markets, I have prepared rooms and dosages for you both."

"Sir, to be frank, we need to know that drug is foolproof before we take it," Will said. "Without a doubt it sounds like it's got some power to it, and based on what Petrok has said, your modifications to Chung's formula are good, but until its market ready, we will have to keep our heads on the task you're assigning us." Will leaned forward. "But after," he said, smiling for the first time, "we can give it a go for you. Especially if your offer comes with a partner more than willing and able."

Duke laughed, throwing his head back, clearly thrilled at the ego boost and buying Will's eager agreement to try out the man's sex drug.

"Oh, my dear Mr. Bryson, I assure you you'll have more than enough willing partners." He sobered up after a few more chuckles and poured himself a glass of water. "Water?" he asked, and filled two more glasses at their nods. "Ah, gentlemen, and my dear Ms. Petrok, I believe this project is going to be successful. Very successful," he said, after taking a sip. "So much so I am eager to get things ironed out in DC. Ms. Petrok, I'm hoping you can handle that end for me while your associates begin training. I think some of the weather might hold us back, but I have enough vehicles with the capability of moving this snow out of the way to get you to the airport. And I believe some of the training you could offer would be snow and hazardous conditions, am I right?"

"Yes, sir," David said. "This type of weather is a good test to your men. If they can survive what I put them through, they'll be more than ready for whatever you have planned."

"Excellent! Let's begin early next week, shall we? Ms. Petrok should be back, and until then you can examine my compound. Let me know what else you'd need to make a fighting force every country in the world would envy." Duke grinned, clearly pretty damn pleased with himself.

David grinned as well, not because sick bastard wanted him to, but because that meant he had a few more days with Paris, then all the nights he wanted.

"Will do." David stood, offering his hand and shaking Duke's again. "I'll stay in town for a few nights so I can acquaint myself with the perimeter. As soon as that's solid, I'll shift to quarters here so I can send out men to do routine checks."

Duke frowned but nodded. "Damn, that's good, Mr. Jansen. I hadn't thought of that."

"That's what you're paying me to do, sir."

"Right!" Duke laughed again and smacked him on the shoulder, then squeezed Will's hand. "Damn good to have you on board. Ms. Petrok, you've done well, *very* well."

"Thank you, sir, we aim to please." She tipped her glass of water at the joke, but set it down without taking a drink then walked to the door, probably as eager to get away from the man as David was. "I'll see about that transport and contact you from the air."

"Very good. Gentlemen, if you need anything I've supplied you each with a phone and my number is programmed in. You're mission here is one of my top priorities Anything you need, anything at all, it's at your disposal."

"Thank you, sir." Will took the lead. "We'll be in contact soon."

David stayed quiet. Will and Petrok said a few more things, then they headed back toward the garage.

"That went well," he muttered.

"Shit, you're going to DC? And Walters has no clue we're here, does he?" Will added in a low voice.

"Right, you heard him. It's fine. You're big boys, you can handle it here. Train a few of these Ken dolls and try not to get them killed. Easy. I'll contact you if I need to," she said, but seemed distracted. "Remember your rooms are free of bugs, and so is the garage, but not much else." She pointedly cast the hallway camera a glance. "And I worked hard to make that privacy a part of your deal with Duke. Still, I'd check your rooms daily."

"Right," Will growled as soon as they hit the garage. "This is a full disclosure operation, no secrets, Petrok, that kind of—"

"Calm your shorts, Will. Tazz. He's going to be a problem." She held up her hand at their immediate denials. "Yes, he will. He's with his little woman, but he's gonna realize that the storm surrounding his location isn't going to keep him safe for long. Walters is going to be sent after him, and Tazz has to know that."

"And? We have to warn him," David said.

"No, we don't. Walters is an idiot. He's gonna screw up, and if I know Tazz, he'll kill him for threatening Kristen."

Will let out a frustrated snort. "Kristen? Who the hell is—?"

"The woman," David answered for her. So Tazz had found his future and wasn't letting go. David's thoughts filled with Paris, her shining smile and sweet but hesitant teasing. This morning he'd thrown out McDonald's as a breakfast option just to see her wrinkle her nose, but she'd nodded eagerly and told him she loved Egg McMuffins. *Hell, is that even possible? What woman loves those and admits it?* "Tazz doesn't have a crystal ball to see the future, Petrok. We need to warn him." He worried for Paris now, and his buddy, Tazz. If something happened to Paris... *Hell, one night in her arms and you're already worrying about that? Slow the hell down, man.*

"No, it's not safe. I've tried calling him, so don't give me that look. He's not answering. If we go there, we draw the wrong attention. We foul up his chances. He's on the other side of this mountain, already under the same storm we're about to get, if I'm reading the Weather Channel right. Let Walters will take some of these men, not you two. You're both in charge of training, so don't do it right. Take your time, I mean, how long can this last? Another day, possibly a week, tops."

"What?" Will demanded. "That's your plan? Have us hang out here with our thumbs up our asses?"

"Sure, if that's what gets you off," Sonya snapped, not missing a beat. Hell, Will had to have grown a bigger set than David sported, talking to her like her that all of a sudden. "Just work on looking like you're busy getting them ready for training. Buy me some time. Go slow. Duke won't ask. He's too busy with his other operation and by the time he does wonder, this will all be tied up and handed to Carson with a nice little bow."

"Shit," Will cussed. "That's too damn easy and you know it."

David agreed. It *was* too easy. That meant it was going to be messy. "What aren't you telling us?"

"I'm telling you everything. Believe me." She tossed her hair over her shoulder and stared him in the eye. "You have all you need to know."

"The sex drug." David exhaled when she nodded. "Did you take it?"

"No!" She was so shocked then pissed that he grinned despite the fact that they were in some deep shit. "If you thought Chung's was fun, do it. Otherwise, steer as clear as you can of that crazy shit."

"Hell, Chung's is still messing with me, so not going there," Will said from his position over by the entrance to the garage.

She frowned at that, but nodded. "Right. Let's hope it's not permanent."

"Shit, I hope not," David said, although the drug hadn't impacted him as harshly as it had the others.

"Naw, no way, Chung said it wasn't." Will rubbed his buzz cut, not appearing to buy his own words. "Just go do the perimeter thing, in case he's more intelligent than we give him credit for. I'll go check out the men and gear. We'll need to make this look good."

"Right." David considered the day and what he had to do, and realized with a burst of excitement he could take her with him. She might even like hiking the outskirts of town. Hell, they'd made love like crazy last night, but it'd really been an early to bed kind of night. They'd both woken up early, too, but that didn't mean she'd be tired. She hadn't been this morning, skating circles around him. Still, he tried not to sound too eager. "Petrok, check in, girl. No going silent on us."

"Of course not. This isn't my first rodeo."

He laughed at that, and smacked her on the shoulder like a guy, earning a dirty look he ignored because he knew she didn't really mind. "Nope, it's not," he told her.

"Will, I'll catch you later." He stopped at Will's grip on his arm. "What?"

"Just use your head," he warned. "The one up here." He flicked David on the forehead with his finger, almost earning a punch in return.

Instead David smiled, feeling as if he'd caught one hell of a lucky break.

"Always, man, always," he muttered and took off at a light jog. If he hurried he could pick up some sandwiches and take her out for a hike and eat while the sun set. If she liked Egg McMuffins, chances were she'd like sandwiches, too.

Has she ever had sex in the snow?

* * * *

Paris stuffed everything back into her suitcase, and tried to convince herself this was the right thing to do. David was fun, *too* much fun, but more of him and she'd be worse off than when Greg had dumped her. *Heck, I already like him more than I ever liked Greg, so what now?*

Stay and have more amazing sex, then watch him walk away? On to the next –

"No, he's not like that, not at all. He's a good man," she said to herself, but she had to force herself to believe it. "He is. He might only want sex, but that's okay since you practically climbed into his bed."

Practically? I did!

"Oh, God." She stood there, struck dumb by what she was saying, let alone thinking.

"I did. I did fall right into his arms, bed, sex," she murmured and sat down as the strength left her legs. "And not just with him but with his friend, too!" She buried her face in her hands. She'd loved every minute of it, so was that wrong? *Does that make me some kind of sex freak?*

Maybe. She laughed, but it sounded hysterical even to her. *Not like the way David makes me laugh.*

"Oh, God."

If I miss him this much now, what's going to happen once this weekend is over?

She stood at that and paced the room. The place smelled like him — them. She'd made the bed and cleaned up but she could still remember the weight of his body on hers. The feel of his rough whiskers along the inside of her thighs when she'd climaxed from his mouth and tongue in the shower. By the time she'd paced the room, she'd decided she needed to talk to Sara. She did one more back and forth. *I'll stay. I can't just go... Right?*

"Hey there, princess, how about a picnic —"

She screamed and threw a pair of socks at his head. They bounced off and he grinned, catching them before they hit the floor.

"Whoa, whoa, girl, what's the —?" He zeroed in on her suitcase, her, then the clean room and right back to her. "Going somewhere?" he asked, hands on his lean hips.

He seemed so aggressive and, well, stern that she giggled then covered her mouth when his frown turned to a truly impressive scowl. He was bigger when he was angry, she noticed, then grumbled to herself for noticing and getting hot all over at the thought.

"You were gonna run off?"

"Run off?" She twisted her sweatshirt sleeve in her fingers. "No, not run off, I was…" She paused when he dropped his arms and stalked toward her like a hungry wildcat. "Tidying up?"

"Oh?" he murmured and scanned the suitcase filled with her tossed-in clothes, bathroom toiletries and hair products. "Well, let me help you then," he said smoothly and pulled her clothes out. He opened a drawer of the bureau and tossed them in, shutting it a bit too firmly because the mirror trembled.

"David! If you break that mirror—"

"You get seven years of bad luck, I know. Now, explain why you were leaving."

She swallowed at the earnest expression in his blue eyes. He quirked one eyebrow at her when she didn't speak then rolled his hand like she needed to start.

"I kinda don't know what I'm doing with you. I mean, I'm supposed to be *here*." She started pacing the room, tugging on her sleeves. "I said I'd wait for Sara, but I am not that type of girl, I mean I don't, well, fall into bed with a stranger, let alone two!"

The last came out on a wail that she wished she could take back, but what was done was done. She hung her head and tried to think past the embarrassed pulse of blood roaring in her ears. Obviously this was more than sex, why else would David get so upset with her for leaving? *Or maybe it is sex and that's okay. Or maybe it is sex and more and that's okay, too.*

David touched her shoulder then turned her to face him. She didn't look up until he began laughing softly. Then she glanced at him to see the silly man grinning down at her.

"Stop thinking so much, I think there's smoke coming out of your ears."

She rolled her eyes and growled. "David, be serious."

"Okay, okay. First, I know all that, and I'll be honest, princess, if you did fall into bed with men like that, I doubt I'd be racing back to take you on a hike and picnic, possibly getting several speeding tickets on the way."

She blinked at the overload of information. "You got a ticket?"

He winced. "Maybe. If they have those cameras, but that's not the point."

"It's not?" She swallowed at the way he traced his thumbs over her collarbones and massaged her shoulders.

"No."

She nodded. "Okay, just spit it out, already. I guess I need to hear what the point is."

"You need to keep up. *You're* the point. *You.* Not any of the other women you imagine I shack up with, you. So, just breathe, and trust me, it's going to be all right."

She wasn't sure about that. "I don't think you shack up with women."

"Or a woman. There's no one else—"

"I know that," she said, even though she *had* worried over it. "I mean, I thought there wasn't. But it's not that, David, it's just—" She stopped when he shook his head, smiling briefly when she paused.

"Paris, I promise, this is gonna be fun. A hike and a picnic. I picked up sandwiches and some fruit. You said you liked fruit. I got some ice tea as well. It'll be fun."

"I don't doubt it." She still wasn't certain she should do this. He'd been gone barely an hour, but she'd been so certain leaving was the way to go. *Kinda. Sorta.* Okay, maybe not, but... *What happens when he's gone?*

"David, what about, I mean, aren't you supposed to be at that place?"

"Not yet, and when I do have to go, I kinda hoped you'd go, too."

She must have looked as floored as she felt, because he suddenly hugged her close and brushed a kiss to her hair. "Just go on the picnic. I'm gonna show you the mountains, while I see them, too, but hey, it'll be fun."

"You said that." She pressed her head to his warm chest.

How can I be so attracted to him already? So quickly?

"Thank you, I would like to go," she added while he held her. "I'm sorry."

"No, don't say that, really, I get it. Okay, I push hard, what can I say? It's my downfall maybe, I'm pushy and impatient."

She frowned at that, not agreeing. "I don't think so," she said shyly, and wiggled until he loosened his death grip. "I think you're kinda nice."

"Gee, thanks."

She snorted and shook her head. "But never serious." He ducked and kissed her. Once their lips touched, every doubt melted away. Or whatever remained of them once he'd returned, larger than life, she admitted. She sighed and tightened her fingers on his shirt, deepening the kiss on her own. Just like he always did, he took over making her toes curl. He dragged her leg up his thigh and fit his erection tightly to her pussy. Passion erupted all over again, but at the same time, that subtle doubt that all he wanted was sex rose to the surface.

He broke off the kiss, surprising her, and tugged her braid. "None of that or you'll be dragging me back to bed. First we hike and I see if you like turkey and cheddar or roast beef and Muenster better."

"You are too much." There was no heat to her words, instead her heart fluttered at the way he was treating her — as if he really wanted to spend time with her. Thoughtfully, like he had last night and this morning, too. "I like both," she added.

"Ah, good," he said with an exaggerated-sounding sigh. "Because I got a veggie and a ham one, too, in case."

"You did not!" she exclaimed, but he shrugged. "You did?"

"I'm a big guy, I eat a lot."

She could attest to the 'big', she still felt the memory of him making love to her. The sensation had her on pins and needles, wanting more, but not sure if she should.

He gathered her coat and picked up the pair of her socks she'd thrown at him and tossed them at her. She caught them and smiled at his whistle.

"Nice catch, how about you get ready? I'll go warm up the truck. Get your gloves and hat, too, it might snow."

She nodded and watched him confidently gather a few things from his bag then bend to kiss her.

"I'll be quick."

"No hurry, it'll give me time to make sure the truck's warm."

His thoughtfulness eased the doubts so much that she smiled and blew him a kiss he pretended to catch as he eased out of the room. Immediately quiet descended. He filled a room. That's what David did. He took all the darkness away and replaced it with his big personality.

She smiled and covered the happy laugh that rose. He did like her. He liked her as much as she liked him — she hoped. Either way, she was staying. She got her boots on, then raced to the bathroom. She rearranged her things and quickly adjusted her braid, tugging it like he did, and smiled wider at the happiness that overflowed her eyes.

Happiness. He did that to me, made me happy. Just breathe. Go with it, and him.

Chapter Six

David started the truck and immediately hit the steering wheel.

She was gonna leave. He couldn't believe how right he'd been. She had to think he was after tail and nothing else. Any other time, any other woman, and she'd be right.

Not this time.

He hit the steering wheel again with the palm of his hand. He had to show her a bit more than how much he wanted to make her scream. She never did scream—she had no idea how insane that made him, knowing she was so lost to the pleasure she couldn't even gather enough breath to shout.

But sex isn't gonna get her trust, dumbass.

No it isn't. Use your head.

"Yeah, both, maybe." He watched her rush out of the side door of the hotel and scan the parking lot. She was so damn pretty that his breath stalled in his throat. Men dreamed of women like Paris. She spotted the truck and him in it. A happy grin broke out on her rosy face. His stomach nosedived as if he'd just done a tricky jump from a low-flying plane. Had anyone ever seemed so happy to see him?

As soon as she got in she scooted over and kissed him, giving him some of her cinnamon flavor. Her toothpaste was minty but she had cinnamon gum—he knew because he'd snooped. Oddly enough, she'd not gone through his bag. He'd left a few things on top of his pants to test her, but he could tell she'd not seen them or she'd be one nervous girl.

"Was that quick enough?"

"I don't mind waiting, but yeah, you're fast," he assured her after he cleared his throat. "Warm enough?"

She took off her jacket, showing him the white scoop neck shirt she'd been wearing when he'd caught her worrying her little head off. He liked it, especially since it was low cut and hung off one shoulder, normally, but now gave him one hell of a view. She bent farther down, having a battle to get her jacket off, but blessing him with a glimpse of a dazzling white lacy bra and her plump breasts rising over the top. He had to adjust his hard-on or get a zipper burn.

"It's hot in here," she said, still struggling with her jacket.

He helped her, hiding his grin when she glanced at him. "Yeah, I thought you might be cold."

"Um, it's like ninety," she complained, turning the temp down with a suspicious expression. "What are you up to?"

"Oh ho, so you think you have me figured out, huh?"

"No," she said defensively, "but you are sneaky."

Sneaky. He winked at her. "Damn right."

"You like that, huh?" she said and bumped his shoulder, cute as heck. "Drive. It's going to be dark before we even get anywhere."

"Whoa, princess, no back seat driving. I got this covered. It's barely noon here. Now, can you hand me a sandwich?"

"What? I thought those were for a picnic?" she asked, giving the time a quick peek to see if he was serious. Then she gave him a puzzled frown. "Where are we going?"

"You'll see. Snacks are in the back," he reminded her.

She gave him another once-over, making him grin, then glanced over her shoulder to the back seat. He turned, too, but to back up out of his parking space. "I'll take a tea and that big one," he reminded her.

With a sigh, she got up on her knees so she could lean over the seat, trying to get the bag. He resisted the urge to pat her cute butt because he knew that was what she expected. When she sat back down he got a suspicious glance before she unwrapped the sandwich so he could hold it and drive. Pretty neat, too, he thought. She also opened his drink and waited for him to take a big bite and hand the sandwich back in exchange for the drink.

"You are hungry, aren't you?" she said and laughed. "Wasn't breakfast enough?"

"That was hours ago."

"Mmm." She took a bite of his sandwich.

"What did you do, besides freak out and try to leave?"

She choked so badly that he pulled over, a bit worried he'd killed her. She finally gasped for breath and smacked him on the chest, without any heat but pretty damn adorable. He kissed her, relieved he'd not damaged her. "Damn, you scared me."

"You are impossible. I mean, who says stuff like that?"

"Me?" he offered with a grin, sliding onto the road and taking his sandwich back. "Better get the turkey one."

"It wasn't the roast beef sandwich, mister. It was you. I was busy. I showered, then went to the store—"

"What? Why?"

She chewed her bite of sandwich then said, "Uh, I needed a few things?"

"Oh, right, well, I can take you—"

"It was up the street, David. I can walk."

Oh yeah, she was still sore over almost choking to death. "Well, if you need me to, I can stop by to see about the car," he offered. Will, much to his irritation, hadn't been able to fix it. They'd had it towed to the local mechanic's shop thinking it better to have it there, than at a potential bust.

"No, that's okay, really, I like to walk, hence the hike is a great idea, although those clouds don't look so good."

He took another bite and tried not to get all crazy happy about how willing she was to work with him. She also didn't seem to hold a grudge, because she elbowed him with a grin to get the sandwich back. He handed it over and took the tea, watching her more than the road. She seemed to be over her anxiety now, but he wasn't keen on testing that out by leaving her alone for too long. He got it. One hundred percent got it. He hadn't found out why she'd allowed last night, with Will, but he would. He bet on some jerk hurting her, or something along those lines. She was too...damn sweet for it not to be.

"Do you think it will snow before we get there?" she asked, sipping the tea after and smiling. "Oh, this is good. Peach?"

He cleared his throat again and nodded. He'd stood at the grocery store staring at the display of drinks, not sure what to get her. The peach just seemed to fit, plus he liked it. "The clouds are trouble," he agreed, when he could take his eyes off her.

She even ate cute. But what about her wasn't captivating? Not a damn thing. She was even one of those women who must have gotten wise enough to get laser hair removal. He wasn't sure if all guys liked that baby soft feel on a woman's privates or not, but he went nuts over it. But why, he wondered, had she? Some guy? The thought made him madder than hell and he didn't even know the man.

"So where are we going?" the woman driving him nuts asked.

He was seriously losing his mind if he already wanted to pound someone for ever being near her.

"Just up here," he said, checking the navigation system. "Yep, right here. Hey, so why are you bare? You know, on your pussy? Why did you go that way?"

She choked again, and he went to pat her back but stopped when she plastered her hand on his chest and coughed as if she had black lung. "Shit, I'm sorry, whoa, I need to think longer than a second, huh?"

"No," she gasped, her eyes watering. "Maybe longer than an hour, okay? I mean, where did that come from? Who doesn't nowadays? It's just...cleaner feeling. David! Watch the road!"

He swerved to stay on it, grinning probably like a fool. He might not be good at this shit, but he was getting answers. She liked the clean feeling? He hoped like hell she liked what he did, too. This morning he'd given her three orgasms before he'd let her feet touch the shower floor again. He'd die a happy man doing that every day, too. She was addictive.

"Sorry, sorry, yeah, got the road," he said in a rush when they skidded a little.

She gave him a wild-eyed stare but exhaled with a hand on his arm. "Yeah, sure you do, so any other questions before I take a drink?" She squinted at him until he shook his head and silently took the sandwich back. He took a big bite, pleased as hell by her answer.

"So why do you shave, you know, down there?"

He swallowed his mouthful too fast, just like she knew he would. Half gasping around the sub roll, he shot her a dirty look that made her smile so wide that she glowed.

"I like it, less trouble," he added with a wink. "I didn't know you noticed."

"Oh, I didn't, I guessed."

"Brat!" He couldn't believe he'd fallen for that dig so easy. She was a genius, obviously quick as a whip, skated like a dream and made his heart race by just smiling. What was it about her?

"I'm not a brat, and is this it?" she asked, getting up on her knees to see where he'd pulled over.

"Yep, this is it." He checked the time. Almost one in the afternoon gave them a good three hour walk. "We hike for a few hours, around that bluff and over that rise, and get back here by a bit after four, tops. Sound good? Too far?"

"Please, I can hike you into the dirt," she said with such bravado he had to kiss her.

He did, pulling her to him, still on her knees when he did. He let her go before they got too wild, but quickly smacked her butt. "We'll see about that, princess."

She tugged him back by his jacket collar and kissed him. "Yes, I guess we will. You carry the sandwiches and try to warn me if you're going to ask something super personal."

"Right," he said. "I got that real quick." He got out, and caught her as she moved down. "And you, huh?"

"And me," she agreed with a pleased, shy grin as she scooted down his body.

"Yeah, unless I kill you by choking." He set her down on her feet.

"True, very, very true," she whispered, then shocked him by swatting his butt when he turned.

"Woman," he cautioned, but she simply giggled, cute as hell, and took off. He didn't mind, since that meant he got a good view of her gorgeous ass in her jeans. "Are you going to be warm enough in that fleece?"

She paused and turned. "Sure, it's not that cold, but I think it's going to snow."

"Makes it warmer, right?" He shrugged his backpack on and adjusted his holster so it was hidden. Of all the things she'd asked him, she'd never once questioned him or Will about their weapons. But then, they'd both been upfront with her about what they did, at least mostly. "Listen, this is safe, walking with me. I'm just assessing the area."

"For bad guys?" she asked.

He held in his grin because really, he shouldn't laugh at her so much.

"Not a chance," he assured her and slung his arm over her shoulders. "Besides, I'm a big guy, remember?"

His boasting earned him a light thump on his stomach then a frown. "You are way too hard, too."

"That I am," he promised. "That I am, but that's for later."

Her eyes widened then she giggled, holding her mittens over her face.

"Oh, I know you're blushing—that doesn't help at all. Come on," he urged, not wanting to stop getting to know her now that he'd put sex off the menu. At least for the next six or so hours. Maybe longer, he surmised, if he held off until after dinner.

"You like to make me blush, don't you?" she accused, taking her mittens off and tucking them into the pockets of her fleece. "I think that explains a lot, mister," she added with a calculating expression that didn't quite make it past her smile.

"Ah, come on, already you have me down? Give me a few more days before you box me up and send me off, okay?"

She giggled then shocked him by tickling her fingers inside his coat, right to the sensitive spot along his ribs.

"Christ almighty, woman!" He jerked away and laughed harder when she collapsed against him, holding her sides. She was so pleased, though, he had to give in and hug her again. "Crazy woman, are you a psychic as well as prettier than a picture?"

"David," she whispered, stopping laughing to stare at him. "That was so sweet."

Embarrassed, he tugged her around and started walking. The snow was deep, but it was easy to walk through.

"You like to hike?" he asked, settling his stride to match hers.

"Yeah, it's nice, getting outside and exploring the woods, and these mountains are beautiful. Do you like to hike?"

"Sure, I guess."

"Oh, that sounds convincing," she muttered. "Well, what *do* you like to do?"

What do I like to do?

Suddenly, he didn't know. He liked to read, he liked to relax, but that was lying around and watching movies, not very interesting.

"Read? Watch movies? What? Race cars?" she asked.

"Not into dangerous sports, other than you."

She rolled her eyes.

"I read some, watch movies, boring now that I think about it."

"Because you should have some dazzling, exciting life, like, maybe being some warrior or something? Hero?" she asked, then grinned. "You already do those things, so why would you want more excitement?"

"Well, I like basketball and hockey," he admitted, remembering he did like both sports. Watching and playing. "You like to skate."

"I do," she said with feeling. "It's always been the one thing I've been good at."

He frowned over that, puzzling out her meaning. It was obvious to him she was smart, funny and had a sweet streak a mile long. But that sounded both sincere and a bit embarrassed.

Before he could pin her down, she asked, "What's your favorite movie?"

"*Iron Man 2*," he said, then followed up with, "Three is pretty funny shit, too, though."

"Both were good," she agreed. "I liked it when he got all panicky and also when Pepper kicked butt. That was good."

"Yeah, then she freaked out," he reminded her.

"But that's what made it so real, not that it was real, but if I did that, I'd freak out, too."

He bet she would. She was so small he doubted she'd ever even gotten in a girl fight. She'd sure freaked out on him. "So, why did you do it? Last night?"

Her body stiffened under his arm, but after a few minutes of avoiding his question, she finally sighed heavily.

"You wouldn't understand."

"Try me," he urged, biting the side of his cheek at her disgruntled sigh.

"Have you ever done something knowing it wasn't the thing to do, but unable not to?"

He frowned and thought about that. Before he could answer she went on, "Not last night, I don't regret that for a moment." Another sigh, then she said quietly, "I mean, when your instincts warned you not to trust someone, and you blindly go on and do it, pushing aside all your misgivings and just going along with them?"

The way she'd said that made him worry he'd pushed too far. Trusting she was honest, he puzzled out what she had said instead of what his own worries were. He could think of ways his instincts had guided him in combat, and when his orders had gone against them. Too many times he'd had that chill that things were not right, and gone on with a mission. The Sentinels were proof of that. But she meant something else entirely.

"Like bury my head in the sand and go out on some insane mission because my commander ordered it?" he teased.

She snorted and hit him on the stomach.

"What was that for?" he demanded, but knew. "You mean you let someone pressure you into something you didn't want, and didn't even admit to yourself you didn't want it?"

Her pace slowed and she sought out his face as if to check that he was serious.

"Like you knew there wasn't a reason to trust but you wanted to so you did, even when deep down you didn't want to? That's why you slept with me last night?" He threw that out there, knowing that wasn't it at all. His guess was she was talking about someone else, maybe a whole lot of someones she'd trusted in her life.

"No, that's where you're wrong. With you my instincts said to trust and I went along with you with my eyes wide open, not sensing a thing other than" — she waved at him — "you, and how good you are."

"Good?" He snorted, but deep down he liked that. Liked it a whole lot.

"You know what I mean. I guess I needed to break away from the cycle, you know? I'm not used to doing things for me, but I did with you and it turned out okay."

He laughed at the doubtful end of her bold statement, as if he might suddenly prove her wrong. "Princess, I'm damn glad you did, have I mentioned that?"

She rolled her eyes again, but he could tell she was happy with his response. He wanted more details, but he settled for what she'd given him so far. It made sense to him in a way it might not to other people.

He'd been raised in foster homes, one after another, and each time he'd opened the door and walked in, it was always with the same misgivings mixed with hopefulness that this time he would be cared for right. Each time he'd been wrong, until he'd stopped hoping and started building a wall to keep safe.

"Oh," she cried and ducked.

He watched her pick up a solitary stone from the edge of a small creek bed. "It looks like a heart!"

He examined the gray and black rock, and sure enough it did.

"Here, you keep it safe, okay?" She laughed and gave him the stone. "You'll be better at protecting it than me."

His heart thudded painfully at her words, and that easy he wanted it—her heart. What would that be like? To keep her safe?

"David!" she whispered, pointing up the path.

He spotted a doe, then two more behind at the same moment the deer must have spied them. The three deer bounded away, knocking snow down from the tall pines as they startled.

"Beautiful, huh?" he asked, and pocketed the little stone.

"Yeah, so beautiful. Thank you," she added when they started walking again.

"For?"

"For taking me hiking." She glanced at his face. "And maybe for a few other things."

He grinned and settled her closer to him. She kept pace pretty well, taking her time to position her feet when it proved slippery a few times, but going at a good, solid walk.

"So, let's talk about you."

She stumbled and laughed. "Okay, let's talk about me. What do you want to know?"

"Well, I already know a few things. You like to skate. Let's see, you like pineapple and you like to look nice."

"I like to *look nice*?" she repeated. "Who likes to look *messy*?"

"Well, some people might," he teased. "You paint your nails. They're cute. You also dress nice—"

"I don't, not really. I wear jeans and dresses but I don't dress up, dress up, like some fashion model or bling-bling girl."

He lost her at that, because he wanted to see her in a dress. And 'bling-bling' girl? She hadn't brought a dress, but maybe he could buy her one. He liked the thought of buying her things.

"Why do you think I like pineapple?"

"You wanted a pina colada last night."

"How did you know that?"

"I watched you," he said simply. "You tapped the pina colada but went for the rum and Coke."

"You guys were ordering beer and that makes me feel full, plus run to the bathroom every ten seconds, but I thought a frilly drink was too girly."

"You are girl, hence, you're girly."

She laughed, catching his teasing her on her use of 'hence' earlier pretty quickly.

"Right, I am," she said, but didn't sound upset by that. "I'm kinda used to being a girl, being born this way and all."

"Yeah," he breathed and turned her to brush a kiss to her lips. "And I'm damn glad you were," he told her. They'd done well. He guessed they'd covered the mountain in just under an hour. "Look, now isn't that worth the hike?"

He turned her around to face the brilliant scenery and she leaned back into him with a sigh. "It's really beautiful, isn't it?"

"Yeah," he agreed. He wrapped his arms around her, sure she meant the view, but he was talking about the woman in his arms. The mountains were spectacular though. The heavy bold peaks covered in white but still clearly rugged and dangerous. The trees softened the wilderness but out here, it would be easy to become lost in all the white. "You've not asked me about— Wait, I'm going to ask something personal, are you drinking anything? Eating?"

She laughed and tipped her head up and to the side to meet his eyes. "Nope, go ahead, what now?"

He cocked an eyebrow at that and instead of asking why she hadn't asked about Will, took an easy question out of the bucket list he had going. "Why haven't you asked what my favorite sex position is yet? And if I tell, will you?"

She blushed pinker than he'd ever seen her and dropped her head in her hands. "You are really trying to embarrass me."

"No," he lied. "I'm not, just curious, you know, for the future. Let's keep walking, come on, you can share with me. Promise."

"I'm not discussing this. Can't we talk about what you do for work? That sounds exciting. I'm sure that's rude, but it does. I mean, you're wearing a gun now!"

He skimmed her face and only found genuine curiosity and a little admiration in her eyes. That shouldn't have made him feel awkward, but it did.

"I am, but only because I have to, not because I think there's a threat. The only thing dangerous out here besides some hibernating bear we might wake up is those clouds."

She glanced at the sky and squinted. "Yeah, that's going to be a lot of snow. Maybe a blizzard. I heard that the other side of these mountains lost power and is buried under a few feet."

If he were snowed in with her, he'd not be able to get over the thrill. It could only get better if there were no television and no lights, so all she had was him to keep her entertained.

"Do you play cards?"

"Cards? Like gamble with my money?" she asked, glancing at him.

"Naw, not like that, but five card stud?"

"Monopoly," she offered then smiled. "But I know how to play twenty-one, isn't that what it's called? And oh, that game where you try to make a straight or... That's five card stud, isn't it?"

"Yep, it is. Good, maybe we can play cards, you know, if we're snowed in."

"What? This is Wyoming, they're used to snow. They have plows for this stuff."

"Stuff, huh? Well, I think some of that *stuff* is going to hit soon." He spotted the unmistakable tread of a snowmobile. "Who rides up here, I wonder?" he muttered, examining the tracks coming out of the woods on their right. They were up pretty far. Whoever was out here was far from town. A rancher, maybe. He'd not noticed any animal tracks, though, so if it was a rancher, what was the cowboy doing up here? Maybe hunters. Or, hell, some kids out joyriding on snowmobiles.

"I have no idea, but they packed it down for us."

"Yeah, I guess they did," he said and followed the trail with his eyes up through the denser forest to their left. "You ever snowmobile?"

"Sure, when I was little. My uncle had them."

"Yeah, they can be fun," he murmured, his concern over the tracks building instead of diminishing.

"Well? Left, or keep going on this? Did you bring water?" she asked.

He nodded and turned to show her his pack. She unzipped it, then reached in for the bottles he'd stored away.

He glanced around at her to see she'd found the sandwiches, too. "Do you want one of these?"

"Naw, not yet. You help yourself though."

"No, I'm good. I ate most of yours," she offered and waved to the snowmobile tracks. "I vote for the tracks. Easier to walk on, right?"

"All right," he agreed, taking the water and waiting while she zipped his pack up. She hummed a little under her breath and he recognized the song she'd skated to, one by John Legend. "You have a good ear for music."

"I do?" she asked, handing him the water. "Why do you say that?"

He took a drink and wiped his mouth. "Well, you can hum a tune, that's not easy."

"Oh, that, yeah, I like that song."

The sound of snowmobiles coming down the track had him moving her aside and up onto a higher trail. His instincts warned that this wasn't the time or place to meet anyone, especially with her here with him. He helped her behind a tree in case the crazy drivers weren't watching ahead of them. Most accidents on snowmobiles and four by fours were caused by stupid people. Today wasn't the day to meet any either. He had plans and they didn't include dealing strangers.

Seconds later, the noise got loud enough to require headgear. He glanced at Paris to find her covering her ears with her mittens.

The first snowmobile roared by, carrying a man in white and gray camo with an illegal gun slung over his shoulder. David urged Paris down and around the other side of the mound of snow, following and making sure to keep her out of sight. She didn't ask what he was doing, and when five more men followed the first, he held his breath as the last one called to the others and stopped. The rest kept on, leaving the lone man behind.

Fuck. From where he was he could clearly see the tracks he and Paris had left behind. He'd been sloppy, damn sloppy. He eased Paris farther down, moving as slowly as he could so that the guy would have no warning if David had to attack. Paris went, not asking questions, but frowning so hard, he tightened his hand on her arm. The man on the idling snowmobile gunned his engine and took off after only a minute more.

David swallowed hard and waited until he couldn't hear the vehicles, then waited longer. Paris didn't move and she didn't speak, which he was grateful for, but when he did glance over at her, she was pale, clearly scared by his behavior or the men, possibly both.

"It's okay."

"Are you...?" She swallowed and frowned harder. "Are you sure?"

"I am. Damn sloppy, I got sloppy. But we're okay. We go down, though, not the way they came. Follow me."

"Wait one second," she said firmly and tugged his sleeve. "What do you mean? You got sloppy and now we go this way? What does that mean?" she whispered with some heat.

"Princess, any other time I'd fill you in, but right now —"

"Not moving until you explain." She sat down and crossed her arms, and her legs.

If he'd been hit upside the head he wouldn't have been more surprised. He squatted and tipped her stubborn chin up.

"Look, I can see you're upset. Hell, I think you have every right to be, but now you and I are walking, and when I'm certain you aren't in any danger I'll explain. Until then, come on and trust me."

She rolled her eyes, but stood when he pulled her up. She skimmed his face for something, but he didn't give her time to find it, instead he ushered her down and to the left of where the men had come through the dense woods. The snow wasn't as deep because of the heavy trees holding it up but it was harder to hike because of how densely the forest grew. He held up branches for her and thankfully she hiked, not angry as far as he could tell, but nearly bursting with curiosity.

"Those men were armed," he said quietly. "That means they were patrolling this area. There are reasons people patrol. Most are to keep intruders away. Or to keep whatever they are doing secret."

She nodded, but didn't ask whatever she had going on in her head.

"I was up here getting a lay of the land, not thinking to run into that kind of thing or I'd never have brought you," he said with some heat. "Now I need to get back and instead of…" He paused, about to share his idea for snow sex, but thought better of it. "Having dinner with you, I have to go check in with Will. I might be gone all night, or I might only be an hour or so."

"David, does this mean you might get hurt?"

Her concerned expression tugged at his heart. "Hurt? No, come on, this is Wyoming."

"Those men had bigger guns than you."

He laughed and felt the tension ease from his shoulders. "Princess, no one has a bigger gun than me, and you shouldn't have been peeking at another man's gun."

"David," she whispered and shook her head. "I'm serious. Those were big guns."

"AK-74 millimeter, illegal in this country."

"See?"

"Come on have some faith. I was a SEAL. I can do more than some guys on a snowmobile who didn't know I was ten feet away."

"You were a SEAL? Oh, God," she muttered and covered her mouth with her fingers.

"Well, it wasn't that bad." He didn't even earn a smile at that, so tried another angle. "We'll get you down to the hotel and I'll bring you some dinner, okay?"

"I'm okay! David, it's *you* I'm worried about." She added an exasperated huff to her words.

"Oh ho! I knew it. I'm growing on you after just a few days."

"David," she sighed. "You *are* growing on me and it hasn't even been a day."

"It's been a full day, about an hour ago," he informed her.

She froze then shook her head. "Just don't get hurt, okay?" She'd stopped under a pine tree and looked so pretty with her light blue hat on and her blonde hair tied back in a braid he couldn't resist tugging it.

"I won't. I try damn hard not to ever get hurt because I'm a terrible patient."

For some reason that made her wince and hug him tightly. Amazed, he held her, wondering what he'd said right, or maybe wrong, this time. She exhaled and pulled away and smiled softly, but it didn't match the worry in her eyes.

"Okay, so no getting hurt, and if you're wondering, that scared me."

Hell, he was an ass, wasn't he? "Sorry, Paris. If I'd thought—"

"Shh, really, I'm fine, you're the one going to do... What? Wait, don't tell me, okay?" She patted his chest with both mittens and smiled brighter, but it was forced. "We'd better go."

"Yeah, but I can stop, you know, get you something for dinner, something warm to eat—"

"David, the hotel has a dining room," she said with a little more of that heat he thought was damn cute.

He didn't want her down there, alone, eating. That was a single guy's dream—meeting a lonely hottie in the hotel. No way, no how was that okay.

"Yeah, but I don't want you down there alone."

"What? Do you think those men will be there?" she whispered, as if they might be nearby and scoop her up.

He cocked an eyebrow and grinned. "You watch a lot of movies, don't you?"

She ducked her head but he saw her smile. "A little, maybe."

"Those men are long gone. I simply don't want any other guys thinking you're available."

That sank in for two seconds then she turned on him and pointed a mitten at the center of his chest. "Just because I went off with you and Will doesn't mean I—"

"Whoa there, take a breath. I didn't think it did, but I don't want you alone eating dinner either."

"Oh?" She arched a pretty eyebrow, and put a whole hell of a lot of oomph in it for such a sweet woman.

"Yeah," he muttered and turned her around to get her moving. "I'll leave the sandwiches and we'll have a picnic in the room when I get back, okay?"

She didn't respond, but when he glanced at her she was smiling, pretty damn happy about that. The anxiety in his gut eased off and he let out a slow breath. He might suck at this communication shit, but he was more than willing to try, especially with Paris.

"You can't leave all the sandwiches, you didn't really eat. But a picnic in the room sounds fun," she said, after a while of walking quietly. "I think we might have to, because look" — she pointed to the left, where the trees broke a little — "it's snowing. Maybe we *will* get snowed in."

She sounded so happy about that, and when she hugged his arm she laughed, that the rest of his worries went right out of the window. One thing was for certain, she liked him. So what if he had to rush off for more of this damn mission? He'd hurry and maybe they would be snowed in together.

"Yeah, I imagine that would be all kinds of fun. You'd probably beat me in strip poker, huh?"

"Oh, I don't know about that." She laughed then added, "But there's some good movies we might watch. Or just, I don't know, we'd think of something," she said with a sigh he wanted to ditto because he hoped that something meant she was as horny as he was.

He curled his arm around her waist and brushed a kiss to her temple. She fit him.

"I like something. I bet I can think of a whole lot to keep you entertained with something," he added, caressing up her ribs to just below her breasts.

She stiffened then trailed her hand down to pat him on the ass. "I bet you could."

Jesus. How could he walk away from this and go chase down men on snowmobiles?

"Princess, you keep that up and I'm not going to be able to leave, you know that, right? Then I'll have even more work to do tomorrow."

Reluctantly, he thought, she nodded, but with an evil little smile kept her hand in his back pocket.

Chapter Seven

Will glanced up from filling out the last of his stack of forms and frowned. "Jansen."

"We have some complications." David threw his gloves down and shrugged off his jacket.

"You're right. We do. I ran into Sara, Paris' friend."

David paused half way out of his jacket. "And?"

"She was pretty freaked out, but seemed to calm down when I offered her a ride to town."

"Wait." David got the jacket off and sat down. "You took her to a hotel?"

"Yeah. Not the same one, she wanted near where we had the car." Will shrugged then spilled the rest of it. "She was given the drug. She was pretty upset, but by the time we got to town, she'd gone quiet. I think she might have had only a small dose, but unasked for. I talked to the boy. He's aware how wrong that was." Will left off the ass kicking he'd given the younger man. Sara was sweet, much like Paris, but…somehow different. He'd dropped her off and left, not trusting himself around her.

"She's okay, though?"

Will nodded.

David exhaled. "Paris will be —"

"She knows where Paris is, and was glad you were with her. Said to let you two have some time, even."

"She did?"

Will ran a hand over his hair. Sara had smiled only the one time — when he'd informed her that his buddy was staying with Paris. She'd been genuinely happy, he could tell. "Yeah, she said she'd be fine in town and since the car isn't ready, she'd simply wait."

"Hell, that's nice of her. Sure she doesn't want to talk to Paris?"

"She said no."

"All right." David rubbed his face with his hands. "Look we got something else to worry about. I ran into a team of six, armed, and on snowmobiles. North side of town. About five miles out from here."

"Shit, and who were they?" Will asked, tossing his pencil down on the desk and stretching his back.

"I have no idea. Not trained too well. I was ten feet from them and they had no clue. Paris was with me."

"What?" he asked, startled that Jansen would ever take the girl on a hike, in the snow. He knew David had it for her, but did his buddy have it this bad? Paris was a keeper, though. He'd not considered his friend — who steered clear of the type — would go down that road. But one glance at David and he'd known the man wanted Paris to himself. He hadn't needed the subtle — or not so subtle — rebuff on his offer to join them.

Jansen grimaced and ran his hands over his face again briskly after. The signal meant he had his head in his ass. The fact he was this screwed up he showed it surprised a laugh out of Will. Hell, Jansen was sunk, hook, line and all.

"Damn, you sorry bastard, you have the worst timing. Hands down, the absolute worst timing."

"Tell me something I don't know," Jansen snapped and jerked a chair around and sat down in it with his arms hanging over the back. "She's in the hotel now, but we have to go check this out and there's what? Two hours of daylight left."

"Did you even sleep last night?"

"Yes, I slept, what do you think? I fucked all night?"

"Well…" Will considered the pissed off expression on Jansen's face and held his tongue. He'd left when the two of them had made it pretty clear they'd forgotten all about him. Not that he'd minded. Jansen needed some downtime. The man was too intense most of the time to loosen up. Not that meeting Paris had lessened that. "No, I guess you're playing it slow, trying to show a bit more…tact?"

"Paris isn't the point. Besides, if we go out now, we might be able to follow them in the snow. The tracks are pretty clear. You set?"

Will stood and rubbed his buzz cut. He needed to get it trimmed, but he could maybe go a few more days. "I'm ready. The men are useless. The facility is good, though, and with some training we could have them mission ready in six months."

"Hell, really? That long? What are they? Gym bunnies?"

"About," he agreed. "What do we need?"

"Just what we've got, not a big deal, I think. We follow this and find out what's going on. Should we ask Duke if it's his damn men out there?" Jansen asked.

Will paused and thought about the men he'd seen so far. None of them could navigate the mountains, and they sure couldn't handle a firearm. "We can, but I doubt it. Let's call en route, because that storm and the sunset are fast approaching."

"Right." Jansen grabbed his jacket.

The rooms were warm, almost too much warm. It was probably because a lot of the men were training in the gyms and wore shorts, but the place must all be rigged for one central heating system, because it was damn uncomfortable. He'd marked that up as an issue, along with the gym. He didn't plan on being here long enough for it to be a real problem though.

Jansen scanned the room, then him. "Looks like your day sucked," Jansen commented with a smirk.

"It was my turn, I guess." Will smacked Jansen on the back. "I did have that babe down south, so maybe this is payback."

"Paris is more than a babe, Will."

Will lifted his eyebrows and scanned Jansen's profile as they walked. "Right, about that. You're sore about last night?"

"What?" Jansen asked, shoving the door to the garage open. "No, hell no, that was hot, besides, you know as well as I do that we pushed her."

"But it was only last night," Will remarked, earning a frown. He agreed they'd pushed, but she'd gone, and willingly. His bet was because of the man scowling at him right now. David had been her focus. He might as well have been a couch for all she'd noticed. Although she hadn't been rude, or even aloof, just consumed with David to the point he'd watched the two of them and gotten himself off on the show.

"Maybe, yeah, unless something comes up," David said vaguely.

"Like what? My dick?"

Jansen slugged him, hard, in the arm, but Will grinned and took it. "Sorry, but hell, you never go hot after a girl, it's a bit, well, fucked up."

"Why? Can't I find someone that's more than a one-nighter? And weren't you the one just telling me you were tired of this shit and wanted to hand in your gun, find a nice girl and all that?"

"Sure, hell yeah, you're due yours, man." Will took the passenger side so Jansen could drive and wondered what had Jansen so jumpy. "How's it going, then? You still dig her?"

"It's been a day. Sure, I like her."

"Nothing coming up as a red alert?"

His buddy scowled at him as if he'd lost his mind and started the truck before he shook his head. "Not a damn thing."

Jansen said that as if it that was bad, which Will could understand. Jansen was a loner. They were close, but there were things about his buddy he didn't know, and things about him he knew he was the only one *to* know. Jansen had been raised in the foster system, and that kind of shit had left a mark. He trusted very few, held on to every damn thing he ever bought, or earned for that matter, or found, and he didn't form tight bonds with many. Will was one of the very few men who could say David Jansen was a friend. But David would come to anyone's rescue. In a fight Will knew that Jansen would have his back without question.

If he was turning that toward a woman, well, Will considered the implications and hid a grin. Paris better be ready for what she got because Jansen when he did go in, he went all-in and he didn't believe in candy coating a damn thing.

Will glanced at the tight grip Jansen had on the wheel and wondered how that approach was working with the lovely Paris. She wasn't either of their typical women—she was sweet, and her shyness wasn't faked—if he had to guess what motivated her to let them share her, it'd been too much alcohol, their personalities and maybe a sadness he'd seen in her eyes. A break-up maybe, but that wasn't all, maybe it was David. She'd been drawn to him in an obvious way, maybe even too obvious for David to see.

"So she's not upset with you having to drop things to come back here?" he asked.

"Naw, she didn't appreciate the guys on the snowmobiles, though."

Will guessed that was an understatement.

Paris was a pretty, a gorgeous woman really, with a sweetness about her that made him more than a little jealous of Jansen. He was also man enough to appreciate that he got to have a small slice of the whole.

"I'm glad for you, man. Don't blow it," he cautioned.

"What makes you think I will?" Jansen growled.

"Well, you're you." Will laughed then felt sorry for the poor bastard. "If you've not scared her off by now, I'm guessing she's into you. Even your damn habit of asking whatever the fuck pops into your brain, so don't stress out so much. Relax. It's not many guys that get what you've been given—a chance with a real keeper."

Jansen glanced over as if checking out if he was pulling his leg. He seemed to soak that in, even loosening up enough to relax on the steering wheel.

After a minute or so he sighed. "Yeah, she's kinda all of it, isn't she? I mean, hell, I held her last night, just kinda watched her sleep." He shrugged and smirked.

"It was damn nice. I mean, no wonder all those suckers called home every chance they got back in the SEALs. Those guys were nuts though," he added.

"Why?"

"Well, first, why the fuck would you go out there and get your ass shot off if you might not be able to come home to that? I mean, what were they thinking?"

"So you'll just call it quits? End your service because you met *the one*?" Will asked, stunned.

Jansen grimaced. "She's worth getting a day job for, hell anything so it's not six months, sometimes a year before I see her again. That shit is a recipe for insanity. Already I can't think straight," he added in a mutter.

Will shook his head. "Man, you just don't know what it's like, that's all. You're never into a woman, ever. Now it's broadsided you. Like basic training all over again, Jan."

"Fuck you, Will. You're just sore she liked me more." Jansen laughed.

"Maybe, maybe," Will admitted but an image of Sara, ducking her head so her hair hid her face when she'd sat in his truck floated through his brain. She might have signed on for a wild weekend with her boyfriend, but she hadn't been prepared for how wild. She'd been frightened, and not too happy with the sex drug, he could tell. What would she think of a man who not only had been on a similar drug, but still fought the effects she'd only sampled in a limited dose? The thought burned his gut, so he switched that line of thinking off. Sara wasn't the woman for him, not now, not ever. Neither was Paris. "How much farther? I'm not thinking a night hike isn't your plan for the evening, is it?"

"She's getting a picnic ready for us, in case the storm snows us in."

"We are never snowed in. What are you talking about?" Will asked, watching Jansen pull over and grin at him.

"She doesn't know that." He sounded happy. "And you can carry my weight for a few days," he tossed in, grabbing his gear from the back. "It's not like you really have to train those men. It's just for show. Besides, I had your back enough when Chung's had you upside down and sideways."

"Thanks for the reminder, buddy," Will muttered, not liking the reference or the reminder that he still couldn't beat the Sentinel Drug.

"No problem, I've got your six," Jansen called. "Here's where I'm guessing the men were headed. We follow the tracks" — he pointed to the left, where Will could see the break in the forest and the snowmobile marks in the snow — "I think we'll find more than we bargained for. I hope Petrok's on your speed dial."

"Is your new girlfriend?"

Jansen grinned. "She doesn't own a cell phone."

Stunned, Will stood there staring at his buddy. Jansen winked a lazy blue eye and twisted his toothpick to the side of his mouth, nodding, pleased as hell. "She likes McDonald's too."

"You're shitting me." *Dream come true.* A woman without a phone, always texting, checking it and demanding constant contact was a rare, if not extinct, species. The McDonald's thing he didn't get, but no phone? Hell, was that even possible? "How the....I mean, fuck, why not? Did you give her one?"

"I gotta get to that, but nope, she said she hates that people are so into technology they can't seem to think of a thing to say to each other face to face."

Holy hell. "You're one lucky man, Jan. If you screw up, I'm going for it."

"Believe me." Jansen gave him a hard stare. "I'm not screwing up."

"Right, well, let's get this over with so you can prove it."

Jansen snorted, but Will shook his head again, following him. The man just might get it right. If she spent the day with him and she still hung around…

"Two hours, then we have to head back," he called, gaging the time on his watch.

"Yep, that was my guess. Do you think she's tired? I mean, we got up early, then skated, then hiked. She might be tired."

Skated? "Jansen, just move your brain back to the mission for two hours," Will growled. If this was Jansen in love, he'd hate to see him if she returned the feelings.

Or if she didn't.

The thought made him frown. Jansen didn't give up once he took something on, but he didn't take something on unless he knew he could handle it. What did that mean with love? Love was a tangled mess of emotional ups and downs with no road map. Was Jansen prepared to navigate his way through that?

Will assessed his buddy and guessed he was.

* * * *

David shifted his pack and tightened a strap, but didn't take his eyes off the camp below them.

"There's twelve men," he murmured in his com. Will was on the opposite rise, having circled around the makeshift camp. Whoever the men were, they'd come prepared to stay a while.

"Got it. There are two more to the left of you, ten o'clock."

Scanning the ridge below him, he located the two. "That makes fourteen. Spot any insignia?"

"Not yet. I'm scanning the men and sending to base."

This could mean more people knew what Duke was up to than they'd thought. More people with the money to take what they wanted, rather than wait for Duke to sell it. That meant money, power and enough connections to get this kind of force in here under the radar. Duke had been given the green light because there were bigger fish to fry. Whoever this was, hadn't hit their radar.

Until now.

He settled more firmly on his stomach and pulled his rifle out, piecing it together silently. He unfolded the tripod and adjusted his scope. Through the lens he could make out the faces of individuals, but none were familiar to him. He'd seen sheet after sheet of criminals in the underground human trafficking ring, more in the arms dealers dung heap and file upon file of threats to the US. None of the men below him set off a warning signal. They dressed like local cult members or some such.

"Anything?" he asked.

"Not yet. Carson is running them."

That could mean many things. The snow had started to turn thicker, a much damper fall too, so it might drop a few feet—as predicted. The soldiers below them weren't leaving. There were six tents, one in the center. Some of them were hanging lanterns, and one guy was making a meal. It even smelled good. His stomach growled, reminding him of Paris. What didn't remind him of Paris? Even the snow gradually covering him reminded him she was probably pleased it was snowing—so she could have a day inside with him.

"The white-haired man, your center, standing with two in green and brown, he's wanted for arms dealing in the Congo. He has a warrant out, along with the two he's talking to. The one coming up to them is Jason Sanders, head of the EBC, Early Believers of Christ, a cult out of Jasper."

"Well, isn't this fun? What does Carson say they want?"

"He's checking. We're to mark their location, get pics and stand down."

"Right." So mark their company and send in sat locations. That meant another hour laying low. Two tops.

"Move your ground two hundred yards to your right and cover that area facing you and I'll do the same. Two hours, we should be good to go."

"Three, then."

"Good catch, Jansen," Carson buzzed in. "Keep your heads up. I'm sending this to Petrok. She's touched base with the sellers in DC. She'll be back by tomorrow. This could be wrapping up real fast. No way can we let these boys near Duke. Be ready to take them down when shit flies south at Duke's."

"A two-prong approach?" David asked, still scoping the group below him.

"Yes. You're in town, move it to Duke's. I want you both within inches of each other and ready to hit these men."

A man walked out of the central tent, lifted his head, and David nearly squeezed the trigger on his sniper rifle. "Twelve o'clock. Rick Martinez." Second to Savage on their list of men to kill on sight.

"Hold your ground, Jansen." Carson's order was sharp and clear, but through the com, David could also hear Will swearing.

"Orders, sir?" he asked, after a minute of watching the scumbag.

Shit. Fuck. Son of a bitch.

"We stick to the plan. I'll send in a team. You will hit these men when we hit Duke. I'll station men nearby in case they move. You be ready for my call. I want you on lead."

"Will do, sir," Will called in.

"Ditto, sir." David gathered his gear, marshalling his reasons for dragging Paris to Duke's. Now more than ever he wanted her as close to him as possible. Martinez was scum, and if he was camping out, it was at Savage's orders. If Savage was involved... David wanted Paris safe. She'd come, if he pushed hard enough. *But would she be safe?* Already someone could have blown their cover. If someone had spotted him, with her, she could be in danger even now.

He forced himself to stop that line of thought. She was safe, and she'd be safer with him.

"Ten minutes, Jansen."

"Check, ten."

The snow made it easy to move unseen. No one searched up high on a perimeter when it snowed. Still, he had to work hard to keep his mind on the mission. In the stillness of the early winter evening he could even make out the men talking in the distance. Someone put on music and a few were breaking open beers. So the cult drank and listened to music. He'd never heard of the group, but then, he'd never focused on domestic terrorists.

Will checked in twice, changing their location but after an hour they were done taking photos and sending them in. The men below them hadn't set exterior scouts, secure in their location and, he guessed, were betting on the heavy snowfall keeping everyone away.

"Finished."

"Done, meet at the northern point," David muttered. He'd stowed his rifle and gear. The sun was down now and the day was catching up to him. Not that he'd be too tired to convince Paris to come with him to Duke's. But should he?

Just thinking of her, he had to pause and shake his head. Now was not the time. Even if every other second his mind thought it was. *That's how you get your ass shot off.* His focus back on the silent woods, he waited until he was certain there was no sound before he began quietly making his way to the meet-up location. Half an hour later, he found their small cut in a pine tree and waited ten feet from it, under the cover of another fallen pine still heavy with greenery.

Will was five minutes late, coming in silently enough that David had to strain to hear him even when he saw him. Snow did that. It also worked for the other guys. They nodded and took off again, still moving silently as they put distance between themselves and the campers. This far out, they would claim they were lost hunters. Both had the fake licenses and maps to prove it, but their rifles were a bit sketchy since neither had a hunting rifle on them. The plan was to say they were scouting, which was valid, but if the guys were worth any amount of money, they'd not buy that line.

"Savage has to be in on this," Will growled for greeting.

"I agree. I was also thinking an insider at Duke's might be dishing intel, giving them details. But they could wait at a hotel. Why camp out here?"

"They like it?" Will laughed then shook his head. "I shit you not, some of those cult guys are nuts. Nothing they do would surprise me."

"Yeah, but they also like comfort, and as nice as those tents are… I'm not buying it. Something else is up."

"Probably, but we're on it now, so it won't matter, right? Carson thinks it's all tied to the drug. The sex drug. It could be used for human trafficking. Think, man, if they had that, it's like Cat, the date-rape drug, right, but the woman is willing, *more* than willing."

"Sick shit, man, sick shit," David muttered. "And you wonder if I would drop all this for the right girl."

"You never seemed interested in the right girl before," Will said.

"I guess because I hadn't met her." Jansen shrugged when he said it because it was more truthful than he really felt comfortable being.

"Yeah," Will said, sounding tired.

Their truck loomed out of the thick snowfall. "Here we are. You tired? Want to stop by, say hi to Paris?"

"What, me? No way man, that's all you. Just drop me off, I'm dead on my feet," Will said. "This cold gets to me. Give me the desert any time."

Jansen grunted. "I like it," he muttered but he doubted Will heard him. Maybe he liked it because Paris liked it. "Do you ever play hockey anymore?"

"Hockey? Nah, not for years, you?"

"Nah. It's a good game, though."

"Yeah, it's a great game." Will gave him an odd frown.

Paris liked skating — he could get back into hockey.

"You gonna start the truck, Jan?" Will grumbled.

"Yeah, sorry man, just thinking about—"

"Paris. Yeah, got that. Man are you in. I kinda feel sorry for the poor girl," Will muttered. "She has no idea what you're like."

David started the truck and let it warm up. "What I'm like?"

"You're like a dog with a bone. I hope she likes that about you, because you do not give up what you got. I bet you have things from when you were a kid still."

"Sure, everyone does."

"Not everyone. You still have that shark tooth you broke off the tiger shark in Vietnam?"

"Of course, that was amazing. Who wouldn't keep it?"

"And the card from Sergeant Brown's wife? When you got him out of the jail down in Bisbee?"

"What's your point? I keep stuff."

"Paris isn't stuff, man, she isn't stuff."

No, she wasn't, she was... Much more than stuff. Maybe even worth more than all he'd saved up. "Yeah, I'm aware. For one, she won't fit in my back pocket like that note from Brown's lady, or on my neck like that tooth."

Will laughed and rubbed his hair. "Right, right, well, good to know, you got it all figured out then—good."

Like hell he wanted to say, but he pulled out and did a U-turn to head back down to the compound. Like hell, because even thinking of juggling this mission and time with Paris, and not freaking her out by demanding too much from her had him sweating. He needed to shower before he went near her, too. Maybe shower in the room, then coax her in with him...

"Just remember, we're not out of this yet. Mind on the mission. You heard Carson, you're to come in."

"I heard him. I'll think on whether to bring her or not."

Will grunted. "I'd keep her out of this. Two days, tops, we're done. Jansen," he added, "if she can't wait that long, then there's your sign she's not for you, man."

"She'd wait, but I'm not sure I want to. I'd be more settled with her close, where I know she's safe. If Martinez is here, Savage sent him, or he's also close by. I want her near so I can protect her."

After a minute or two of driving, Will nodded. "Yeah, that might be true. Those men have to come into town to get supplies. Women disappear all the time. Maybe closer is better, but if she's there for you, she's there for you, man. You got to get your head on straight, otherwise you're of no use to us. Half in is half a foot in the grave."

David exhaled, knowing what Will said was true, except Paris would wait for him, she'd be unhappy, he thought, but she'd do it. *Why make her unhappy? Worse, why endanger her by not being near her to keep her safe?*

"Yeah, I got your six, no worries," he said automatically.

Only he did have worries. What if this all went to shit and he couldn't reach Paris?

No cell phone. As thrilling as that was, he needed to set her up with something in case things did go south. First, he needed to bring her in. And that, he sensed, might be harder than getting in her bed to start with.

Chapter Eight

Paris took one look at David and giggled. Then covered her mouth. He had snow on his shoulders and head, more on his arms, and probably some on his back. He took a step toward her, and she jumped off the bed to the other side so it was between them.

"Stop right there, David Jansen. No way are you trailing all that wet cold snow —"

"Is that so?"

She tried to be stern, but got tackled to the bed, a big, wet, cold man on top of her grinning as if his football team had just won a winning touchdown.

"I can't believe you just did that!" But she could. And more, she liked it, the feel of his cold weight pressing her down and the long, hard cylinder of his erection letting her know he'd absolutely missed her.

David kissed her. He was cold and smelled like snow, and she couldn't get enough of him. It was sweet at first, but like every other time his lips met hers, it turned hot really, really fast. Surprising her, he pulled up and shook his head.

Confused, she tilted her head on the bed, examining his handsome face. He didn't say anything, not even when she tickled her fingers along his neck and into his damp hair.

"Uh-uh."

"No?"

"Nope. Not going there, princess. I have news," he tacked on, but he said it so gently her radar went off big time. "Now" — he lifted up and pulled her with him so she was standing. A little wet, a bit rumbled now, but for the most part dry — "I have to go in, and stay in, but only for a few days. The trouble is those guys."

"Those guys?" she asked, waiting for more.

"Yeah, those guys are terrorists. The kind that deal in women and guns. I want you with me, not here, where you might be the next victim of a human trafficking sicko."

Her eyes rounded out, she was certain.

David reached out and tipped her mouth closed with his finger, then winked.

"I'm serious, and I guess, judging by your stunned expression, I've said too much, but I want you to come with me. This should be over in a few days. I have an apartment, no one else has ever been in it," he added for some reason. "And no one will be but us. You can hang out with me, and if I have to go, I'll make sure you're secure."

"Go?"

"Yeah, we're waiting on some men, then we take this team down. Easy, really, but we've been there so we're lead."

"We?"

"Will and I," he clarified, then tugged her closer by her hands. "Paris, you okay? The one word thing is cute, but you can ask away. Anything, okay, I'll just help you pack."

"Oh, no, I don't think, I mean, go with you? Is this a military base?"

"No, not at all. It's run by a wealthy civilian, but right now, we're undercover doing some training for him." David winced. "I don't want you near him, either, but again, it will be two days, possibly three."

Two days. With him. Everything he said felt as if it was playing pinball in her brain. She watched movies, who didn't? And this was right out of one of those, only she wasn't a movie star and didn't want to be on the six o'clock news either. Suddenly her friend, the reason she was even here, popped into her head.

"Wait, is Sara safe?"

"Hell, I forgot. Will gave her a ride to town. She's safe—"

"Here? In the hotel? Why not—"

"I think her boyfriend pissed her off," David said way too fast. "She's fine, and willing to let us have a few days."

She covered her mouth again and blinked. "Oh my God, she's willing to let us have a few days?"

"Yeah."

The avalanche of information had her head spinning. She'd taken time off to come with Sara on this wild vacation, but...if Sara was alone now, was that okay? Worse, what if these bad men found her and hurt her? "David I need to talk to her. I mean, is she safe, here?"

"Yeah, of course." He paused, rubbed a hand over his face, then gripped her shoulders with both hands. "I will make sure of it, okay? I worry if we spotted these men, they might have gotten a glimpse of us, and worse, you. She was at the base, and Will drove her to the hotel near the garage, but didn't go in with her. There's no connection, you see? But you... I need you safe. Otherwise I'm going to be of no use to anyone." He finished with a great deal of heat.

She nodded, simply because he seemed to need her to agree. "I need to talk to Sara, though."

"But you'll come?" He squeezed her upper arms when she nodded again. "Good, that's good, princess. It'll be okay, and Will is cool, he won't try anything, you know, if you don't want."

"Will...? He won't... Oh my God! David! I can't go see him, after what we did, I mean, I did." Panic set in and she tried to back away, thinking of all the reasons why she couldn't go now that she'd said she would.

"He knows it's a hands-off situation now, or only my hands on. Don't get all upset. I can't think of a better story to tell than how we met." He pulled her in and hugged her as if he thought that would ease her mind.

"Oh my God."

He hugged her closer. "I'm kidding, I'm kidding. Now, come on, get dressed, we can have this sleepover at my place, huh?"

"It's kinda scary, David. What you're doing, it scares me."

"I won't be doing it much longer. Trust me." He kissed her on the temple. "I promise to make it all okay."

He said such things so easily. "Promises are meant to be kept, you know. You can't just throw them out there all the time."

"Didn't I do pretty good on that first one?" he murmured, his voice going low and deep like it did when he was turned on. Between them she could feel the hardness of his penis, getting harder by the second, too. He had more than fulfilled that first promise. But this was different. International gunrunners? Human traffickers? She was just an ice skater from Canada. What did she know of such things?

What did I know about ménage à trois before David Jansen? Or sex? Or, love, even? Trust him. Trust him.

She tilted her head and met his blue eyes. He seemed to be waiting on her, with a look in his eyes that made her wish and hope for much more than just a promise to make this okay. Slowly, she nodded, feeling as if she'd just jumped off a ledge into a pond instead of dipping her toe in first.

His smile was worth it, though.

"Good, that's good, princess. Now, come on, I'm horny as hell, and even though I swore to myself to hold off so you'd stop thinking I was just trying to get in those sexy panties, I can't wait much longer."

She laughed until tears came out, but she nodded, too, because she was just as horny as he was, or maybe not that much, considering the size of his growing erection. "Do we have time," she whispered, "for something here first?"

"Anything you want," he said in a husky voice. "Just whisper it in my ear, and it's done."

"Oh, God, that's sexy." In the end, she didn't have to whisper at all. David managed to take her breath away too fast for her to be able to anyway. But that was good, since he also made it all okay, before, during and after.

It wasn't until she was loaded into his truck, and they were pulling back in the entrance she'd driven through with Sara, that she realized she'd not once protested coming with him, up until he mentioned Will.

"You knew I'd come with you," she accused, feeling more than a bit as if he'd managed her. Not that it was a bad thing, but he was sneaky and very, very good at it, too.

He gave her a half smile and patted her knee. "I did hope, but no, I didn't know how hard you'd resist. Here, see that door?"

She followed where he pointed and saw that he'd parked along a wall. Near them she saw a small door beneath an awning. This was quite far from where she'd pulled in and dropped Sara off. The place had to be enormous.

"That leads right into the apartments where we are. That over there" — he pointed to a Jeep — "is in case you need to leave. I'm not saying you should, or that I want you to, but we always have a backup plan. That Jeep has keys on the runner above the right front tire. It has a full tank of gas. The plates are fake. That means untraceable."

A shiver ran along her arms, and she froze with her hands partway to her face. She'd felt such a thing before. Once. Right before her career as a skater had ended.

"David, why are you telling me this? I thought you'd be here, with me."

"I will be, but I never go with one plan, I always have three or more set up in case one goes to hell. Don't be scared, Paris. If you're scared, I can take you out of here, drive you to the next town over, or maybe two, and you can wait there."

"No way, no way. First, Sara, okay?"

"Yeah, I called Will, and he took her to a hotel two towns over. He'll check on her again, maybe tomorrow, okay?"

"He moved her from town?" She'd taken longer to get ready after their wild sex, but she hadn't known he'd called Will. Maybe cell phones were good. As if reading her mind, David pulled out an iPhone and handed it to her. "What's this?"

"It's your new phone. My number is in it, along with Will's. We'll get Sara's in there as well. If I need you, you pick up. I don't call to chat. I call if there's a problem. Or I'm maybe, I don't know, running late, okay?"

She nodded. He seemed worked up over this and she worried he was planning to take her two towns over instead of letting her stay here.

"David, let's go in, okay?"

"Yeah." He brushed her hair back gently from her face and sighed. "You remember where the key is?"

"Right front tire."

That seemed to ease some of his tension. "Good, that's good. Come on, it's late enough, maybe no one is up. The room is clean, too."

"Okay," she murmured, smiling.

"I mean, no bugs, coms," he added when she glanced around, her smile gone.

"You mean this place is...wired? Can they hear us now?"

"Nope, not out here. The garage and our apartments are all free of taps, too. Will has a room next door. No one else in on our floor. We made it secure. We're also bottom level, near the exit."

She shivered, feeling as if things were getting out of hand. "David," she whispered when he opened the door. He got out and turned to help her down. "Is this what you do?"

"It was. This is it, I promise. All done. I'm done with it all."

There wasn't anything to say to that, so she let him lock the truck and usher her inside, down the few feet to his door, and then inside. The place was empty, and clearly brand new. It even smelled like paint. He urged her farther inside and winked when she glanced at him. He'd made a little picnic-type area in the living room, complete with pillows, blankets and food. Tears rushed her eyes, but she sensed he'd not like that one bit, so she turned away and laughed.

"Oh my God, that is too cute," she managed, busying herself with her jacket and mittens. She could sense David coming up behind her and sighed when he hugged her from behind.

"It's okay, I know you're freaking out, and if you didn't, I'd be worried you were some super spy or assassin."

"What?" she laughed, turning in his arms to stare at him. He helped her with her jacket, then wrapped his arms around her waist.

"I know one, don't laugh, she kicks ass and takes numbers. Tiny like you, too, but not as pretty or as sweet," he added with a low laugh and a truly wicked intensity in his blue eyes. "How about we see if you can really play cards, huh? Maybe make some high-risk stakes, like… Strip poker? Or maybe the winner gets to see how sweet the other is?" He nudged her with his hips and his sexy lips curled up in a smile that was all male.

A rush of pinpricks shivered up her back. He meant oral sex. The winner got to…go down on the other? *Oh God. I love it when he does that, but would he like it if I tried?*

"Sounds like that's a yes," he murmured, walking her backward.

"I suck at poker," she said, feeling like she might be taking the bull by the...well, horn.

"Well," he said as if considering that. "We could switch that around then, how's that? The winner gets to lie back and let the loser see how sweet they are?"

She laughed, so caught by his humor and his dirty mind, she couldn't help it. The idea of giving David a blow job thrilled and scared her. His expression dared her though. He just looked so primed, and so sure she'd balk at that.

"Well, do we have to play or can a player forfeit?"

He sank onto the couch and took her with him. She landed right between his legs, on her knees. If he'd planned it, he was very, very good.

"Well, maybe we could have some pre-game fun, how's that?" He reached down and unbuckled his belt, watching her as he did. He got it open then worked first one button then the next one free. His erection angled its way up and out, the thick stalk so sexy she had to swallow past the lust she experienced at just the sight of him. He stopped and dragged his T-shirt over his head, revealing his chest muscles. The head of his cock sat dead center with his flat navel, an enticing peach shape she wanted in her mouth so badly that her mouth watered.

"David, I've..." She swallowed again and met his eyes. He was watching her as if he'd been waiting for her to look at him.

"Never done this."

She nodded and bit her lip nervously. "But I want to."

"Oh, princess, that's more than enough, believe me," he said with such relief in his voice that she giggled. "Not funny. A man isn't built like a woman, beautiful and hotter than hell. So hot he has to fight to keep his hands off her. This" — he pulled his erection all the way free and grimaced at the thick length as it settled against his toned abs — "isn't the nicest looking thing to put your mouth on."

She laughed, so caught off guard by his words she couldn't help it. Even when he tweaked her hair, she couldn't stop. "Oh God, that's not true. I...want to, I have been thinking about it, wondering, but..." She sighed and wiped at her tears. "I might suck at it. And not the way you want."

His face flushed, and if he wasn't a former Navy SEAL and a big, tough man, she would have said he was embarrassed. "You've been thinking about it?"

"Yes," she said honestly. "Since that first night."

"Last night."

"It seems like ages ago," she admitted.

He nodded and pulled her closer. "It does. Like I've always known you, but then, not. I want to know stuff like this, you wanting to suck my cock, that's the kind of thing a man wants to know, Paris."

She nodded, reaching down when she did to touch him. He was such a man — so much more comfortable, she thought, in his own wants and desires. Maybe it hadn't been her all along with Greg, but him. Maybe he'd had hang-ups. He'd certainly never walked around naked, or made her a picnic on the floor when it was snowing out.

"I also like touching you, especially here." She closed her fingers around his velvety warm skin, getting a thrill when her fingers didn't touch.

He groaned and covered her hand with his. "I was so damn jealous of you touching Will."

"You were?" she demanded, shocked enough to stop smoothing her hand up and down his erection.

He nodded. "I know, it's stupid, since I pushed you into last night, and it was hot, man was it hot, but yeah, I wanted you all to myself. Maybe next time with Will I'll be better—"

"Oh no, no next time. I only wanted you," she whispered. "I really only registered you. Is that mean?"

He drew his eyebrows down, but shook his head as he lifted her up to kiss her. He had such a great nose. Whenever he kissed her, he breathed against her, heating her face lightly. She wanted to memorize every line of his face, every expression, in case she only had this time, right now, with him. She couldn't help but touch his bristled jaw and surrender to his kiss.

"Hell no, that's fucking perfect, sorry, I mean, that's—"

"Good, now, where do I start? Here?" she asked, sliding downward to place kisses along his chest, then one at the tip of his penis. It felt like warm satin against her lips, surprising her. David groaned heavily, so she guessed that was a good way to begin. She stroked upward, moving the super thin foreskin up and down. He groaned again and spread his knees wider.

"Take your T-shirt off, Paris. I want to watch your breasts *and* you while you blow my mind, sucking my cock in that pretty mouth."

Sucking my cock. The roughness of his words, plus the dirty meaning, exploded along her body, turning her into someone bold, sexy and in control.

She sat back on her knees and pulled her shirt over her head, leaving her lacy bra on for now. She knew it pillowed her breasts upward and tantalized him. This morning in the truck he'd gotten a hard-on just watching her bending over to get her jacket off.

Now, David's face flushed and he spread his legs even wider, and shoved his pants farther down, giving her more room and releasing his heavy balls, too. God he reminded her of a sexy barbarian sitting like that. All man, to the point that in just staring at him, she tingled all over. If she wanted to, she could have stood, gotten naked and mounted him without a complaint from him. But this, on her knees, with him eagerly guiding his big cock down at an angle for her, wasn't an experience she was letting pass her by. When this was all over, if it ended in a few days, she wanted every moment to count.

For both of us.

She leaned on his thigh with one hand and took hold of his big cock in the other. Then, when she knew he was watching, she kissed along the underside, memorizing the size and texture of every inch of him, along with the way his expression tightened when she reached the heavy sac.

"Oh, Jesus, yes," he sighed when she licked the thin skin there and traced the puckered skin between the two balls. He smelled like a mixture of male musk and the strong scent of soap he'd used in the shower. She kissed then licked along the tightening line along his balls. He shifted with a heavy groan. It was exciting, but sucking was what she wanted. Him, in her mouth, and as much as possible. There were ways to take a man deep, she knew, but more from girl talk than experience. Greg hadn't really liked her going down on him and so she hadn't. But she knew there wouldn't be so many jokes about deep throat and so on if men didn't really, really want that.

Those jokes might not have considered a man built like David, but she was going to do her best.

She licked back up the groove on the underside of his cock, which made him groan heavily and flex his thighs. When she reached the head, she pulled the stalk down and sat up taller. She sucked the musky taste of him past her lips, then sank her mouth down, opening wider to try and fit him in and still be able to suck gently.

"Jesus H. Christ, Paris."

He was hard, big, and she couldn't take him all. Not the first time. She pulled up then, with a gasp for necessary oxygen, slid his cock back deeper.

It was addictive. So were his low moans and the way his grip tightened on the couch.

She managed more each time, and each time she got him wetter, so he was easier to handle. David groaned steadily, massaging her shoulder then her head then her shoulder as if he couldn't stop. She rose up slowly the next time and stroked along his cock with her hand, smoothing the moisture, then drove her mouth back down, twisting her head when she did so she could get him past her gag reflex. It was amazing, and it worked. He slipped deeper, a bit uncomfortable, but worth it.

"Sweet Mary, mother of God, woman!" David yelled. His thighs tightened to steel around her and his hand landed heavily on her head. "Paris, you're an angel, a fucking angel, you're killing me here."

She took encouragement from that response and stroked up his cock with her hand and slipped him free from her mouth. She gasped for air then did it again.

"Jesus, Jesus, Paris."

Each time she managed more and more. Each time, David shouted, growing more and more aroused. On her third pass he stiffened and pulled her up.

Breathless, he nodded urgently and cupped her hand around his cock, then urged her mouth back on him with a grip that trembled.

"There, there, princess, do that," he demanded, thrusting his cock in and out of her mouth in shallow passes. It was so hot she had to squeeze her legs together to ease the ache in her empty pussy.

David sounded out of his mind with how close he was to coming. She concentrated on short, tight sucks, making sure to get the sensitive spot under his flared hood with her lips and hand. She also reached down with her other hand and whispered her fingers over his tight sac.

"Paris, ah hell, Jesus and Mary!" The first burst of cum filled her mouth, but the second and third went so deep she didn't have to swallow, merely hold on as David shuddered through an intense orgasm. "Ah, God!"

When he fell back with another groan, this one softer, she slipped him free and kissed the rosy tip again.

"Ah, sensitive, sensitive, princess," he whispered, grabbing for her hand. Another spill of creamy fluid dripped from his cock.

Watching him, and feeling as if she'd just done very, very well for her first go-round, she licked along the drip and sucked him right back inside her mouth.

He winced but bit his bottom lip, clearly liking what she was doing. "Paris."

She leaned back and let him slip free.

"You have to do that again, often, okay? I mean, that was life changing. That was your first time?" he asked breathlessly, pulling her up to press kisses all over her face and neck.

She nodded, more pleased than she could explain that she'd done so well with her bad boy.

He leaned his head back and groaned. "I'm ruined. Absolutely ruined."

If she laughed hard, it wasn't her fault, besides, David joined her then, of course, tackled her to the picnic blanket and made a meal out of her, before he let her do the same to him again.

Chapter Nine

David played with Paris' blonde hair as she laughed into the iPhone.

They'd spent the night on the floor, or most of it. He'd lifted her up, still sleeping, and carried her to bed around ten, but she'd stayed that way and he'd had the pleasure of falling down on the bed and gathering her into his arms. He'd woken the same way. He could get used to that.

"I'm just glad you're safe," she said. "But why did you take a bus home? I don't understand that part." She glanced at him, turning rosy with a blush. "I mean, I wasn't ready to go, but you could have waited."

He was puzzled by that as well, but when Paris got off the phone, he'd ask her what was up. She seemed upset, but more embarrassed than worried for her friend. He was concerned though. Maybe her boyfriend and the drug had bothered her more than Will had recognized.

Paris laughed and covered her face with one hand. He guessed Sara was teasing her and couldn't resist kissing the warm softness of Paris' cheek. He'd left another mark on her neck, but she'd left an amazing one on his, so he was kind of proud of the strawberry.

Now if only this mission would be over, all would be good. As if on cue, his phone vibrated and he checked the caller ID. Will.

URGENT was scrolled in capitals on the screen.

"Paris," he said quietly.

She glanced at him, and seemed to read him fairly well. Not surprising, since he'd spent every waking and sleeping moment with her since he'd run to her rescue.

"Well, fine, that's good," she said into the phone, nodding to him. "I have to go. I have plans, you know, so I'll talk to you soon, okay?" She listened for a few seconds more, then hung up. "She sounds...odd. I mean, why would she go home? Are you sure Will drove her to the hotel and she got in and registered?"

"Will said she was safe, maybe she didn't want to interrupt us. Will did tell her about us, so maybe she was being thoughtful," he assured her. Paris frowned but let him tuck her hair behind her ear.

"I don't know. I mean, she left her car."

He frowned. That did bother him, but he assumed that meant she'd thought Paris could use it to drive home. The phone buzzed again and he pushed his concern aside for now. "Sorry, but Will is on his way over."

"Okay," she said, and he pulled her closer. She was practically on his lap already, but he wanted her to feel secure. She wiggled her gorgeous ass, giving him ideas for later, until she was comfortable, then said, "I'm okay. It's okay. I have her number now."

"Okay," he teased, earning a swift kiss, not a cute swat for once.

He had to admit, to himself at least, that the feminine crap about not hitting guys because that showed violence was acceptable was a load of bologna. He would never lay a hand on a woman, no matter how many times she hit him. And Paris hitting him was like a butterfly winging too close. Every time she swatted him, he got a little love drunk on her. Crazy, but maybe that was the way these things went.

He kissed her fingers. "You hungry?"

She smiled. "No, and not tired. I don't need a walk, or have to pee either."

"I get that maybe I've been overbearing, but come on, I don't treat you like a puppy or a child."

"A puppy no, but a baby, almost," she teased, then leaned in close to whisper, "Unless I'm, you know, doing adult things, like sucking your cock until you're saying your Hail Marys."

God damn, that was hot. Was it possible that he'd not only met a sweet, wholesome woman who didn't like cell phones and matched him in bed, but also liked sucking his cock as much as he liked her doing it?

He tugged her blonde hair, probably the equivalent of her hitting him. "Brat, every time you say that, I want it, immediately if not sooner, and now we're having Will over."

"What? No way, it's my turn, remember?"

A knock, followed by Will popping his head in, dragged David's attention off her soft, amazing mouth. He sat back and grinned at her. It was her turn, but he loved that as much. She always made such soft, passionate sounds and the way she tightened her legs around his head was dynamite. Some men didn't get going down on a woman, but for him, it was a rock-hard turn on. With Paris it was off the charts hot. He'd stroked off more times while he'd been driving her wild than he ever had with anyone else in his life. They'd watched a movie today and explored the woods near the compound, once Will had said it was safe. He'd also shown Paris a few more things to do on a hike than merely walking.

"David," she whispered, sounding embarrassed. "Behave."

He focused on her blush and not the clear memory of her hugging a pillow to her face just this morning while he brought her to orgasm with his lips.

"Believe me," he murmured, and shifted her to hide his hard-on. "I am."

She tucked her hands on her lap and ignored him, looking pretty innocent except for her blush.

"Hey, Paris, Jansen, sorry to interrupt," Will said uncomfortably.

"Hi, Will, you aren't interrupting." Paris stood, giving Will a quick hug.

David narrowed his eyes and pulled her back down. "Yeah, you were. What's up?"

She gave him a frown. "We were not busy." Her blush brightened at the hard wedge he had her hiding.

Will folded his arms over his chest and took on a stance that meant trouble. David gritted his teeth, sure now that his buddy was going to say something he wouldn't like.

"There's a situation."

David tightened his arms around Paris, then realized it and loosened his hold before he hurt her.

"I think we'd best talk outside, or in my room," Will added, meeting his eyes.

David shook his head even before he felt Paris stiffen. "Nope, not happening. What is it?"

Will gave him a hard stare as if he'd lost his mind then ran his hand over his buzz cut when that got him nothing.

"Maybe I should go—"

"No, you're staying." David pulled her firmly down. "This affects you. I won't lie to you. And I'm not about to hold back what's going on now. What is it?"

"Duke set up a room for us and..." Will paused, then added, "Our friend."

"Who is Duke?" Paris whispered, threading their fingers together.

"He what?" David asked. "How did he know she was even here? These rooms are secure."

"He knows, man, he doesn't bug this room, but there are cameras at the gate you drove through. The guards suck but they logged you in, with a friend."

"Just tell him thanks, but no thanks," David growled.

"It's not that easy," Will muttered. "If it was, I'd not be here. It's either take the drug and go off with one of his matches or—"

"His drug?" Paris made to move off him again and he stopped her by being bigger and stronger. "David Jansen—"

"Just calm down, Paris. There's no taking the drug, Will."

"Jansen, this shit is serious. If we don't do this, we need a reason. And fast."

"Just let me think," David muttered. "Paris, trust me, okay? We're here on a mission. I told you that already. We're here to take this man down, but he's not dangerous to you."

Her eyes rounded a little, but she bit her lip and nodded, cute as hell.

"Jansen's right, he's not dangerous to you," Will assured her. "If you want, we can send you off, which, Jan, might be the way to fucking go with this shit."

"Watch the language," David growled.

Paris squeezed his fingers and whispered a kiss to his jaw, her way of indicating all was okay, but he waited until Will's eyebrows lowered from his hairline and nodded.

"Right, sorry about that, Paris," Will murmured.

David relaxed—somewhat.

"As long as he believes we're two highly trained special operatives here to get his men in shape, he's on our side," Will added. "But he makes a drug that I don't want in my system. And if we don't do this, that's exactly what I'll end up having to do. *We'll* end up having to do."

Shit. Will was right. If Duke was pushing this, he'd begin to wonder why they weren't all over it. The mission could go down at any time now, if they blew this now it could go on for months more. Maybe longer.

Paris was too quiet, but he could tell she was waiting on him to say something. *But what?* The truth, he guessed with a sinking feeling in his gut.

"What Will means is the man makes a sex drug, kinda like Ecstasy, but a hundred times more powerful because it screws with a person's DNA. It's supposed to make a couple, like tight, in almost every way, but it's also marketable as a rape drug, you know what that is?"

She nodded, mute and wide-eyed.

"And that's another part of this mission. We're here to make certain that drug never reaches the market." He wasn't sure if telling her all this was the right thing to do, but he wasn't backing down now. If Will was right, though, he couldn't let his buddy shove some sex drug down his gut so he could perform with a stranger. He sure as hell wasn't doing it and chancing harming Paris. He'd already had problems with Chung's cocktail. Who knew what Duke's modifications would do to him?

"What would this do to you if you took it?" Paris asked the same question he was thinking about.

"Duke got his hands on a drug we'd piloted. It was supposed to make a better soldier." He laughed without much humor. "It did that, but a hell of a lot more. It screwed with us. I got anxiety and headaches. Will and a few others suffered from a dose of sexual drive that couldn't be tamed," he offered when Will nodded, unhappy as hell. "That drug is off the shelf and the formula, we thought, destroyed. Duke got hold of it, and modified it."

"You took this...drug?" she asked, worry clouding her gray eyes.

"Not Duke's, no," he assured her. "The other." He shrugged and squeezed her hand gently. "Yeah, it seemed like the thing to do at the time. But there's no way Will can take Duke's modified version. And I sure the hell don't want to take it and chance who knows what with you, and I'm not making love to anyone else either." He added the last so forcefully she blinked. Then, surprising him, she leaned into him and kissed his cheek tenderly.

"Good, I don't want you to. If it's still in the trial form, it might do horrible things to you. Both of you," she added quietly. "What can I do to help?"

At her words, Will relaxed. Hell, even David took a deep breath. She was clearly worried about him and Will. *Golden. She was golden.*

He kissed her temple and met Will's eyes. "You're certain there's no getting out of this?"

Will shook his head once. "I'd not be here if there was."

True. David firmed his resolve and lifted Paris up and turned her so she stood before him. She was so beautiful. He took her arms and stroked down them to hold her hands. Even her wrist bones were tiny. *Fragile.*

And we're going to share her, for an audience, no doubt. Maybe she was better off never meeting me, but I can't let her go now.

"You want me to...do this? Pretend you are both on the drug, with me, and we're...together. Like the first night?"

He nodded.

Will cursed softly. "Paris, it's not that easy. He'll want to see, there will be cameras."

David hung his head, cursing softly at the shock on Paris' pretty face. "I should have taken you away from this."

She didn't say anything but she reached out and hugged his head to her chest. "No, you shouldn't have. I would have missed you and worried until you showed back up. Besides, didn't you say you wanted to try public sex?"

"He said what?" Will cried, then cursed some more. "Paris, I swear if there was any other way out of this—"

"I know, you'd do it. Both of you would," she said with a little squeeze to his head. "Now, stop being scared, because that is my job, and start being heroes, that's your job. We can do this. I can do this, but only if you two keep up at least the appearance of being big, strong and soldiery, okay?"

David laughed and finally pulled away to meet her eyes. She was smiling but the fear was there, darkening the gray to blue. He loved her so much in that moment that the goddamn words nearly spilled from his mouth. He tightened his hands on her slender arms.

"We can do that. Hell, I'm even good at it. You? Will? Feeling big, strong and soldiery?"

Will didn't say a word for a full minute, just hung his head and exhaled. Finally he met their eyes again. "I'm always big and strong. Soldiery you might have to explain, Paris."

She laughed, but it was quiet, and didn't really reach her eyes.

"We get through this, and I promise, it will soon be over, then we can see how many more wild things you can do to me, okay?" David teased.

She hugged him, for some reason, as tightly as her small arms could, he thought. He stroked her back, not sure if what he'd said was good or bad. After a minute or so, she turned her head and whispered in his ear, "You'd better keep that promise, David Jansen."

* * * *

The room wasn't just a room, it was a sex shop, complete with silk scarves and a floor- to-ceiling mirror that David knew let everyone walking by get a full view of whatever they did. There were even a few couches and chairs meant to give enough room for a couple — or more people — to have sex.

He hated it immediately.

Will tipped his head and rubbed his buzz cut, but David could see his hard-on outlined under his BDUs.

David tried ease his jealousy, and managed it fairly well, he thought, until Paris rubbed his arm.

"We have to do this," she whispered in his ear. "So looking like you want to kill your friend is not helping him, is it?"

David scrubbed his face with his hand then nodded. Will let out a long, pent-up breath and seemed to relax. No doubt, his buddy was dealing with more of the side effects left over from the drug in his system. It came and went, he'd once said. David still got headaches, so he guessed it was the same for Will and his cock.

Paris kissed him on the jaw, running her fingers over his chest after. "I'm scared."

She spoke so low he had trouble hearing her, but he did. She got his full attention, though, and he saw it there, in her eyes.

"Don't be, princess. Just be you. I have a feeling this is going to be fun, how about that? Ever been tied up, you know" — he nodded to the scarves on the wall — "with silk?"

Will took one long black one down and trailed it through his hand, giving Paris a grin. She shook her head but turned to David for what to do.

"Just let me see you burn, okay? Nice, hot and sexy," he whispered, taking her black dress and pressing it down off her shoulders. It went slowly, revealing inch after inch of her. By the time she used his shoulder to steady herself and step out of it, his cock was leaking a steady stream of pre-cum.

She was naked underneath. The dress wasn't hers, but one of Sara's she'd left behind. The dress turned Paris into some sexy model from New York, but naked, with the glow of oil he'd massaged into her skin after their shower, she stunned him even more.

"God damn, you're gorgeous, Paris," Will murmured, clearly impressed. The hotel had been dim, so David got that. Paris dazzled under the room's lights. "You're one lucky bastard," he added.

She smiled and turned, giving him permission to tie her hands behind her back. She watched David while Will tied her, her eyes so light blue they were like chips of the sky.

"Jesus, Paris, you're more than gorgeous," David whispered and tugged his shirt off, then ditched his boots and pants right after. Her breasts were high and jutted up for his mouth with her hands behind her back like this. Both nipples were hard, and he could tell she was aroused from the blush that stained her pretty face.

Will stood back, undressing a bit slower, no doubt giving him time to settle Paris.

David didn't waste the moment, he kissed her, igniting her that quickly. She was already breathless, but at his kiss, she moaned into his mouth, but when he lifted from her lips, she whispered, "Do you think anyone is watching?"

The worry in her tone made him madder than hell, but he hid it, or tried to and carefully caressed her cheek. "It's just me. Concentrate on me, and I'll make you come so many times, you might insist on this from now on."

She laughed, then sucked in a shocked breath when he stroked down her lean stomach and lightly brushed his fingers over her bare mound, then gently circled her clit. "Oh, David," she whispered, leaning her head on his chest.

"I'm on fire here, princess," he warned her. "If anyone is watching, let's give them a real show."

"Because of the public sex?" she asked, then surprised him by nipping at his jaw. "Or me all helpless and tied up?"

He laughed, hearing Will chuckle, too. "Yeah, you helpless, beautiful and at my mercy." But that wasn't really it. It was her. She did this to him. Paris. "Now, how about you go to your knees and let me try something new?"

Her cheeks turned rosy, and he urged her down, watching so she didn't hurt herself as he helped her. She smiled as he brushed a kiss over her cheek. "Damn you're sexy when you follow orders."

"David Jansen," she whispered, clearly embarrassed.

He held off teasing her any more. He stepped back and admired the view of her on her knees, impressed again with just how stunning she was. He made her wait a little, sensing she was shedding her fears and getting hot over what they were doing. She met his eyes, daring him to stay away, not that he needed the encouragement. He wasn't going to be able to keep his hands off her for too much longer. For some insane reason, ever since she'd so completely got how badly they needed her, he'd been on fire for her.

She seemed to sense it, and matched him with an arousal he could see made her shiver every few seconds simply from him watching her.

Biting her lip, she shifted her legs, no doubt trying to ease the ache between her thighs.

"That's it, get hot for us This is going to be fast, but, baby, we're going to turn you inside and out," he warned, bending over to kiss her pink lips.

She shivered once again, especially when he straightened and urged her head up with a grip on her hair. When she lifted it, Will walked over, his cock out and ready for her.

"First, suck his cock. Give him that amazing mouth of yours while I give you something else to think about."

Her breasts quivered on her deep exhalation. She'd been holding her breath, he knew, and the message that sent had his cock pulsing for her. No doubt her pussy was soaking wet, more than ready for him, and they'd just started. He crouched behind her and speared his erection between her legs so he could make certain she liked his orders. He smiled and bit down on her earlobe, then smoothed his hands possessively over her breasts.

"Paris, did you hear me? Suck his cock, princess. It's big, but you can handle that, can't you?"

She moaned and pushed back along his body. He positioned himself, but waited. When she opened her lips, Will took hold of the massive hard-on he was sporting and filled her mouth, then withdrew, urging her to keep her lips open, and did it again. David let her taste Will for a few seconds then thrust his hips. He glided inside her easier than he ever had before.

"Ah, fuck, yes, she's wet and loving it. Don't stop, Will," he added.

Will gritted his teeth until his jaw bulged, but rested one hand on her head and with the other he gripped himself so he could feed her shallow thrusts.

David did the opposite.

She was primed, so ready to climax that he knew she wanted something more from him. He'd never fucked her like this, but at the first hard pass, then the next, he could tell she loved it.

Will groaned and threw his head back, a clear sign he wasn't going to last either.

It wasn't Will, or the idea anyone could see them, or the sharing, it was Paris. *Warm, sweet Paris. She loves me. She has to. Why else do this, help us like she is, if it wasn't because of the same thing I feel each time I touch her, or look at her?*

He drove into her harder. Sweat poured down his ribs and back, slicking his skin as he brushed along hers. Will groaned breathlessly, clearly nearing the end. Between them, Paris knelt, delicate, beautiful Paris, giving them more of herself than any woman ever had. David only hoped he could earn every ounce of her love, because he couldn't image losing her.

He quickened his pace as he felt his climax growing closer. She trembled, and pulled free of Will, then with a soft gasp he felt her tighten on him, coming so hard he had to follow her or be unable to move from the grip of her pussy. He threw his head back and shoved his hips upward and his cock deep for her. Along his erection she clenched harder, clearly lost in a powerful orgasm.

Will groaned, and David knew he was climaxing along with them. It was good, so good, in fact, he wasn't willing to let it end. This was supposed to be for show, but finally, finally he got it. *Got her.*

He loved her. It didn't matter that he'd known her for only three days. There wasn't a chance he'd let her go now. She tipped her head back and gazed into his eyes, and he knew she didn't want him to.

More confident now, he caressed her upper arms and kissed the curve of her neck where it met her delicate throat. Tonight he'd show her just how wild they could get and hopefully make every dream she had come true. At least in the bedroom. Later, once they were alone, he'd start ensuring all those other dreams were reality too.

* * * *

Paris woke with a wince. Someone must have forgotten to tell her she'd be tender from the top of her head to the bottom of her feet this morning. Or whenever this was, she thought, opening one eye and frowning. It wasn't daylight, so what woke her?

"Paris, wake up."

She groaned. "David, I'm—"

"Thank God, I've been trying to get you up for five minutes."

"You have?" She rolled over.

"Princess, as much as I want to let you sleep, I have to go. We got the call—Will and I have to go. You have to stay here, but when we're through, we're getting out of Dodge."

That woke her like nothing else could have. He might as well have shouted 'fire'.

"Ouch!" she cried when she sat up too quickly. There were very, very sore parts of her. She blamed the man even now hovering over her.

"I'm sorry, princess. We got carried away, huh?"

She grumbled but really, she had no business grumbling. She'd loved every minute of it. She'd thought, at one point, in the middle of David's hundredth—*possibly*—orgasm, that she'd seen something wonderful in his eyes. Love, maybe.

"Where are you going?"

"The men," he rushed to say. "The men on the mountain. We'll be back in a flash, but we have to go." He kissed her.

She gripped his hand and held him in place. "Wait, wait, wait." She used his arm to get to her feet, winced again at the tug on *very* overused muscles and faced him.

She wore his T-shirt.

He was completely dressed. Fatigues, gun, winter gear and a pack.

He was ready for war.

"Oh God." She hugged him, but froze when alarms went off. A wire hanging around his neck buzzed and he lifted something on the end of it to his ear. His eyes widened and he grabbed her hand and dragged her to the bathroom.

"I got that. Copy. Ten. Give me ten." He paused, caught her eyes and grimaced again. "Five, I need five."

She covered her mouth with her fingers and waited.

"Copy. Five." His face turned hard and he pulled the earbud from his ear. "Princess, I have five minutes. Those alarms are our guys. I have to go out and meet them, then hit those bast — guys in the hills. This place is going down, but so is the other. I have to go. I promise you" — he gripped her arms, kissed her once then continued — "I will be back. This will all be okay. I promise."

She nodded, too stunned to do much more.

"Remember the Jeep, remember the phone. If it gets bad here, you go to town. Wait, there, I will call."

She nodded again, and he blurred. Shocked, she realized she was crying. "David, please, don't go, I feel, I mean, I think something will go wrong." Her skin prickled with warning and her leg ached from the memory of the last time she'd ignored her gut.

"Princess, nothing is going wrong. Nothing, okay? Now, let's get you dressed. Do it, now, but kiss me once more before I go win this war. I'm being all soldierly, right?"

She choked on a laugh, but hugged him tightly. He kissed her then disengaged, scowling when he did.

Something buzzed and he swore, then kissed her once more and turned and walked away. She felt like he'd just thrown her to the wolves.

Instead of freaking out, which she knew he expected, she sniffed back the tears. He was still gone, and worse, she was cold and alone. The alarms blared again, and she got busy.

First she dressed, then washed her face and brushed her teeth, then packed. She even packed his things, then straightened up the apartment. It felt as if the place was deserted now that he was gone, but she cleaned up and finally turned in a circle. The phone he'd given her caught her eye, but she didn't go to it. He was busy. Being a soldier. He'd be back.

* * * *

David stared down at the mess of the camp and cussed until Will came on the com and told him to calm his shit.

"I can see you blowing a gasket, what's wrong?"

"I hurt my damn leg," he muttered. Not happy about it, but too worried about Paris to be macho and lie.

"Same leg as Afghan?"

"What other leg would it be?" he griped. "I'll need a medevac and you need to go check on Paris."

"I'll be there in ten. Let me close this down, hold tight."

David pulled out his cell phone, turned it on, and against all regulations he called Paris. By the sixth ring he knew something was wrong. He pulled up Carson's number and dialed it.

"What the hell are you doing calling me on your cell phone during a mission?"

"I need you to send in men to check on Paris."

"You're talking to me on a mission to — ?"

"Sir, if you don't send men in right now to check on her, I'll not only blow the rest of this mission, I'll come and shoot you in the goddamn leg for pissing me off."

Silence, then a low chuckle. "Jansen, glad to see you finally grew the hell up. I'll have someone check on her. She's in your quarters?"

"Yes, she's there, and not answering her phone."

"Hold tight."

With that damn statement, Carson hung up. David waited ten minutes, got his leg under him and limped over to pick up a tree branch to help him down the slope. He'd done his job. They could damn well do the rest. Martinez was dead, David's bullet in his brain. He only wished Savage was here so he could do the same to that bastard. At the thought of him, David stumbled. What if Savage was at Duke's even now? What if he had — ?

"Jansen, what the hell are you doing?" Will demanded over the com.

"I can make it down on my goddamn own," he growled, firming the stick under his arm.

"Like hell you can, I'm on my way. There's a medical team coming in on a copter, hold your position or they won't — "

A sound to his left caught David off guard and, with the leg, too slow to react. He misstepped and for a split second considered that staying put would have been wiser, then the impact of a bullet winged his arm and he dropped like a stone down the edge of the bluff. The landing was hard enough to knock the wind out of him, then his head connected with the frozen ground and the world went all kinds of crazy on him.

Paris, just stay put. If she doesn't, how the hell can I make up for not saying I love her before this shit hit the fan?

Chapter Ten

Paris twisted her sweatshirt sleeve and paced the room. David still wasn't back. In the movies these things went by really fast. This wasn't the movies, though. Tears kept building up as her fear for him grew.

Suddenly, without knocking, two men opened the door, glanced at her, at their clipboard, then stepped inside.

"Who are you? Are you on the list?"

List? She shook her head, unsure what to say. If they were military, they didn't dress like David. One was wearing a suit, the other a sporty green golf shirt and jeans. They shared a look she didn't like because it was clear they thought she was here to entertain David, and not because they were dating either. *Are we dating?*

"Come with us, then," the suit said.

"Where?"

"We'll brief you when it's your turn," he responded, harshly, as if she'd done something criminal. She glanced at the phone, but it was too far to reach.

"Let me get my things." She edged toward the phone.

"Not necessary. Just please come with us, miss," the jeans and sporty shirt said. He waved to the door as if she was going to go in the wrong direction and waited for her.

David, now would be a good time. Now. In the movies these things are fast.

Less than ten minutes later, she was seated in an area with ten other women, some of them crying, others simply staring into space as if they were absent from their bodies. A dozen men were gathered at the other end of the room, checking out the women, and once in a while reading something on a chart then zeroing in on one woman for a while.

She waited twenty minutes and couldn't stand it a minute more. She stood and instantly two men walked over.

"I have to pee." She had David to thank for helping her out of that little shyness.

The men frowned.

No way was she sitting back down. "It's that time of month and I need a new tampon."

That got them both stepping back, and one frantically glancing down at her hips as if she'd start pooling blood.

"The bathroom's in there." He gestured.

She walked calmly to where he'd pointed, opened the door, went in, and locked it behind her. There was a window, and they were on the ground floor.

The Jeep has to still be out there, please, please, please.

She washed her hands, for some insane reason feeling dirty from just being near those men. The window opened easily enough. With just a little push, the screen came off. She was out and in the snow before two minutes had passed. She checked her watch, still only three hours or less since David had left. She glanced around and no one was near, but she had no jacket on and no idea where she was. She had money, but no phone, no purse, no wallet, since yeah, she'd lost that before this trip had even started. She didn't have Sara's or David's numbers memorized. Now what? She couldn't walk to town. She couldn't go back to his apartment.

The two men who had picked her up had walked down the hall away from the exit she knew, then turned…but which way did that mean for the Jeep? She spotted no cameras and took a chance and ran for the corner. There, across from her, was the Jeep. No one was around, not even a dog. There hadn't been that night either, but this was a raid or something like that. In the distances she could make out voices, and loud trucks. She'd have to drive the Jeep out of here unless she hid in it. But with no jacket…

I won't get anything if I don't try.

Instead of running, she walked as if she had every right in the world being here. She reached the side of the Jeep without an alarm going off, but she could hear men shouting and trucks moving around closer to her. The key was where she'd been told, and she used it to open the door. She thought about her phone, but knew the chances of sneaking back in, getting it and coming out were slim. She got in and, fingers trembling, started the Jeep.

Five minutes later she drove out of the compound and didn't look back. There was no shout, or reaction to her leaving, so she tried to calm her breathing, but eventually she pulled over and off the road, hid the Jeep and jumped down to vomit on the ground.

She was still shaking when she drove into town and parked in front of the hotel she'd stayed at last time. They still remembered her, and let her pay in cash again.

She cried herself sick that night, so worried and confused she couldn't think straight. The next and the next day were the same. Every morning she thought this would be the day, he'd show up now. She even called her uncle and told him she'd be a few days late. She'd hoped Sara might have called, or even come home, but he'd not said a word, and she couldn't ask.

"Sugar, you sure you're okay? You sound rough. Have you caught a cold?"

"No, I'm fine, it's just a few more days. The kids won't mind."

"No," he laughed. "They won't and I'm fine. You have some fun."

Fun. She covered her mouth so he'd not hear her painful sob.

"Take a week, I'll call the rink. I'm sure those kids are all out building snowmen by now anyways."

"Right, okay, thank you, Uncle, I appreciate it."

"You just have some fun. I'll see you when you get here."

His voice had made it worse somehow. The one person she could always count on to tell it to her straight. She didn't even have the nerve to tell him that she'd met someone, but he'd...disappeared. It was easier to think of that, than to think of him being dead.

She called the hospital and asked if a David Jansen had been admitted, but was told no, so she called two more hospitals. She looked up bases nearby, since he'd said he used to be a SEAL, but she couldn't figure out how to find him in the confusing websites.

After the third day, she took the Jeep back up the mountain, scared, but unable not to go. There were new, ten foot tall wooden gates on the place, and an enormous lock on them. She got out and took a deep breath, releasing it after without crying. If he was okay, he was gone. If he wasn't... She brushed a tear off her face and thought of all the wonderful things about David Jansen—his smile, his easy humor and the way he'd been so thoughtful and sexy. Right there was where she'd turned and met his lazy blue stare. He'd been half smiling, something she knew he did on those rare occasions when he was unsure.

SEAL. You were in the SEALs. But how do I find out if you're still alive, if I don't know where you live?

She walked up to the tree she'd parked near. This was where Sara's Honda had died. Surely he'd show up again, just like before.

Unless he's hurt, or worse, dead.

Or he'd been sent out on another mission and what they'd shared was over because that was all there was. *Just fun for a weekend.*

No, I can't believe that. It was more.

* * * *

"What the hell do you mean you can't find her?" David asked. His hand shook, making the grip he had on the phone shake the whole damn thing, but he held on, listening to Will's lame excuses. Five days he'd been out. Five days and she was gone without a trace. How was that even possible?

"She's not at the compound. I'm checking on it. How far can she get?" Will said.

Pretty damn far. "I tried her cell phone."

"Affirmative. So did I," Will clarified. "Again, don't worry, I'll find her."

"Sir." A nurse dressed in scrubs came up to his gurney. "We have to get you prepped for surgery."

"Just wait," he muttered, and held off her demands long enough to focus on the biggest issue here. Finding Paris. "I want her safe, Will. Sound and secure. Find her. Something had to happen—"

"Or this life is too hard on good girls, Jan. Think about what you were asking of her. You were shot, that bullet had to come out, and you hit your head pretty damn hard. We shut down Duke's. She was not there. But—" He exhaled again and the background static calmed down enough for David to hear men talking near Will. "I found her phone, on a table in the apartment. Maybe she just left."

David's head felt as if it was going to explode from the stress he was putting on it. But he pulled himself up to a sitting position. He even managed to hold the nurse back with one arm and his side with the other. The phone he cradled between his ear and his shoulder. "I know damn good and well she didn't just leave. I made a promise. A promise is meant to be kept, Will. She wouldn't have simply left because I was hurt. She had no idea I'd *been* hurt, and even if she had known, she wouldn't have left me over it. Shit, buddy, think. There were more jackals out there then we knew, someone could have gotten hold of her. Whatever, I'm not talking when you're being too damn dense to get it. Get a car here for me, the leg can wait, I want to check the goddamn compound myself."

"What? Hell no, get that leg—"

"I'm coming in. Get here and pick me up or send someone," David barked and shook off the nurse.

"Get me a leg brace, the kind with the metal on the sides, that buckles on," he ordered her. She backed up and finally nodded. "I'm going to be waiting, half an hour, I want that pick up."

Silence, then more cursing. David got his pants on and only had to sweat through the pain for a few minutes before his leg calmed down. By then, Will had as well.

"I'll be there."

"Good." Real good, because there was no way he wanted some MP witnessing him losing his shit if Paris had left him. It'd been more, a hell of a lot more, than a vacation.

Chapter Eleven

Six months later

"I've got this," Paris called over to Margaret, her co-teacher, then skated to where two of her students were having a mini catfight. With the way they acted, soon they'd be ready for the Olympics.

Immediately she felt bad for her thoughts and slowed so she arrived a second after Susie had rushed off crying. The blonde ten year old would get over it, but the real trouble was the stoic child left behind. Macy met her eyes and immediately glanced down at her scuffed white skates.

"Hey, Macy, what's wrong? I thought you and Susie were getting along better?" Paris asked, giving the girl her space by circling her on her skates.

Macy was dressed in her pink leotard, pink tights and pink socks today, complete with pink ear muffs with little cherry stems and smiley faces. She was adorable, until you met her eyes. Then she just looked sad. Lonely. Paris knew that feeling.

"You're not answering me. I thought we talked about this." Paris hated reminding the child of painful memories, but with Macy's problems on and off the ice, Paris had made the girl promise to try harder. Talking, for Macy, was one of those trying harder points.

"She was making fun of Kay."

"And?"

"And, I don't like it. Susie is so spoiled, she has everything, and now she wants more, my time with you, and if she can, she wants to make Kay quit."

"Kay's not quitting," Paris assured her.

"If she can't afford it she will. Her lessons cost—"

"Her lessons and the cost are not your concern, are they? You are your concern, and your behavior on this ice. Right?" Paris watched Macy tighten her hands into fists at her hips. "I teach, you learn. I teach Kay and she learns. I teach Susie and she tries. Keep that in mind, the next time she says something. You are learning. Why? Because you want to improve. Kay wants to improve. That's why you are here, not to check a box that says you take figure skating lessons. Now, are we clear?"

Macy's hands relaxed while Paris talked, and by the time she was done, the girl had steadied her breathing and nodded, quickly wiping at her face.

"Clear."

"Well, let's go then, show me what you've been practicing"—Paris glanced at her watch—"because Kay is up next, and she won't waste ten minutes of my time with silly girl stuff."

Macy wiped at her face once more and a smile peeked out before she put on her serious face. "I've been practicing the Layback spin for my dance."

"Oh, very good. Did you warm up?"

At Macy's quick nod, Paris motioned to the now empty ice. "Let me see you do a quick circuit or two."

It took her longer to say it than it did for the girl to take off. If Paris had to choose, Macy would be the student to make it to the gold. She simply lived to skate.

And I skate to live. Ironic, isn't it?

Macy did a few smooth circles of the rink without a hitch, clearly ready and eager to show her hard work.

"Okay, show me from the beginning," Paris called, and skated slowly out to be close in case Macy needed her. "Start with the Attitude spin and then proceed to the Layback, but watch your back arch and remember, concentrate on the ice, your body and your breathing."

The girl nodded, clearly excited, and began her performance from the start, keeping her form tight and her body loose and carefree. The first Camel spin was perfect. Her leg was parallel to the ice and her head forward, arms close to her legs. She did a perfect build up into an Upright spin but under-rotated her Axel jump and wobbled, but shook the mistake off. Immediately she went with a beautiful twist, back bent, head partially down, but not quite in position with her arms above her body.

Paris clapped and smiled at the work she knew Macy had put into her practices to get her form so close to perfection.

Macy slowed down and glided to a stop in the middle of the rink, breathless and glowing.

"Beautiful, absolutely beautiful, Macy!" Paris called, skating to her and taking her hands. "You have really practiced, haven't you?" She ruffled her hair. A slice of pain filtered through her remembering a certain man doing the same thing to her, but she stopped the memory. Thoughts of David Jansen weren't allowed on the ice.

"I have," Macy said, still breathless. "I wobbled a bit and didn't get the bend right, it felt off."

"You did great, but let's work on it. The Layback is famous for a reason. It's tricky. Now let's see if you can't let me show you a few things, okay? Follow my lead now," she called, beginning to build up speed to help Macy see the form as it should be.

Macy did, and by the time all her lessons were through for the night, Paris was exhausted, but it was a good tired.

Paris was just about to leave the rink, when she spotted a familiar pink and white mitten on the ice.

"Macy," she muttered, but smiled as she skated over. The cool air of the rink and the wet smell of the ice comforted her. Usually she stayed after and skated, neatly avoiding any of the other girls asking her to join them for a drink, or, worse, finding a man.

She'd found one, thank you, and he was now gone — leaving only the dreams that still plagued her. Lately even skating hadn't helped. Tonight she felt more restless than ever.

Or horny.

At the thought, she felt her face heating. Maybe. But if she was, she wasn't going there. Not after Wyoming. Not after doing things that still made her ears burn just thinking of them. Sex where anyone walking by could see being one hot memory that still made her shiver. Just thinking of David's lazy grin could make her heart race, let alone his low groans and whispered promises.

A rush of sensations and emotions tried to attack but she shook them off and turned her iPod on. What she thought of as their song, *All of Me*, flowed around her.

She sped up, taking the rink in faster and faster circles until she built up enough to let go. The power surging through her made all the hopes and crushed dreams fade to the background and the beauty of the dance surface. It took over, transporting her out of the ugliness of the world. And the loss of one man.

Skating did that for her.

One man had as well.

Then he'd left and destroyed yet another dream — one she'd never known was a possibility. What would it have been like if David had survived? If they'd been able to build a life together, with kids, and pancakes and lazy Sunday mornings in bed?

The pain found its way through, but she used it and skated through the heartache. He'd been too young, too full of life and fun to die. But there was no other explanation. There was one thing she knew for fact about David Jansen. It might not be his address, or when he'd left the service, or even if he had, but she knew David kept his promises.

Tears blurred the rink, but she didn't need to see to glide across the ice. She just needed to feel the music and let her sorrow out — once again — and hope that she could finally be free of one man she'd given her heart to.

* * * *

David wanted to pace the hallway leading to his former commander's office. He stifled the urge, but not the anxious pit in his stomach.

Paris. She'd not left him like he'd thought. *All these months, I wallowed in my misery when I should have asked Petrok for help.*

All this time Paris thought…what? I'd left her or I'd died, or…I'm a lying promise breaker that can't be trusted.

He rubbed his hands over his face. He knew first-hand what a broken promise felt like. For years foster parents would load him up with promises then break every one of them.

Carson's door jerked open.

"Sorry to keep you boys waiting, but we have a situation," Carson said as way of hello. The welcome was immediately cut short by his phone ringing. Carson grimaced but answered it with a sharp 'Carson here' and another scowl.

Carson was an ex-SEAL and one hell of a tough man, but today David saw the age weighing on him. The words, *we have a situation*, didn't sit well, not with David, and by the lack of emotion on Will's face, him either.

"I don't have time for this," he muttered to Will. "Paris is up in Canada thinking God knows what about me after half a fucking year of me twiddling my thumbs."

"She's fine, you'll get her back," Will added. "You were drinking more than you were twiddling. She'll listen, just explain and you'll have her back."

Will I?

Two days ago Petrok had ripped his heart out with the news Paris hadn't deserted him, but had waited for him. The Russian ex-spy had then filled him in on not only *why* Paris had left, but *what* had happened to her, and more importantly, *where* she lived. Paris had been scared and alone, without much money and no car. She'd waited six days for him then taken a bus out of town.

Alone.

He'd located the bus driver easily enough. The old man even remembered her. He'd torn David's guts to shreds by telling him she'd spent her time crying in the back, thinking no one saw, but the old man had nodded and told him, he'd seen.

He'd been sure she'd simply left—that he'd read her wrong and it hadn't been love he'd seen in those pretty gray eyes.

Petrok had set him straight.

Six months. Six months I let her think I broke my promise.

By now she'd probably forgotten all about him, worse, had moved on to someone else.

Just the thought had him fisting his hand on his crutch until the metal protested. He needed to get on the road now. He needed to see her. Just see her smile, or hell, yell at him. Anything but sitting here and doing nothing to get to her.

He shoved his other hand in his pocket to fiddle with the rock heart she'd given him on their hike. He'd worn it down a little, he thought. It was smoother now, not so jagged on one side.

Will I get a chance to get back into her heart?

"I'm gonna need you for a little longer," Carson said after pocketing his phone.

"Sir," David began, "I get that you need men, but I'm of no use to anyone right now." He indicated his crutch. "And I've got a girl to get to in Canada—"

"That, my boy"—Carson pointed his finger like a gun at David—"is where you are wrong. On both counts." He ducked back into his office after that hopeful sentence, and they had no choice but to follow.

David caught Will's eye and nodded at the unspoken question there. They'd go in, but if this was another mission, they were walking. Will led and he followed, spotting an open laptop with Petrok and her soon to be husband, if David had to guess, Cody Johnson on screen.

His tension lessened. Sonya and Cody knew how important getting to Paris was to him. If anyone would understand a man who had really only had four days with a woman and knew she was the one, it was those two. Heck, they'd had a whirlwind of a time and were already talking marriage.

Will Paris forgive me enough to marry me?

Cody was as sappy over Sonya as David was over Paris. Heck, even Sonya had softened a little.

The two had fallen in together soon after the Duke operation, then she and Cody had worked together to bring Walters down. He and Will had been called to help, because they'd been in the same area. David had been too drunk most of the time to leave his room, let alone the state. Will had stuck around for who knew what reason. In the end, Walters hadn't gotten past Sonya, let alone the ex-Ranger, Cody. And David had managed to fall on his bum leg—again.

But seeing the couple on screen, in Carson's office, could mean only one thing—they needed something. Or, worse, the Sentinels weren't as over as he wanted them to be.

"Jansen, Will, don't look so grim. Man, are you two fighting again?" Sonya grumbled.

"Hey, Sonya, Cody, long time," he called and turned one of the chairs around to straddle it, then carefully leaned his crutch on the conference table. "Kinda thought you two would be on some island honeymooning it by now, 'cause I'm on my way to Canada."

"Don't we wish," Cody grumbled good-naturedly.

"Petrok, Johnson," Will grunted, taking a chair next to him. "Why are you on screen?"

Carson coughed, the code sign for 'stop asking questions I'm about to get to'. The guy had to be in his late forties, but with his hard physique David had a difficult time pinning his age. The white hair threw him, but he had a few gray hairs himself, so who knew how old Carson was. What they all knew though, was he was the man to get the shit end of the stick on taking over the special ops team nicknamed the Sentinels. Carson had a record for getting a job done that needed doing, so maybe that was why. The hard-ass even worried Sonya, and no one, to David's knowledge, did that.

"They're here because Petrok's been briefed about the buyers Walters contacted before he was killed. She's worried about one in particular. She's also found something out that might concern you," Carson replied, taking a seat opposite them. He didn't even bother to move so he could see the screen, which meant he'd already been filled in on whatever the issue was.

"Well, by all means, don't keep it to yourself. Share," David said, stretching his knee. The thing still bothered him and the crutch he used made it damn embarrassing. If not for Will offering to drive him to Paris, he'd have been long gone, but on a plane, and he hated flying commercial.

"Leg still bad?" Sonya asked instead of answering.

The redhead was one tough cookie, but David had never tried to take her on. He owed her too much. Right now was not the time to start either.

"Yep," he admitted. "It's been what? Two days since you saw me last."

Cody whispered something to her, which made her grin. The woman had once been a spy—and not for them. David had never seen her happy. She was more than happy now—she was all set. Cody fit her. Kind of like he thought Paris had fit him. As soon as he found her, she would again, too.

"Petrok." Will leaned forward in his chair and put on his mission face, which meant a total lack of emotion.

Sonya was smart enough to see it, too, and got down to business.

"Right, so that counts you out of this mission, Jansen, you'll have to wait on the sidelines, but Will, you're going to have to go in. The man we're after—"

"Hold it, hold it, what are you talking about? We are done. Out. You were a charity mission, Red, nothing more," Will said quickly, frowning over at David.

"Explain, Petrok, what mission and why?" David said, instead of agreeing with him.

"Savage."

The one word stilled the already quiet room in a way only bad news that suddenly got worse could.

"Fuck!" David slammed his hand down on the desk, nearly upsetting the laptop, but he was too far gone to worry. "Now he shows up? You've got to be—"

"Settle down, Jansen," Will muttered.

David spared his partner the briefest of glances. "Walters contacted that slime, didn't he? It wasn't Duke. And he has what? The drug? Chung's or Duke's?" he asked, although both fucked up the person who took them. "And you want me to settle down?"

Walters had been one sick bastard by the end. David knew from Walters' autopsy results that most of the man's sickness was from overuse of Duke's drug.

Chung, the scientist behind the first DNA trial, was examining the results, but David had read them. It wasn't just the report either. He'd known just from looking at the man he'd been in trouble. Thin wasn't even close to what Walters had become—hell, he'd seen scarecrows with more meat on them. The guy had once been a rock, if not a bit too buffed for his own good. When David had turned him over, he'd been shocked down to his boots at the changes.

"Yes," Sonya said, "he did. Savage received several samples, and the footage from Duke's compound."

Will leaned forward. "What footage is that, Petrok?"

David gave Sonya credit. She didn't back down when confronted with an angry Will, she simply said it like it was. "All the footage, Will. Every room was filmed—except the apartments you two were given. Outside of that and the garage, the entire compound was rigged for show and tell."

She let that settle only for a minute before she added, "But that's where this gets worse, fast. He has names to go with the rooms. Your names were fake. So no worries. But someone put Paris Masters down on that guest list, and it wasn't Duke."

A chill, as if a goose walked over his grave, rushed David at her words.

"Who would have done that?" she asked.

"Are you telling me Savage has Paris' ID and location?" David asked so quietly most wouldn't had realized how angry he was. But everyone present knew, and by the serious frown on Carson's face, he'd expected nothing less.

"I am," Sonya said, with sympathy. "He's had this list from the start, but now he's collecting the people on it. My guess is he wants to discover for himself what the drug was like before he markets it."

"Fuck," David groaned. He grabbed his crutch and would have stood if Will hadn't laid his hand on his shoulder.

"No. Sit."

"What? Are you insane? He knows where Paris lives!"

"But my guess is he hasn't collected her." Will turned at the finish to face the screen.

"No, he hasn't. We had men go...well, fetch her. From all accounts, she's not happy."

"What? What do you mean you sent men?" David demanded.

"When you two went off radar, this all exploded on me! I did what I thought you'd want! They picked her up yesterday," she added with a bit less heat.

"Where—" He paused and swallowed. Off radar? They'd gone to get a new truck so his damn leg would fit in it all stretched out. Less than twenty four hours and they were off the radar? "Where is she, Sonya?"

"Back at Duke's. We have the entire perimeter secure and she's safe, but somewhat vocal about how unhappy she is. Didn't see that coming," she muttered. "She seemed too nice, or," she added with a glance at him, "way too patient for that."

She isn't happy.

The last day, at Duke's, she'd asked him to stay, cried for him to stay, but he'd had to go. He'd promised to come back. She had to believe he'd broken that promise, or worse, he'd died.

"I have to go to her," he said, then louder, "I'll go take care of, you get me if you need me—"

"Or when your leg heals," Carson said. "Get that taken care of, Jansen. You don't want that kind of thing hassling you all your life."

"Yes, sir." He stood.

Will got to his feet as well. "Just be honest. It might help, and remember, she's not used to this—any of this—so just be honest, like you were before."

"Just get this bastard and hurry up on it, too. She's not safe until you do."

With that he turned and, leaning on his crutch, made it out the door before they saw him sweating in a panic.

Hell, panic? I'm a mess.

What if she wasn't just vocal, but pissed off at him and already settled down with some big Canadian Mountie?

She'll just have to forgive me, that's all. Then he could see about making a promise that was going to last a hell of a lot longer.

Chapter Twelve

"There is only one answer that's going to please me right now," Savage said, making certain the man in front of his desk understood him. "Bring me the drug. And, this time, I want David Jansen's dead body at my feet."

"Yes, sir," Murphy said on cue, nodding to reinforce the affirmative.

"If you find me Petrok and Bryson, your fee is doubled. But Jansen's the man responsible for this shit," Savage shouted and threw the empty bottles of Duke's sex drug at Murphy's face. "You and your men have had six months. Six fucking months. If I have to show you how to run this operation I pay you to run, than why would I need you?"

Murphy shifted but kept his Irish mouth shut.

Behind him, Marcus, his South African killer, also stayed silent, but Marcus wasn't stupid. He'd let Jansen get the mark on Martinez, so his days were numbered simply because he'd been there when Martinez had died. He'd been instructed to protect one man—Savage's brother—and he'd failed. Failure wasn't tolerated.

"I want this done. As quickly and quietly as possible. Now." He turned and buzzed in the man he'd left to wait outside. A few seconds later, Ashton Potter walked in. He lifted an eyebrow at Savage, most likely for the plastic surgery he'd had done after the Duke fiasco. The heat surrounding his club had been too much for him to retain his own identity. The new face was just shy of Hollywood and resembled an assassin he'd killed last year for double-crossing him on a deal. The irony was possibly only understood by him and Martinez—if his brother had still been alive to enjoy it.

"How's the new drug coming along?"

The chemist sat and crossed one leg casually over his knee. Not much dismayed the MIT graduate, not even, it would seem, Savage's new look.

Savage leaned back in his chair. The younger man pulled a file out of his briefcase and placed it on the desk.

"So far the subjects have tested well. Now that we are picking up the people who were on the Duke drug, the process should be much smoother. By the end of the month, I think we'll have a product."

That surprised Savage, but he didn't show it. Potter was good at what he did, and charged a fortune for it. He wasn't a wimpy college kid, but a genius, who, Savage gauged, had no morals or conscience. The kind of man he dealt with, but from a distance. If Savage went after someone, he killed the man—sometimes face to face, other times using the same methods as Murphy and Marcus. But Potter wouldn't go for someone like that. He liked suffering, and the more he caused, the more interested he became.

A serial killer in the making. Or maybe already made. Didn't matter to Savage. One way or another, he was getting what he wanted, and Potter seemed more than happy with what he received each week in subjects to work on and digits in his bank account.

"That soon," Savage murmured, cutting off his thoughts about the oddity of the man and shifting his focus to where it should be. Making money. His new club was run on high-priced women who did whatever the client wanted, but this drug would make him a billionaire if it did half of what Duke's had done.

Inhaling, he tapped his desk with a pencil and nodded. "Good. Send me an update when you have one," he added, standing.

Potter stood as well. "There's just one more thing I'll need."

Savage paused from pulling out a Cuban cigar from the box on his desk.

"And that is?" he asked, nodding for Marcus and Murphy to leave. As soon as they had, he offered a Cuban to the kid. Potter took it, staring at it as if it were a science experiment, then pocketed in the front breast pocket of his suit. As always, he was dressed in the latest fashion from his hand sewn shirts to his handmade Italian shoes. Every detail of his appearance was neat and orderly, down to the part in his brown hair. Savage knew he also kept his home and lab the same way—OCD off the charts, one of his girls had told him after a night with Potter. Kayla had also threatened to quit if he ever let Potter near her again. If even half of what she'd said he'd done with her was true, none of his girls were ever going near him again.

"I need these women." Potter flipped the file open. "Paris Masters and Sara Stevens."

Savage clipped his cigar and lit it, drawing on it deeply before he answered. They'd already brought in almost all the other 'volunteers' from Duke's compound. Masters was on the list but in Canada, a stretch for him right now when he had a new club to organize, a drug to get on the market and some scores to settle. But the other girl, she was an unknown.

"Get me both of them, and you'll have your drug."

"Leave the file. I'll see what I can do."

The sick bastard smiled tightly. "Good. I'll see that your drug is ready."

With that, the little prick walked out.

Savage contemplated the doorway Potter had walked through. If so much wasn't riding on the drug, he would have killed Potter for what he'd done to Kayla. Business wasn't good though. A full shut down and bust hadn't helped his clientele feel protected, neither had his promises for more of the drug, then not delivering.

If Potter wanted Paris Masters and this other girl in exchange for the drug, he'd have Murphy bring them both in. Two women's lives weren't worth losing billions. Not even close.

* * * *

Paris paced the length of the room, giving the mirror, which she knew was a window that someone was behind *and* watching, a dirty look as she did. It wasn't her first experience with two-way glass after all.

Or this place.

No one had come back in, but then, she'd thrown their water at them when they had. It had to be illegal for them to snatch her from her home in Canada, cross the border and bring her here—this place of all places.

She heard footsteps leading up to the door and turned, arms crossed. Whoever it was, she was ready to snap someone's head off. It opened and the last man she expected to see stood—or leaned on a crutch—giving her a somewhat tentative, but cocky grin.

Her mind went completely, utterly silent.

"Hey, princess, I hear you're not—"

"David Jansen, I should kill you," she said, then ran to him and hugged him as tightly as she could. Tears blurred everything, even the six months of heartache, as his solid body and warm pine scent settled around her. *He's here. He's here.*

"Whoa, there, no killing me before I get to explain."

His voice sounded deeper than she remembered. Rougher. Then his words registered. "I am so mad at you, so very, very mad at you! You left me, here, then dragged me back…here!"

"I'm sorry, hell, I didn't mean for them to do this, I didn't know they were doing this," he said, sounding oddly choked up.

Probably because I'm squeezing his neck too tight.

She let go and stepped back, giving him a once-over. He was dressed in combat clothes, the kind of dusty brown camo that men in the military wore. He wore it better than the men behind him. But he *looked* better, too.

Don't go there. He left once. No more second chances.

Even as she thought it, she knew such a thing could never apply to David.

"Why am I here?" she asked, a sudden suspicion and the memory of the last time she'd seen him rising to the surface. "Where is Will?"

"Look, you're not supposed to be in here," he said firmly, and waved off the two big MPs behind him.

She glared at them. They'd been the ones to pick her up at home and drag her to the SUV then drive her down here. Maybe she'd been very unwilling to go, but they shouldn't have manhandled her like that. "Will is, well, he had to go clean up more of this mess. But I'm here now."

That caught her attention. Will hadn't come. She explored her feelings on that and found no hurt, just worry over him. David was here, that was why, too. David the blue-eyed, cocky soldier who made her knees grow weak with his sleepy eyed smile. The man who'd made her choke on sandwiches from his insane questions. The man who'd woken her heart, then ripped it out.

"So it's just me," David muttered and reached up to rub a hand over the back of his neck with a wince.

After this long, it's just him. That's all he has to say?

Go slow, don't jump in. Steady, just slow down. Don't give your heart out so quickly – again.

She folded her arms and assumed a bored posture.

"Oh, great," she muttered. "At least you're not dead. Although I'd love to hear how you searched for me, because that would be a truly tall tale since I was right there, in the same hotel room, in town, waiting for you."

He widened his blue eyes, but quickly gave her his big confident smile, the one that had got her into his bed – and Will's arms – all in one wild week of such passion she even now woke up aching for more.

Adjusting his crutch, he said, "Look, princess, it's – "

"Don't. I don't like it here. I want to go home. I have work I'm missing. This place stinks and those men were rude and very, *very* uncool dragging me out of my house the way they did. Who knows what this will do to my uncle, and I really, *really* don't appreciate being ignored for months, then shoved back into this as if no time had passed. You—"

"Whoa, that's a lot of pent-up anger. You'd better calm it or you might just end up burning your wick at both ends."

She snapped her mouth shut then speared him with the glare she reserved for very spoiled brat skaters wanting her to let their lazy skating slide. "My wick and ends are none of your concern. You left me here!"

"I didn't leave you here!" he exclaimed with heat. "I left, and when I came back, you were gone!"

Shocked, she stared at him, unable to believe all her pain and loneliness was that easily explained. *He came back and I was been gone? That was it?*

"We told you to stay here, to wait—"

"What? Are you saying it's *my* fault? That if I'd just stayed here everything would have been okay?" she asked, waving at the entire compound. "Everything would have been *fine*?" she shouted.

"Yes. If you'd stayed put, none of this would have happened—"

"None of *this?* What do you know of *this*, Mr. Smarty-Pants G.I. Joe? Nothing! You would have left too if you were suddenly surrounded by sick perverts thinking you're their next play toy!"

"Holy hell," he breathed, and his crutch crashed to the floor. He hobbled over and suddenly she was in his arms again, and just like before, it was okay. More than okay, so much better it was good enough she felt tears spilling free. "I'm sorry, Paris, sorry, hell, I never would have left you here to deal with that, if I'd known."

"I know, I'm sorry, I didn't mean to shout at you—"

"Hell, I'm listening, shout away, as long as you tell me you're okay and you missed me, but come on, Mr. Smarty-Pants G.I. Joe is the best you got?"

"What!" She pushed at his chest, but he only kissed her temple and didn't let her go. He'd tricked her, hadn't he? God, she shouldn't have felt her heart melting at that, but she did.

"Just come on, say it, whisper it if you need to," he murmured, stroking her back. All those times he'd said that then done everything she'd whispered came back with a full body shiver. Even her traitorous breasts grew heavy and achy at the sexy tone of his voice.

"You got hurt," she said, instead of dragging him into the room and whispering exactly what she wanted from him. She moved back enough to inspect the brace he wore on his leg and knee. "And you shouldn't stand on it, either!" she exclaimed and picked up his crutch.

He took it, but she could tell he wasn't completely buying her nervous attempt at changing the subject. It was too soon, and she was too close to falling for him all over again. The last time she'd barely survived. David had shown her what real heartache meant—she wasn't ready to lose again, so soon. But God, he had great reasons, and such an earnest expression mixed with his bad boy grin, she wished they *were* alone.

"Yeah," he sighed heavily and eased back on his crutch a few steps. He seemed to catch on that she wasn't falling so easily this time, or else the sneaky man knew he'd have her alone soon and God only knew what he had in mind. Another traitorous tremble dove down her spine at the thought.

"What happened to your leg?" she asked.

"It was an accident. One of the reasons I couldn't make it back in time to catch you before you ran off," he accused. She opened her mouth and he tacked on, "I hurt it again recently climbing down too fast from a cliff. Another mission, not a big deal, but I was careless."

"You're using a crutch, it's a big deal," she surmised. *He hurt himself? That's why he didn't show up?*

His grin grew in his eyes. "You know me so well already, don't you, princess?"

The comment sizzled between them and filled her with such possessiveness she tightened her fingers on his camo jacket. "I guess so, mister, so fess up. You're hurt and it is a big deal, isn't it?"

Laughing, he surprised her by slipping his hand along the back of her dress and squeezing her butt.

"David!" she whispered and thumped his chest. "Stop that. We need to talk," she said, still cautious of the men who might or might not be watching or listening through that glass. "Especially before we move toward *that*."

He ducked his head and stole a quick kiss before she could break out of his arms. With a heavy sigh, he straightened. "All right, we'll talk, but I'm warning you, I'm not waiting too long."

With that sexy threat, he shouldered the door open wider and beckoned her with his hand.

"Come on. Let's get you out of here and to a room— a clean one, so we can talk."

"What's going on? Really going on?" she asked, easing by him, still nervous he would try something else with his quick sneakiness.

"I'll tell you." He bent low and whispered against her ear, "when we talk."

The ticklish sensation of his hot breath, and hot body, apparently very ready to make up for all those lonely nights, had her feeling as if she were walking on air. She tripped, since, of course, her brain was focused on the man and the things she wanted to do to him, let alone him do to her. She'd been getting ready to go meet a banker for a loan to purchase the local ice rink, so she was still in her heels and wrap-around blue dress.

"Until then, let's just keep the ideas flowing silent-like," David added. "And, princess, you look beautiful in that dress. You're going to be more beautiful when I lift you up again for a better look, but damn, I missed you."

The honesty and teasing hit like a double whammy. She'd missed both so much, and him so much. She knew exactly what he was talking about seeing... David was so strong he had been able to hold her up as if she weighed nothing and make love to her. He had a chest she'd never grow tired of touching, let alone the other parts of his anatomy.

She pulled her mind off David's incredible body and swallowed to ask, "A clean room, what does that mean? And please don't tell me it's near the last one. *Either* of the last ones."

He grimaced at that, and she felt bad. He'd been hurt. That meant he hadn't been able to find her, especially with her phone back in his room.

Before she could apologize, he said, "It means it's an unused wing of this disaster and safer than anywhere else I can put you. *Us*, put us right now," he said. His expression could only be described as hungry. "No one is near there, and no one has clearance to be there, in case, you know, you get loud."

She felt the familiar blush warm her cheeks. She had never been loud. Even when David had done things to her trying to make her scream—she'd been quiet, which seemed to amuse him, and she hoped please him, too. He'd certainly gotten out of control with her when she had whispered and moaned quietly. Her blush turned hotter at the memory.

David noticed it and nodded. "We talk, then we'll see about being loud—"

"Don't you dare," she murmured, seeing the passion, banked for now, in his lazy blue eyes. The two MPs waited down the hall, but when David approached, they nodded respectfully.

"I want your reports."

"Yes, sir," both said smartly and saluted.

She rolled her eyes and blew her hair off her forehead. "Nice. You get the 'yes, sir', I get the 'get in the vehicle'," she mocked.

"Just walk." He guided her past the men and down a hall. "They were doing what they were sent to do, Paris. Protect you. I'll admit—"

"Protect me? From what?" She glanced back to see the men already heading off down another hallway.

"We never thought someone would come after you. Hell, we didn't know where you were, not until this past week, and then we were—"

"Someone is after me? Why me? Why would anyone be after me?" she asked, and pulled on his sleeve to slow him down. He amazed her, but she also doubted the way that he was using the crutch was okay. It seemed to keep his weight off his hurt leg, so she guessed it worked. But he went at a pace that had her hurrying to keep up.

"We should talk about it when we get to the room." He led her along several deserted hallways, then farther, until finally they came out of the hall and into what reminded her of some huge, ritzy hotel lobby from a Hollywood movie set. There were sad, neglected plants in huge planters lining a wall of windows, and more scattered throughout the marble-floored room. The entire place seemed deserted. She'd only seen two men other than her MPs her entire time here.

"What *is* this place?" she asked, awed by the huge chandelier and long, black marbled topped bar along the far wall. There were bottles of alcohol lining the shelves still. The large, round, plush velvet benches on either side of them were so luxurious she wanted to see if they were as soft as they appeared. The light dove gray velvet matched the dark purple carpet swirled with black and gray perfectly. The place had to have been amazing when it had been taken care of. "This place reminds me of a Stephen King movie set. If I'd seen all this that day, I'd have done something besides jumped out the bathroom window."

He laughed then froze, realizing, she guessed, she wasn't joking. "You jumped out a bathroom window?"

"Yeah," she admitted. At his round-eyed expression, she plunked her hands on her hips. "Listen, Mr. G.I. Joe. You were gone, and I was scared. I did everything—almost—you said. They wouldn't let me get my things, but I had no wallet remember, so I had to go back to the same hotel. I waited six—"

"Paris, slow down, breathe. I'm fucking sorry, there, I said it again, I'm sorry, this time more polite, okay? I was hurt, and Will was sent after a real sick bastard and I couldn't get him to come and hunt you down. I didn't think of the hotel, just saw you'd left the phone behind and thought—"

"You thought I left you?" she asked quietly. Now that she had a chance to see him, really comprehend he was standing here, she could see he had circles under his eyes and he was a little leaner.

"I didn't make it back as quick as I wanted, since I tried to get off the mountain like a dumba— Anyway, I fell on down a cliff and was out for a bit."

Ice shivered between her shoulder blades. "You fell off a cliff?"

He nodded, then seemed to think he'd said something wrong and cleared his throat. "It's no big deal. I got shot and they had to take the bullet out, which took time. I didn't let them operate on my leg," he added in a tone that seemed to imply he thought that would please her. "Once I found out what really happened to you, what those two...bozos did, I punched one hard enough to break his nose." He frowned and rubbed his jaw, considering her, then added, "Maybe the other, too, before they pulled me off."

He stood there when he was done, as if he wasn't sure what she'd say. As if she would criticize him. All the days missing him and he had been hurt. Shot. And thought she'd left him like...well, whatever kind of person does that...

Her brain was too full to come up with more than, "The men who took me from your room?"

"Yeah, those two."

Her heart clenched and she had to fight to keep her hands off him. *He'd punched them?*

"A friend of mine found out, she showed me your bag, and I put two and two together once we got those two talking. She found out your last name," he added with a frown at her. "And that you're Canadian. I was on my way to you."

She twisted her fingers together, unsure what to say. It was all so perfect. David was so big, and right there. All her worries, and all the nights of crying for him, and he'd been just as upset over her being gone as she had over missing him. It all seemed like a dream.

Was it this simple?

Her instincts said yes. She watched him waiting on her, and knew he wanted as much as she did. It was there, simmering in his worried blue eyes.

David cleared his throat and rubbed his face again. "Anyway, yeah, this place is a huge compound. The guy even had a hospital, swimming pool and track. We're going to rooms he set up for later on in his operation. We're safe. You don't have to look so spooked."

"It's not the room I'm worried about, David! It's you. You were hurt and I was…well, I was afraid you'd died, then I kinda got to thinking you'd just moved on," she whispered past the tears. *If only I'd taken the phone. None of this would have happened.*

He winced at her. "I never break a promise, Paris. I told you that."

"I know. And you were hurt."

"I'm fine now. I got shot and fell down a small cliff. I just knocked my head a bit too hard."

She nodded as if that made perfect sense. A tear slipped free, but she quickly brushed it aside. Another followed.

"Just a graze, but the bullet made surgery necessary," he repeated. "That's why I wasn't there, why I didn't find you."

She tried to get herself under control. He was safe now, standing and right here, larger than life. She swallowed down the tears.

"Paris," he said gently, "don't cry, princess. I'm not sure what that means when you do that." He tugged her hair, but he looked miserable even as he cradled her in his arms. "Talking would be good, too. You know, so I know what you're thinking."

"Fine, Mr. G.I. Joe," she grumbled, but kissed his shoulder to soften the sting and hugged him tighter. They stood like that long enough for her to get her tears to slow down. "How bad is your leg?" she asked. "Should you go so fast on that crutch?"

He sounded as if he'd choked on a laugh, and when he pulled away she could see she'd surprised him. The way he scanned her face suddenly had her accepting everything. His disappearance, the long, lonely nights, the misery, all of it was worth it if he was back, *really* back.

"I've got to get surgery, but it's a quick one, and I should be able to walk on my leg in a day, or two after."

"What?" She was an athlete. She knew what an injury could do. David had to be hurt to have a crutch because he was a stubborn man, and no way would he use one for no reason. "You have to—"

"Paris," David murmured, drawing the breath from her lungs with the heat in his eyes. "I missed you so damn much. I don't want to talk." He tugged her hair, just like he used to.

She melted. Every hurt, every tear she'd cried and miserable thought she'd had vanished.

"Oh, God, you're good at making up, aren't you?" she whispered and dragged him by his rough cut blond hair down to kiss him properly.

Right before she could, he smiled. "I don't know, you tell me. This is a first," he told her, then took her breath away with his kiss.

Their passion exploded all over again, reminding her of how it'd been, but this time with an urgency she knew he shared. All those nights, all those days without him, if she were honest, they disappeared. In their place was a need that roared through her. Not just for sex, but for the connection, the intimacy she felt sharing herself with this man — with David.

She pressed him back until she felt him sit. His crutch went down with a loud crash, but she was too busy getting his pants open to worry over it. He had his hands under her dress again, and the feel of him cupping her butt was so good she moaned against his lips.

"I like you in a dress, Paris." He tightened his grip and squeezed then stroked up her spine and back down with the same urgency she experienced. His hot breath against her cheek thrilled her, even as their kiss grew wilder. As soon as she reached his stiff penis she moaned. It was so hard, all for her, she knew. He lifted her by the waist and settled her to straddle his lap.

"David," she whispered, and stroked down him. He was hard, so very solid. She'd missed this, him, all of it. The passion tore through them and she sucked along his jaw, so eager for him she couldn't get enough. David must have agreed because with a groan he took her hands in his and tugged them behind her back and pressed into her with a firm, long thrust. It was slightly rough, and she wasn't ready, but she loved it, his urgency and him.

"Paris, Jesus, I need you," he groaned and flexed under her. She was spread tightly around his erection now, and the sensation was so good, he slid in as her excitement grew. "Let me in, princess."

It'd been so long without him that she hugged his head to her chest and pressed back, trying to take him deeper. His girth made it difficult, but after a few shallow passes he eased more and more of his erection deeper. She knew he wanted more. She could feel the tremble of his muscles against her as he held himself in check. Wetness flooded her at the realization, and at her own naughty thoughts.

"Fuck me, David, hard. Show me how much you missed me," she urged, kissing her way to his lips and watching his blue eyes narrow in sexy slits.

"Paris," he breathed, and wrapped his arms around her waist so she was forced tight against him. He kissed her breasts, sucking on her nipple when he found it, right through her dress. At the same time, he shoved his hips upward.

"Oh, God, yes." She couldn't say more.

It was a rush to climax for them both after. Her orgasm built until her thighs shivered and a moan of pleasure escaped. At the sound, David tilted her closer and started pumping aggressively—giving her such a hot rhythm that she shook from the slap of the impact. Within glorious seconds David called out her name. She felt him grow harder, bigger, then with a long groan, he climaxed with her. Out of breath, she held him tighter as he shook with the power of his own climax.

Long, lush moments later, he slowly eased back onto the soft cushions and sighed. He took her with him, caressing her back until he pressed his hand to her neck and kissed her, holding her there as he destroyed her with soft, languid strokes of his tongue, as if he was savoring her.

Another tingling began around his thick erection. It had been like this with David. She'd sometimes climaxed after he did, by feeling him there, still inside her where he stroked her so beautifully.

David massaged his hands down her back and, featherlight, brushed the tips of his fingers lower. Then he pressed delicately against her ass.

That was all it took. She fell like a house of cards. Her body tightened so hard on him, David grunted and drove in just a tiny bit deeper, which added to the rush and explosion of her orgasm. He continued to nudge her until she cried out softly and broke away to pant against his neck. She stayed like that, so lost she couldn't think, couldn't do anything but hug him tightly and rock along his body, hoping beyond hope that this time he would keep his promise.

Don't leave. Don't leave. Don't ever, ever leave.

Chapter Thirteen

David watched Paris closely, unsure if she was pleased with their crazy sex in the lobby, or worried. She didn't appear upset, but she was quietly washing her hands and face in the bathroom. The room he'd chosen could have been an apartment in the Grand Swiss Hotel or some such fancy resort. All he knew was that it was unused.

If Paris was upset, he wasn't sure he could honestly say he was sorry—since he'd climaxed so hard he thought he'd experienced a double orgasm. He had before, but never so fast—well, he thought, watching her dry her face with a towel—he had that first time. And possibly when he'd shared her with Will back at Duke's.

"Oh, that is so much better. I felt all caked in dirt," she said and walked over, then surprised him by sitting down on his thigh and wrapping her arms around his neck. She smiled and pressed a kiss to his lips. "Did I smell bad, you know," she said with a blush and whispered, "when you were ravishing me in that lobby?"

He snorted and pulled her a bit closer. She kissed him again, seeming to want him close. Some of his anxiety disappeared at her affection.

"You never smell bad," he said, adjusting her so she was more comfortable. He easily remembered those few days, and how she'd loved to sit on his lap, just like this, and talk about nothing more than silliness with him.

She examined his face this time, and tilted her head slowly with such intensity in her eyes he felt his face flush. That was her thing, but he worried about her scrutiny, and about what she was thinking.

"I hope there were no cameras out there," she whispered finally, blushing.

"I do," he said. "Then we can watch how hot we are."

She ducked her head and tucked her cheek to his chest. "You better hope there weren't," she said. "I love the way you make me feel," she added quietly. "But I don't ever want anyone to see us again."

It wasn't she loved him, but it was damn close. That night he and Will had made love to her here, at the compound in the room with the two-way mirror rushed through his memory, and he hugged her tightly to his chest.

"Good." He sounded rough. "I never want you in that kind of situation again either, Paris." He swallowed and brushed her blonde hair off her cheek. He sucked at this part, talking about important stuff. Will was better at all of this—he'd seen the man coax a woman into forgiving him when Will had seriously been in the wrong. Will had simply smiled, said a few quiet words, and left with her minutes later. David had lost twenty bucks on the deal.

With Paris, he didn't want her to feel as if he only wanted sex, and that's the first thing he'd done — within minutes of being near her.

"I didn't plan to start making up so quickly, but, princess, you make it hard."

"I do?" Paris laughed and sat up to face him again. She surprised him by stroking down his chest right to where he was still sporting a semi hard-on for her.

Laughing at the catch, but not willing to be outdone, he pressed her hand down harder and bent to kiss the tight point of her nipple that he could see through her thin dress.

She giggled and tugged at his hair, squirming on his lap in a way that had him more than ready for another round. He let up on his prize and sucked his way up to her pink lips.

"Yeah, always, you should know that."

"Always?" she teased, and batted his hand off hers with a sweet, curious expression. She was so damn innocent about so much, it gave him one hell of a thrill to show her that 'dirty' side to sex. He still couldn't believe she'd used the f-word with him.

"Paris, there isn't a second you're with me I'm not thinking of having sex with you."

"You are not!" she said with such indignation that he laughed even harder.

Hell, she was fun. And he now knew she wasn't always so happy either. He'd seen the pictures Petrok had of her. She'd looked sad, and if he'd read the pictures right, lonely. She had always been happy with him — at least those few days, he reminded himself. He'd make her happy again. If he didn't, she'd just have to tell him what he was doing wrong, so he could.

"Oh, yeah, I am. You should know that," he warned her, tightening his arm around her.

"You said that was the Duke drug," she whispered for some reason.

"Not on me, and we never took that junk. The other stuff just gave me headaches. This is all me, princess." He flexed his hips so she could feel the full impact of the hard-on she was causing to fill out his BDUs. "Having you near me after you left me? I'm sporting an erection that's going to need more than that quickie."

"David!" she exclaimed softly, but giggled and covered her face. "I did not leave you, either, by the way. You left me."

He knew he was embarrassing her, but he also sensed he pleased her. Maybe he wasn't Will, but maybe Paris didn't need him to be. Maybe he didn't need to be a smooth-talker like his buddy. Maybe she simply needed him to be himself.

"I missed you, Paris." He said it softly enough he thought she might not hear, but she lowered her hands from her face and reached out and tenderly caressed his jaw.

"David—"

He covered her pretty pink lips with a finger to still her. A man had to say some things, or chance losing everything, he thought, and took the bull by the horns.

Tell it to her straight.

"It's been hell, not knowing where you were, or what you thought. Worse, if you were a dream, or simply got what you wanted and left, to go back to your life."

His honesty made her eyes glisten, but he didn't stop, it was as if once he'd started, he had to give her it all in a rush.

"We both searched all over for you, including every database we had, and found nothing. Not one thing. You didn't take the cell phone I got you. Hell, I didn't even have your last name. Or that you were from Canada. That was something you didn't mention when you were here."

She tried to talk, but he kept his finger in place, even when she narrowed her eyes and he considered the fact she had nice, sharp teeth.

A knock on the door interrupted him when he opened his mouth, but it was immediately followed by a 'sir' he couldn't ignore.

"Damn it, we're not done here," he muttered and dragged her closer and kissed her as deeply as he could as fast as he could. Releasing her, he examined her flushed face and her pretty wet lips. "Not by a long shot, princess."

He set her on the bed and got up, grumbling his way to the door with the damn crutch keeping him upright.

Roy Moon, a man who worked under Carson, stood at the door, a clipboard in his hand and a sorry expression on his face.

"Sir, we have word from Commander Carson."

Shit. "What is it?"

"He said for you to pack up and relocate. They'll be in DC, and contact you from there. We're to close this place down and leave by twenty-one hundred, sir."

He fisted his hand on his crutch and calculated how long that was. Not long enough.

"Fine, we'll be ready. We'll branch off once we're on the road. The plan is complete silence, so from that point on no contact."

"Yes, sir."

"Thank you, sergeant."

"You're welcome, sir. Good luck with the leg, sir."

With that, Moon saluted and left.

Three hours. Three hours to convince Paris this was the right thing to do. Go with him to Vermont, pretending to be his wife so he could keep her safe. And meanwhile, Will would lay his ass on the line doing the same thing.

He turned to find her watching him, sitting small and alone on the big bed he'd hoped to spend the night in with her. Nothing in his life compared to sleeping with his arms around Paris.

"We have to go?" she asked softly.

The worst thing about answering her was that he was glad they were going—not so soon, but that they were going together—even to pretend to be married. Maybe he'd even convince her to do it for real.

As soon as he hobbled over to her, he sat down and pulled her back on his lap. She crawled onto his thigh and hugged him in the same way she had before, but her expression was wary, something it hadn't been before.

She dropped her gaze and played nervously with his shirt.

Hell, he sucked at this.

Will would know what to say.

How to handle this?

He thought of all the stupid lies he could say to her, all the half-truths and bullshit, but all that he could come up with was the truth. Secure her. That was his mission—to do that he was going to lay it all out and hope like hell she didn't fall off his lap, laughing her ass off.

She hadn't last time he'd told her the truth. She'd proved how much he believed she loved him.

Taking a deep breath, he then held it for a few seconds before slowly releasing it.

"I didn't spend that week with you on a holiday, Paris. This—" He grabbed the bull by the horns, or in his case, the sweet, shocked-looking woman he loved by the shoulders as he said, "Is more than some fling. I just need to know if you want more. And if more from me and me *alone* is enough, because while the sharing was hot, it's not gonna happen again, not unless we both want it, sometimes, maybe, later, but us, it's going to be *us*. I'm not easy to live with, or easy to get along with, whatever, but I know that. I can work on that. And besides, relationships are hard, they're work, but damn it, if that's what it takes so you don't disappear like that again, than that's what it takes."

Paris' eyes widened, then she did the craziest thing she'd ever done. She shoved him. She surprised him so much he landed flat on his back with her straddling his hips.

Any other time that would have thrilled him, but when the crazy woman took hold of his wrists and shoved them up above his head like a wild cat, he almost prematurely ejaculated in his BDUs.

"David Jansen, is this your idea of telling me you love me?"

His cock grew so hard, apparently willing to show her how much that was true, he panted for enough air to keep from tossing her on her back and taking her the way he really needed to.

"David?" she whispered, hovering just far enough above him that her body didn't touch his except where her knees pressed to his sides. The heat of her soaked through his clothing and he knew by the flush on her cheeks that she was turned on.

In all their interactions, she'd never initiated sex. She'd been on board, completely willing every time — *every single time* — but she'd never displayed such sexy aggression before. This was a woman wanting to claim a man — him. The shot of heat that caused had him nearly groaning. Not willing to end this that soon, he tilted his head on the bed and gave her his best smile just to see what she'd do.

She leaned in closer, so close he felt her breasts, and hell, maybe her tight nipples brush his chest, but she didn't move. Instead she drove him nuts by pressing slowly forward until her lips were a scant centimeter from his mouth.

"Well, is it?"

When she spoke, she rubbed her hips down and the sweet, soft mound of her pussy settled over his eager erection for a too brief moment. He was pretty sure she'd taken her panties off.

"Cat got your tongue?" she whispered into his ear.

He swore his body nearly took over. He was so turned on he felt as if he wasn't going to last much longer. She released one hand but he didn't move, not even when she breathed against his ear and slowly caressed down his shirt to the buttons of his BDUs. She took her time, releasing one after another, all the while hovering over him and breathing hotly against his neck. But when she had half the buttons down his cock sprang out so hard it touched his stomach.

"Or maybe you need some incentive?" she asked, then licked a hot path from his sideburn right to his mouth. She didn't just kiss him, she stole his breath away with a kiss that had his cock wetting his shirt with pre-cum at the memory of her doing a hell of a lot more with those sweet lips.

Paris shifted upward just slightly, and he felt the softness of her skin, then the bare wetness of her pussy gliding along his cock. Without moving, she kept him there, right at her entrance, an inch from paradise as she held one hand tightly in hers. She began unbuttoning his shirt slowly, at the same time driving him nuts with the thought of her soft pussy so close to his cock. When she was satisfied, she shoved his T-shirt up then did some crazy thing with her dress and she was practically naked without taking her lips from his for more than a second.

She sucked his bottom lip and, eyes wide open, she eased her body down that precious inch to his cock.

"Don't move," she warned, making him fist his hands but he nodded quickly. "Not one inch, David. When you're ready you tell me, okay?"

He knew damn well she didn't mean ready to come, so he grabbed her hand in his and nodded. Her eyes seemed as if they glowed and she pressed back, taking him in with a long, slow slide. It was amazing. Beyond amazing, it was so hot, he could barely stand it. She was always so slick around his cock, but so tight and silky soft at the same time that he never wanted anyone else *ever* again. Every time was mind-blowing, but this was entirely new. This was what they meant by 'making love'.

"Paris," he groaned when she had him as deep as she could. She didn't move, and the heat of her body drove away all the horrible things he'd had to endure to get to this—a woman he never wanted to be parted from again. All of it, his fucked up childhood, his Navy career, the sacrifices and losses, the pain and suffering, all of it was worth it because now he knew what love was.

Paris. She's love.

He trembled, so close to coming simply being inside her, he had to do something—anything.

Paris took care of it. She eased upward. The pull and drag of her body along his erection was so good he groaned. Then she pressed back and made love to him with even, slow strokes that unraveled him bit by bit. Just when he knew he wasn't going to make it a second longer, she breathed against his mouth and kissed him deeply, not stopping until they were both panting.

"So big," she whispered, pressing back to sheathe more of him. "You're so full of yourself, David Jansen, but you're also so very, very sweet," she added. "That's one of the zillions of reasons I love you so very, very much."

"Paris." He was unable to say more as the rush of cum swirled down his cock and tightened his balls. She continued to kiss along his skin, caressing him with her hands and breasts as she stayed in place, holding him tight. "I love you," he shouted and shot off, coming so hard he swore he'd pass out. His legs shook and his cock jerked repeatedly until he melted back into the bed, only half aware he was still saying those three words as Paris moaned through her own pleasure.

"Holy hell, Paris," he managed when she collapsed, smiling, on top of him.

She leaned forward and pressed her lips to his as if she couldn't get enough. "Say it again, David."

David. There wasn't a person in this world who called him that.

"I love you, Paris, maybe from the start," he added when those three words had her eyes filling with tears. "Don't cry, though. Do that again, but don't cry."

"Oh, David." She hugged him around his neck, crying a little.

He turned her to her side so he could gather her closer. "I need these damn pants off and this brace gone, princess, so none of that, right?"

She nodded and rubbed her face, adorable as hell, on his shirt.

"Why didn't you take my shirt all the way off and how did you get so damn naked?"

She heaved a sigh and frowned at him. "Well, you're too big, and I couldn't figure out how to, and if I asked, I might have ruined the mood."

He laughed so hard she hit him a few more times, but it was so damn funny to think anything would ruin the mood with her, he couldn't help it. He finally had to hug her tightly and roll with her to stop her attack. "No hitting. Rule number one."

"Did I hurt you?" she immediately asked, breathless from beating on him with her tiny fists. "Oh, David, is this where you were shot?" She feathered her fingers over the newest bullet wound with a worried frown that got to him.

"Yes, but no hitting, you might get hurt."

"Oh, man," she grumbled and tried to hit him.

"No crying, rule number two."

"Oh, really?" she said, giving him a look that shouldn't have gotten his body all primed and ready again, but with Paris, he should know better.

"Absolutely, and rule number three, you do whatever I say."

If her eyes could have become rounder he'd have been surprised. She stayed that way for a brief second, then thumped him again on the chest. He caught her hand and kissed her fingers.

"No rules, then?"

She seemed to think about that, then with a smile hugged him around the neck and brought him down on top of her. "I like that. No rules, except maybe that you should say you love me often, like maybe" — she shrugged shyly — "once a day."

"Deal," he promised and kissed her quickly. "Now, can you help me out of these pants? And boots?"

"David, you are too much." She laughed but kissed him quickly on the lips and wiggled until he got off her. As soon as he had, he got the full impact of her sexy body.

"Damn, Paris, I am one sorry fool, aren't I? We could have been making love in this room, not talking all this —"

"What?" she asked, hands on her tiny waist. "And miss you telling me you love me?" She tugged his shirt off and threw it behind her then tilted her head. "T-shirt, too?"

"Yes, we're showering. Not like I want, but there might be a way to make it work."

Her eyes widened, but she smiled eagerly. "I love showering with you. I have days and days of showers when I've been alone that you need to make up to me."

"Oh, ho! Is that so?" he asked, but damned if he didn't like that. She hadn't found some Canadian Mountie. She began working on his boots and took his breath away with the bounce of her breasts with each tug on his laces.

"Yes, sir, you owe me."

"I thought I was making some headway with that, twice," he grumbled, but didn't mean a word of it. He *did* have some making up to do. He knew it, even if Paris was too sweet to realize it.

She got one boot off and gently pulled at the one on his hurt leg. She winced when he stiffened.

"It's okay, just pull," he said, watching the show again with a slight smile that got him busted when she glanced up and froze.

"Are you watching my…me?"

"Your breasts? Yep, I'm watching, Paris. I'm a man."

"Oh, I hadn't noticed," she said, ogling his hard-on. "And didn't we just take care of that? Twice?"

"Baby, you've got to start listening," he told her, sighing in relief when she got his boot off. He'd damaged the leg again on his way to her—again—but hell if he was going to admit that to her or anyone. The surgery, as much as he hated the thought, was a good idea. He'd done his research on the way here. He'd be walking on it the next day, taking it easy, but within weeks he should be solid.

"There, now, seriously?" she asked with a pointed glance at his hips.

He smoothed a hand down to where his erection lay against his stomach and stroked the thick flesh, Paris watching him avidly.

"I'm serious. If you're around, I'm thinking about sex with you. Naked?" He laughed and got a fierce look for it, but suffered through and watched her sit next to him on the bed. She wasn't shy about her body—not now, anyway. At first she had been. Whoever had done a number on her needed his ass whipped, or his head examined. "No way am I going to be able to keep myself under control. Now, can you unwind this brace? See those side latches? Just pull those and it slips off."

She got busy with that, concentrating so hard he simply watched her. It amazed him all over again that she'd said she loved him. It hadn't sunk in yet, he knew, but he still got a shiver over it. Some men said they only knew they loved a woman when they let them go. He could attest to that. He'd not let her go, but as soon as he'd found her gone he'd known exactly where he'd fucked up—leaving her side. He wasn't doing it again.

The pit in his stomach, the completely irrational need to run after her, without an idea of where to go, had thrown him for a loop. He'd been unable to concentrate, let alone do his job. There was a reason he'd hurt his leg the second time—his mind had been on Paris and what Sonya had known about her.

"There? Better?" she asked, clearly anxious she'd hurt him.

"It's good, just fine. Now, here." He sat up, only to knock heads with her. "Damn, Paris, are you all right?" he asked, steadying her. "Baby?"

"Oh," she murmured and rubbed her forehead. "You have one hard head, David Jansen!"

He grinned. "Yep, I do, now"—he shoved his pants off and grabbed her right after, laughing hard when he tossed her to her back and she squealed—"let's see what I can do about making up for all those lonely nights."

"And days." She wrapped her slim legs around his hips.

"Yeah," he whispered, just to see her dazzling smile. "And every second in between."

Chapter Fourteen

Paris woke to the sound of a man in pain. She immediately reached for David. His arms were wrapped around her, and every inch of his body against hers was hot and hard with smooth, supple muscles—muscles that were tensed because he was having a nightmare.

"David," she murmured, trying to turn in his arms.

A fine sheen of moisture slipped along her skin, making them as slippery as when they were having sex. Only David wasn't enjoying whatever it was that had him sweating.

"David," she said a little louder, and moved one arm off her.

"Paris." He tightened his arms almost painfully. "What is it?" he asked, and released her to sit up. She heard something, and in the moonlight saw he'd pulled a gun out of somewhere.

"No, David, I…" She stopped and worried over telling him he'd had a nightmare. "I have to pee," she modified. "And you were dreaming, I think."

"Yeah." He lowered the gun out of sight. "I was. Go on, I won't peek," he teased when she didn't move.

Peek? It hit what he meant a second before he leaned over and pushed her hair off her face.

"Peek, follow you. You know where the bathroom is."

"Yes, thank you, I do." Paris suddenly turned shy all over again. Bizarre really, since the man had seen every inch of her and then some.

Still, she got up and headed to the bathroom, knowing he was watching her. It didn't bother her now. He loved her. *Loves. Me.* She did a happy little dance in the bathroom and froze at the grin on her face then glanced lower. The breath left her on a gasp at the love bites he'd given her. She vaguely remembered the feel of his mouth tugging and the sting she'd known would leave a mark. She'd left a few herself, but hers were much, much lower.

"Paris, stop admiring your body and pee, the bed's getting cold."

"Brat," she whispered, then covered her mouth. He was, but he was hers. She quickly took care of business and washed and dried her hands before racing back to bed. "It's cold. Did you turn the air on high?"

"I did. That way you'd curl up against me," he admitted without an ounce of shame. "You like the white noise, so I thought it would help you get comfortable, too."

"Oh, David," she said, and hugged him.

"Yeah, yeah, I'm sorry I woke you," he added.

"You—"

"Rule number five, no lies—"

"I wasn't lying! You were—"

David tugged her hair and laughed when she hit his stomach. "I have nightmares, sometimes, I guess."

"I'm sorry. Do you want to talk about it? I'm a good listener," she coaxed. "Besides, I've had a few myself."

"You?" he said, adjusting her the way he wanted her on the bed. "Why do you have nightmares?"

She laughed and snuggled closer. "Why does anyone? Why do you?"

"War. I have nightmares from things I've seen," he said and shrugged. "And snakes. I hate snakes."

"I know, me, too." She stroked his chest and, after a deep breath said, "I have nightmares from when I was hurt. Skating."

"You were hurt?" he asked, then tipped her head up. "I read about you. You almost went to the Olympics, then something happened. No one wrote about it, but you and your partner disappeared."

"You read about me?"

"Yeah," he said and shrugged again, something she knew he did when he was uncomfortable. "I did. When I found out your last name, I did my research."

"On me?" She was oddly flattered, but also worried. "What else did you learn?"

"Not much, but I know something happened, Paris. Why not tell me, since you woke me up anyhow. Was it your partner? Did he do something?"

He sounded so rough, she soothed him with a hand on his chest. "It was a long time ago now, and forgotten."

"No, I don't think so. Do you still skate?"

She thought he was asking because he was trying to change the subject then circle back around to the tougher one, so she kissed him. "I'll tell you, okay? But no, well, getting all upset."

He frowned at that, not something he normally did, so she worried a little more about telling him. "I won't tell you unless—"

"Okay, okay, don't get your panties in a bind," he grumbled. "If you were wearing any. I like that you're not, now, go on."

"Okay, but then you share, too, David," she said, then added, "if you can."

As expected, his chest hardened and he gave her a long, intense look that, even in the shadows of the moonlight, she could see. "Deal. Then we gotta get up and get dressed, unfortunately. I'll let you sleep on the jet, okay?"

"Jet?"

"Paris," he grumbled.

"Right, my sad life story. So, yeah." She gathered her thoughts and realized she could tell him. She was certain he'd had worse things happen to him. He was a soldier, after all.

"I was always good at skating. Even as a kid, I was on skates more than off. My mom wanted me to be a figure skater, so I worked hard, and we got a coach when I was old enough," she said, simplifying all the side jobs she'd done to get the money to pay for a coach herself.

Her mom had been too busy with her life, and the men who trailed in and out of it.

"I was good, so I was partnered up with a guy, Alexander. We started dating, it happens, then he and I didn't fit any longer. My coach wanted a different partner for me and it didn't go over too well. Alexander came by the rink one day, just talking, and I was practicing." She paused and checked on David.

He was silent, and watched with a frown she'd only seen him wear when he'd talked to those MPs.

"Anyway, I was stupid to skate with him. I thought he'd gotten over the partner switch and all that. He acted so nice, and well, he wasn't. Not at all. Worse, I kinda think I knew, like, deep down, I knew he wasn't over it and he was still angry, but...well..."

"You trusted him. And this is why you took us up on that offer. Or one of the reasons you let me drag you off to bed. You went with us with your eyes wide open, but not with this guy."

"I went with you, and I still have my eyes wide open, too," she added, all warm inside that he remembered their hike and the talk they'd had.

He brushed her hair over her shoulder. "What did he do, Paris?"

She cleared her throat at David's tone. He sounded harsh. "David, it was long ago."

"Yeah, about the time you were supposed to go to the Olympics, right?"

She huddled deeper in the covers and shivered.

Almost instantly, David grumbled and pulled her closer. "I'm sorry, Paris, it's okay. I guess I don't like where I know this is going. He hurt you, didn't he? That scar on your leg, is that from him?"

She wasn't sure whether she should answer him or not. But when she didn't, he tightened his arms around her and pressed his head to her neck. "I wouldn't kill him, I'd just maim him, a man can still walk and all, just be missing parts. It works. The Russians do it all the time."

"David," she whispered, more touched by his savagery than she should've been. "He's dead. He committed suicide while I was in the hospital."

"Holy hell," David murmured, tightening his arms around her.

"He was sick, he needed help. He didn't know what he'd done, I'm sure—"

"The hell he didn't." David dragged her to sit up. "He was older than you, wasn't he?"

"A few years, yes."

"He knew better. He hurt you on purpose."

It wasn't a question, but she nodded hesitantly, knowing deep inside he was right. "He did. I broke my leg in three places, and he gave me a concussion that damaged my balance for a few months after the casts came off."

"Casts?"

"The thing is, David, I let him. If I'd stopped and thought, really thought, and *seen* him, I would have known he was no good. I don't do that anymore. I see you, I know you're good, that's..." She paused and caught her breath. "That's one reason I know I love you, and maybe the reason it hurt so badly when you broke your promise."

David grimaced and reached up to tenderly hold her face in his hands. "Paris, I didn't break it, I was just late in my delivery. I have you now, and I don't plan on leaving your side again."

She nodded, too emotional to do much more. David took care of it. He pulled her tight to his chest and hugged her. "Good, I'm glad we're good with that plan, princess, because I also bought some rope and a gag. You know, in case I had to kidnap you."

"David Jansen," she cried, hugging him tighter.

He laughed and pressed her back to the bed. "Just once more, before we have to go?"

"Yes, once more," she whispered against his lips, and spread her legs for him.

If she had her way, they'd never go anywhere, so they'd always, always have one more, and then one more, and one more.

Chapter Fifteen

"I need to call my uncle. He's gotta be out of his mind with worry."

David nodded, trying hard to keep his face clear of his thoughts. Which were amused. She was in a dressing room, trying on a few new things he'd practically had to force on her, but she peeked out a few times to see him.

She walked out in jeans that hung down way too low on her sexy hips and a tiny tank top with a pink and blue checkered shirt over the top. It made her breasts look way too big. She'd left the shirt unbuttoned so anyone who glanced at her would see, too. She looked like a sexy cowgirl.

"We can get those. But button up that shirt."

"In your dreams," she murmured, opening it wider by plunking her hand on her hip. "I got two more shirts like this and another pair of jeans."

"How about a few sweaters? It's cold in Vermont."

"Not in July it's not," she assured him. She'd also gotten a few sundresses, not that she knew. He'd already stuffed them in the bag the store gave him to lug around. He'd picked out a few boy shorts and tank tops that she would wear, he hoped, just to walk around in. He knew for a fact she wasn't wearing them to sleep in. He'd also gotten her shoes, and some cute shorts. She'd tried the shorts on and he'd sworn she wasn't wearing them out of the house. She'd laughed. He hadn't.

"I got you some skating clothes."

"You did?" she asked, turning to scan his face. He now knew, or thought he knew, why she did that. She'd only shared part of her story, and nothing about a man named Greg who'd been a first-class sleaze. Greg was two years ago. Two years she'd been alone. He wasn't ever leaving her alone again.

"Yeah, and I already talked to your Uncle Troy. He's a funny guy."

She froze and blinked. It was cute as heck. She'd done that when he'd pulled the SUV over and into the mall parking lot, for a quickie, he'd said. He knew she would have been on board for a quick lovemaking session, but she'd given the mall a horrified glance. He'd busted up and earned a few soft thumps on the stomach until he'd explained what he really wanted was to stop for a quick *shopping* trip.

"He said that if I screwed around and left you crying again, he'd fill my ass with lead. I assume that means bullets, although I'm not sure we use lead any longer for—"

"You talked to Uncle Troy?"

"Keep up, princess, come on. We gotta catch that flight, so we need to get these and go before you want anything else."

"David Jansen! I can buy my own clothes!

"Not a chance. I already got you taken care of."

"David—"

He stared at her and, amazing him, she snapped her mouth closed, then smiled and tossed a pair of pretty pink panties onto the stack of clothes he already had in his arms. A guy next to them stared, but that was cool. He was completely aware of how gorgeous Paris was.

"Fine. So, Vermont. Why there?"

"That's where we're getting married and I'm getting surgery."

She was just about to take a sip of her iced coffee but stopped with her lips around the straw. Her eyes grew wider by the second. If they weren't waiting in a line to purchase her clothes, he was fairly certain he'd be flat on his back again, and this time not with the happy ending he'd gotten last time. He altered his approach.

"I need you to pretend, but as long as we're pretending, I thought, why not? We could stop up at Vegas —"

"Vegas is not *up* from here."

"And do the jumping over the broom handle there."

"People don't do that."

"I know, so maybe we could exchange vows and jump over the —"

"David, do you think because we are out in a public mall I won't give you hell?"

He squinted at her, assessing her flushed face and the cold chips of gray ice in her eyes, and thought better of shrugging. "I am completely serious. I would like to marry you, but if you want to wait and just pretend, that's cool, too."

She stalked away a few steps, stopped, turned, and loaded him up with more of the clothes she'd been carrying, then walked right through the store until she hit the mall. He watched her reach a bench, turn and plunk her butt down. She rested her elbows on her knees and her head on her hands and glared in his direction. Thankfully, he'd already bought the clothes she'd left wearing, otherwise he'd have had to go haul her out of the mall jail or something.

At least she hadn't run in fear.

That had to mean something.

He was next, so he went through the process of paying, then spotted a little chain with a ballet dancer, he thought, on it, until he looked closer and noticed tiny ice skates on the girl's feet. "Is this an ice skater, or ballet dancer?" he asked the older sales clerk lady, handing her the charm and necklace.

"I think it's a figure skater, see the hands up like that, I think that's a figure skater's move, but figure skating is a lot like ballet," she offered.

"Ah, right, it is. But those are skates, right?"

She examined the piece through her reading glasses, then smiled. "Good eyes, those are. It's adorable, isn't it?"

He nodded. "I'll take it, thanks."

"No problem." She rang him up and folded all the tiny clothes in two neat bags. Hell, was this enough? Well, there'd be malls in Vermont. He managed the two bags and his crutch and made it out of the store. He found Paris still contemplating him, with her hands still holding her head up.

"Okay, we're good to go. Maybe we should stop by that drug store, huh? And get you some girly shampoo and so on."

"Are you serious?"

"Well, you won't like my Old Spice stuff, I'm fairly sure."

"David," she grumbled and stood.

He put the two bags on the bench, tucked his crutch tighter under his armpit, then took hold of her hands.

"I'm always serious, even if I'm kidding. But in answer to your question, yeah, I'm serious. I'm not in love with you for a few weeks, or months, or years, then I'm done and off I go. I want all of it. Love, marriage, kids that drive us nuts then turn around and make grandkids we can enjoy, all of it. Cruises when we're seventy, you name it. But we can start small with pretending, if you want. Although I did see a pretty set of rings in that jewelry store over there."

She let out an explosive breath and suddenly threw her arms around his neck. He was still a bit wobbly, but he caught her, and didn't drop his crutch either.

"Oh my God, that was so romantic!"

Paris stiffened then buried her face in his neck because, yeah, that wasn't her gushing at them.

"I mean, oh my goodness, that was so sweet!"

"Thanks," he muttered. "I think she liked it, too," he added.

"Um, well, you forgot this. Sorry, I wasn't trying to listen, just, oh, I'm so sorry."

He took the little bag with the jewelry box from the sales clerk and chuckled. Paris tightened her arms and laughed against his throat. "You paid her to say that."

"I did no such thing!" he cried, but damn, that would have been a good idea. "Now, come on, let up on the stranglehold. I got you something."

She eased up enough to look down, then sniffed and rubbed at her face against his shoulder and shirt before she took the bag.

"Sit down, come on," he urged. His leg throbbed so she had to sit or he'd be falling down.

"Okay, sorry you had to carry the bags alone."

"The bags weren't heavy, princess. Now, come on, cheer up, it's not that bad," he teased.

"No, it's not, it's wonderful. *You're* wonderful. But you just love to shock me, and sometimes I can't tell if you're teasing or serious."

"I know, I know, I can't seem to stop that, but—"

"I don't want you to," she said quickly, then sniffed and rubbed her cheeks again with the back of her hand.

"Open it, it's for you."

She nodded, then pulled the velvet box out and lifted the lid.

"Oh." She blinked, and he winced when a few tears slipped free. He did need to pick better ways of telling her things. He'd worried her, and if she wanted to marry him, asking to pretend now seemed like a dumb-ass thing to do.

"I think if you wear this, you and I are going down that aisle, Paris. So think about it before you put it on."

"Uh, isn't that an engagement ring?" she asked, doing that cute wrinkle with her nose.

"Why can't it be an engagement necklace?" he countered, and pulled the thing from the box. The clerk had taken off the price tag, thankfully, so Paris didn't see that. He had a feeling Paris was frugal with her money.

He held it up, and had to admit it was worth every penny to see the shock on Paris' face. She glowed, and the happy squeal and smile he got was worth ten hundred of the damn things. She hugged him again then turned on his lap and lifted her hair. It took him a vital second to figure out that the squeal meant yes, she'd marry him, *and* she wanted him to put the necklace on her now.

"David?"

"Right." He felt as if the world had just been lifted off his shoulders. He kissed her bare left shoulder and tucked the shirt back into place before he put the necklace on. It was so small and the tiny latch a hell of a tough ticket when he couldn't get his hands to stop shaking. Finally he got it on and she turned, giving him a sunny, happy smile before she kissed him.

Married. She was going to marry him. *For real. Not yet, though. Not a chance.* He wanted to give her the whole shebang. The white dress, the carpet, the flowers, the beach or a sunny garden. Somewhere romantic after.

"Start thinking on that dress, Paris, because when we tie the knot, it's not coming undone. And we're picking up those rings," he said, then at her frown, he rethought the order. "If you like them, I mean."

She squeezed her arms around his neck and laughed. "I will like them. And no way are you leaving my sight again. Not even when you're sixty and going through that midlife crisis thing."

"I thought that happened in the forties?"

"Well, you're what, thirty now, and you're still acting like a kid, so I was betting on sixty being — ahhh!"

He took that bet, and if they hadn't been in a mall, he'd have taken a heck of a lot more.

"I love you, Paris — soon to be Jansen."

Her eyes got all round and shimmery and her smile lit up her face. "Oh, David."

Chapter Sixteen

"This is not a plane, this is a private jet."

"I know, it's for us. Faster," David added, and pushed against her lower back to get her moving. "Back, see the door, we take that."

She did, and stumbled inside to see an amazingly cozy cabin, complete with bed, bathroom and a few windows. David shut the door behind her, threw the crutch down and sat heavily on the bed.

"Is your leg hurting?"

"Naw, just tired. How about we sleep?"

"Oh, sleeping sounds wonderful," she said, sighing.

"You didn't sleep much last night," he added, wincing when she bent to take off his brace. "It's okay, yeah, let's take this off."

The sound of the engines coming to life made her pause, but David nodded. "We have five minutes, no worries."

She did worry, though. Over him, over them, over Sara. She cleared her throat and got the last buckle undone, then slipped the brace free. "David, I'm worried about Sara."

He was in the process of reaching for her hand, and paused. His blue eyes were tired, she thought, and red from lack of sleep. Or all his making up last night instead of sleeping.

"Come here and you can tell me why," he murmured, helping her onto the bed and scooting back with her. "What's wrong with Sara?"

Paris considered what to say. She trusted David completely. "I don't want secrets between us, David," she began.

David smoothed his thumb over the engagement ring he'd slipped on her finger. Her heart did a little jump, and she couldn't resist kissing his cheek.

"I don't either, Paris." He tipped her head up to stare into her eyes. "I won't say anything, if that's what has you worried."

"I know that, but I'm worried you might have to," she managed, then sighed and leaned into his warmth. "I think she took, or maybe she was given that drug, at Duke's."

His chest muscles tightened under her cheek, and for a few moments he stroked her back with one hand and smoothed his thumb on her finger. Finally he sighed and she felt him nod. "I see. Will thought so too. So she's what? Sick?"

"I think so. She isn't eating right, and she's anxious."

"And?"

"She quit her job. She said it was too stressful, but she loved her job, and I think…" She hesitated again. "I think that drug, whatever it was, is doing something to her. Still. Is that possible?"

"Yeah, it is. We should get her to Chung. He's the man that developed the first serum. If anyone can help, it'd be him. Don't worry. I'll see what I can find out."

She nodded and relaxed. David would take care of it. She could count on him, and that was one reason she'd hesitated about telling him. Sara might be...embarrassed. Her friend had always been open with her sexuality, free of a lot of the hang-ups Paris had. But now, she'd changed. That meant something had caused the change. Paris only hoped it wasn't something bad, but maybe what David had said Will suffered from—constant arousal—and not that someone had hurt her. But the way she'd taken off in Wyoming—that wasn't Sara's style. She'd left Paris, the car...everything and just gone. They'd talked and her reasoning had been Paris was happy and she didn't want to rush her. But there had been something else. "Sara is back in Florida. I barely hear from her. I just want to be sure she's okay."

"Don't worry, Paris," he repeated, hugging her closer. "We'll see what we can do, first without her knowing, then maybe if that doesn't work, we'll have to be more...blunt."

Blunt did not sound good, but she'd cross that bridge when they got there. Suddenly the sound of the engines roaring alerted her and she sat up.

"Oh, we're taking off, should we use seat belts?"

"I'm your seat belt, just hold on." He kissed her temple and pulled her back down, then tensed his muscled stomach and lifted enough to turn off the light by the bed. "Go to sleep. Maybe I'll wake you so we can see how good this bed is. After you let me get some rest, princess."

She laughed remembering all the whispered demands she'd given him last night.

Wiggling up enough to reach his ear, she whispered, "Only if you promise to let me give you another wild ride."

"Oh ho," he laughed but sounded sleepy already. "Any time, any place."

"I'm going to keep you to that promise," she murmured, already feeling the heaviness of lack of sleep taking its toll on her as well.

She still heard David's whispered, "Always."

* * * *

"So, this is our new home for the next few...weeks?" Paris asked, staring around the cozy living room and kitchen.

This looks like my home in Canada, only...empty feeling.

"Yeah, imagine that," he said, folding his arms over his chest. He'd come here first, making her wait outside at a post office while he'd played G.I. Joe. "Or longer."

"Or longer?"

She might have offended him a tiny bit by playing on his phone while he'd been gone. She'd beat three levels on Angry Birds Stella, though. He'd deleted the game, so she pretty much knew she'd been in the bad because she was supposed to 'watch' the area. She wasn't sure what that meant though, so after several minutes, she pulled her new iPhone out and minutes later had a few games open. Addictive wasn't even close to what those games were.

"You wanted something more glamorous?"

"What? Me?" she asked, beginning to think this two-story cape house just might be David Jansen's home. "It's okay," she murmured, turning to examine all the knick-knacks lining the bookshelves instead of books. There was a football, a really big seashell and on one of the shelves, pictures of him with various military men. One of him deep sea fishing, posing with a grin and a huge fish, and of course a beer in his hand. She circled the room and ventured back near him, feeling oddly off balance. This *was* his home.

The sneaky man laughed and beckoned her over with a hand. "Come here."

A phone's dull vibration made her smile, especially when his smile dipped into a frown. He scanned the screen and sighed. "Shit, we just got here."

"What does that mean? We can leave?"

"You like the place that much, huh?" he muttered without looking up. She opened her mouth to tell him she loved the place, and he added, "Naw, we stay, the doctor's moved my surgery to tomorrow, though."

"What? Already?"

"Yep. Did you have something else you wanted to do?" he asked, attention back on her.

"I love this place," she said, moving to the kitchen. "It's yours."

He smiled but nodded.

"And we're safe here."

"Yes, ma'am."

"David—"

"You're safe with me. If Savage can connect you to me, then me to this place, and you with me here, well, that's just about genius."

"But he did connect me to Duke's so…he must have seen us," she said, not happy doubting him, but not happy keeping her thoughts to herself.

She noticed that his gaze dipped to her hand, where she now wore a shiny engagement ring. He had their matching rings in his pants pocket. He'd said if she had them she'd lose them. Probably. She'd already lost two phones—one back in Wyoming and another she'd bought in the hopes that somehow he'd find her and call. Although wedding rings were a bigger, way bigger, deal.

"If you noticed, this was a dead end street. My house is also secluded. No one outside of Will's been here."

"So we're safe."

"I believe so. If we're not, the men stationed up the street and in the nearest couple of towns will let us know. There's no where we can truly hide, Paris. Here, at least I know the land and will be warned if anyone suspicious shows up. Now"—he exhaled and dropped his arms to his sides—"is there anything else bothering you? Or can we be done and get to doing something else?"

"I think you and I have had more than enough of *something* else lately," she told him when he met her eyes again. "Talking is important, too."

He pulled her over until she fell into him. "It sure is, but we haven't tried out this counter, or that couch. And we're never going to have enough of *something*, believe me." He stroked down her butt when he said that, and angled her hips so she could feel the semi hard-on he was sporting.

"We can't just have sex all over the place," she said quietly.

"Why not?"

She blinked, because really, she couldn't think of any reasons. Every time David Jansen gave her that sexy blue-eyed stare, or held her in his arms, she couldn't think properly.

"Princess, my house is safer than your momma's arms. You can talk about anything, even how much you like me teasing you with my tongue along the inside—"

She covered his mouth, already aware of what she liked him teasing. *Touching. Licking.* Anything David did to her about summed it up.

"Don't even say it," she warned, but her heart swelled at the laughter in his eyes. He was leaving her again—going to surgery, yes—but so soon. *I just got him back.*

Everything he did was dangerous and snuck up on her—like leaving, that day back in Wyoming. Her stomach bottomed out. Maybe bringing her here was just as dangerous.

His phone vibrated again, a different sound from the last time. He pulled her hand from his face and winked at her. "You know you're not lasting a full two minutes when we start, but let me get this—Will hates it when I ignore his calls."

"Will has his own ringtone?"

David shrugged and kissed her lips. "You have one, too, don't be jealous. Hold off on those whispered demands and ravishing me, okay?" He dug out his phone, laughing at her when she rolled her eyes. "Will, tell me you have good news."

She was so close she could hear Will's grumbled response. She moved to give David room, but he tightened his arm around her and tilted his head so she could listen.

"Not good. So far we've determined it was Savage in Wyoming."

"And? Where is he now?"

"That's the million dollar question. When I know, you'll know."

David nodded, a concerned frown growing on his handsome face. When he was worried, his sleepy eyes narrowed to laser slits, like now. He reminded her of a spy in a movie she'd seen once. She couldn't remember the name but it had been a good movie. The girl had died, so that hadn't been the best ending. Maybe it had been a James Bond movie. David reminded her of the actor, except David was wearing a charcoal-colored casual shirt and black dress slacks, not a tux.

"So, it's a shot in the dark he's even in DC," David said. "You're doing what until you know?"

"We're pretty certain he's here. For now, I'm on standby. Petrok is positive Walters contacted Savage. She's also a hundred percent certain Walters never dug into his past, or probably past the money Savage wired to his accounts."

"What do you mean?" David asked.

"Walters had no idea who Savage really was," Will muttered. "We're hoping Savage still believes he's hidden—"

"In plain sight. How is it a guy like that even owns property in the US?"

Will laughed harshly. "I doubt we really want to know that answer, buddy."

He sounded angry, much harsher than she remembered. Worse than Wyoming, even. David was also stern in a way she'd only seen back in Wyoming.

"We have more than a dozen men working on this," David said. She sensed it was for her benefit, but didn't interrupt to ask. "But if Savage gets wind who's closing in on him, I want Paris long gone, is that clear? Any connection between her and us has to be completely void."

She frowned at that, and would have spoken, but David shook his head once.

"Absolutely," Will agreed without a pause. "We hear a whisper that he's connected her to us, and you're both gone. The men in Canada did a half-ass job, but at least Carson got that lid sealed tight."

"What does that mean?" she whispered

"Sara and your uncle are safe," he murmured with his hand over the phone.

"Besides, Savage doesn't know you, and it's highly doubtful he'll recognize Paris as the blonde woman in Canada he wanted to chat with even if he did run right into her. We have men stationed down from your house. They're doing repairs to the road out there, so it's all on the up and up, right?"

David tightened his arm around her shoulders and she leaned into him for support. He was solid and strong, but this was way over her head.

"Troy got hired on, remember him?"

"Sure, he's here?" David asked, relaxing a little.

"Yeah, just a phone call away, too. You're up for your surgery?"

"Yeah, thanks for the privacy, man," David muttered, but she could see he was pleased Will knew his surgery was in the morning.

"Just stay off it for the first twenty-four. If I have to haul my ass over to pick you up again because you've screwed up with your leg *and* Paris, I'll be—"

"I got Paris under control," he added, squeezing her butt with a big grin.

"Good, that woman's more than you deserve, buddy, but if you—"

"And she's listening, so keep your comments above the belt, otherwise she'll kick your butt first, then I will," David warned.

Paris knew she was blushing. She shook her head at David, but didn't really mind. This close to him, she never minded anything. Already she was starting to feel achy and his suggestion of the couch or counter was quickly building into ideas she hoped he'd explore—if he got off the phone. The danger they were in, mixed with the fear they'd be separated again, built inside of her. All those lonely nights, the tears and heartache were still too fresh for her to chance losing him again. If she knew one thing about David Jansen, it was that when he made a promise he kept it. She'd just have to help him see that from now on, his promise to her was more important than this trouble they were in now.

She'd slept the entire flight in his arms. If she could, she'd sleep the same way for the next hundred years. He'd slept as well. He'd also told her it was the best sleep he'd had in six months.

Will chuckled. "Hey, Paris, I knew you were there, otherwise Jansen swears like a sailor. Keep him off his leg for the first day, then make him walk on it, without that crutch, even if he whines. He's a terrible patient, too, did he tell you that?"

"Hey, hey, no spilling the secrets of my bad behavior," David said.

"I already know about your bad behavior." She sneaked a hand down to his belt. Watching his eyes light up, she worked the buckle open. Tomorrow, she could worry over what they were doing. Right now, she knew exactly what she was doing. Making love to her fiancée the one way she knew turned him inside out.

Through the phone, she could hear Will, but her attention left their conversation and switched to the stiff cylinder pressing insistently against David's slacks for her.

"Right, I guess she has them all figured out. You two keep your heads down, and if this pans out, you're just getting a long vacation."

She smiled at Will's phrase and kissed a path down David's jaw to the buttons of his shirt. His attention turned to focus on her so fast she knew he knew what she was going to do. Or *thought* he did.

"There's no worry over me forgetting that." David winked at her and nodded to his zipper. He was completely shameless, but then maybe so was she. She unzipped him and, watching his face, slid down the counter so her mouth was perfectly aligned. He bit his lip sexily when the head brushed her cheek. The head of his cock was swollen, the slit already moist. Seeing him like this, so masculine, was so intimate she had a surge of jealousy for every other woman he'd ever played his games with.

This was hers, though. *He* was hers. Just as she was his. But today, with the threat of losing him again rising up like a terrible nightmare, she wanted to give him everything she could. She wanted him to always remember her, them, this passion they shared with their love as the foundation.

As she grew more determined, she tightened her hand on his dark erection the way he loved, rubbing just up and over that spot underneath the flared head. Slowly, keeping his gaze locked with hers, she released him and reached for his shirt. His stomach tensed under her hands as he prepared for the passion she knew would explode between them. The buttons of his shirt came free easily enough, then she teased him by licking from his tight navel to that rough patch of golden hair on his chest. Stroking his cock faster and harder, she sucked one hard nipple in her mouth.

His muffled groan covered by a cough thrilled her.

In the background, Will was still talking strategy with him, but she knew none of that mattered. Life had given her a second chance. *Us a second chance.*

When she knew David was dying for more, she stopped her strokes and squeezed until he bit back a moan only by covering it by clearing his throat Oh yeah, he was primed. If she had to guess, he was close to coming already. Not waiting on more, she went back down, sucking on his skin as she did so he shifted impatiently and half muttered, half grunted replies to Will.

"Yeah, I guess you're supposed to make them believe you're a happily married couple."

She smiled at that. They wouldn't have to make anyone believe anything that wasn't true. With that thought in mind, she licked out, slowly catching the drop of pre-cum on her tongue then treating the rest of his heavy cock like a Ben & Jerry's soft serve. David caught hold of the counter.

"It is a nice place, isn't it?" she asked, feeling like a bit of teasing was necessary. It had been months since she'd tasted him and made him shudder in pleasure. She wanted him to always know they shared this—the sex, the fun, the…love.

He blinked and she heard Will say, "Have you been there long?"

"No, just got in. Made it to the kitchen, though," David said, his voice coming out deeper from the passion simmering between them.

"Ah, is that so?" Will asked, then laughed. "I bet you did. Try to treat her right."

"Believe me, I am." David bit his lip.

Paris smiled, and as David's face darkened with passion, she kissed along his tight scrotum. She'd discovered he loved it when she licked lightly along the supersensitive skin. He made a strangled sound and tightened his hand on the counter until his knuckles turned white.

"Hey, check in on your progress, man, we gotta go—"

She sucked the left side of his sac until the ball slipped into her mouth. Gently, but not too gently, she tugged on the flesh then teased it with her tongue. David's hand went for her head and he nearly dropped the phone putting it on the counter in a rush.

"Right, good luck, I heard this doc is one of the best," Will said. "Paris, try not to spoil him too badly."

As soon as Will disconnected, David hauled her up to her feet, turned her, and all six foot three inches of aroused man plastered himself to her back. He also frantically tore at her jeans. She heard a rip, but it didn't matter. A second later he was panting in her ear.

"God, you're a dream come true," he groaned. "Let me in, princess. I need you."

He didn't wait for a reply, but bent her over, legs as wide as her jeans at her ankles would allow, and thrust. The first thick slide made her curl her toes and grip the edge of the counter to keep from crying out.

He wrapped his arms around her for support and breathed in her ear. "Tell me, tell me, Paris. Anything you want. I'll give it."

"Harder, David, I want to feel you tomorrow, when you're gone, I want to know you were there, here." She dragged his hand down to her pussy.

He thrust harder, rocking her in his arms with the force of his hips. Only once before had he made love to her like this, and she *had* felt him for days afterward. This time, she wasn't losing him.

"Again. More," she breathed, arching her butt.

"Always. Tomorrow you won't be able to walk without feeling me," he warned. His words and tone sent a shiver rippling down her breasts, past her stomach, and right to where he pushed in and pulled out of her so frantically. He kept the pace up, making her wetter and wetter for him. The sounds of their love making filled the room. It was so hot, especially with cold marble counter under her cheek and his hot heavy breath in her ear, she began to feel her orgasm building.

"Love you, Paris." He tightened his hold on her hips and, with a heavy groan, kissed her shoulder, whispering her name as he shuddered over her. She moaned and burst into a climax that kept going as he filled her with pulses of warmth.

When they could breathe again, David pulled free, turned her and picked her up. His pants were still on, she knew, but she also knew he wasn't letting that slow him down.

"David, your leg!"

"Princess, my leg can support you, believe me. I think we're going to have a long, long night. Did you have your Wheaties today?"

She kissed his lips and hugged him to her breasts. Somewhere along the way she'd lost her shirt. "I did. Did you?"

He laughed and sat her down on the counter. Immediately he kicked his shoes off, then nodded to her when he undid his pants all the way so they dropped to his ankles. David even had great legs, long, lean and toned.

"How about those jeans?"

"Pull." She was too busy admiring how his muscles all rippled and bulged when he moved to do much more. He had one of those tans that men got when they wore board shorts, so his butt and half his legs were pale compared to the rest of him. It was an interesting contrast.

"Are you checking me out?"

She met his blue eyes and her grin grew. "I am. I'm a woman. We do that, check out the scenery."

He froze, then laughed so hard even his erection shook. It was fascinating. "Paris, you are one smarty-pants ice princess, huh?"

"You stole that from me," she accused.

His eyes glowed with such passion she shivered. Taking her jeans off, he threw them down after and edged between her legs. He settled his hot body as close as possible and positioned her legs so they were held up by the inside of his elbows. She was tipped back but also exposed this way. She shivered at the desire flushing David's face. He edged his hips and angled his erection so he could slowly ease forward as he stared at her.

"You stole my heart, so I guess I'm forgiven."

He matched his words with a hard, firm thrust, lodging every inch of his cock deep.

"Oh, David," she whispered, keeping their gazes locked. "Don't you know? I didn't steal it." She lifted closer to him and caressed the smooth skin of his shoulders. "You gave it to me just like I gave you mine. Remember? Forever."

A smile slowly filled his eyes. "Forever, huh?" He leaned forward so she lay back on the cold counter and started a slow, steady meeting of their bodies. "And always."

"Always," she vowed. "Always and always."

The pace increased quickly. They were too intense for slow and easy, especially with the tension she could feel just below the surface. She gasped when he released one leg, but only so he could massage his fingers over her clit. Within seconds she was close.

"More," she whispered.

David groaned and began giving her what she wanted—firm, hard drives with his body that lodged his big, long cock so deep she would always feel him.

She climaxed again, twice more, each time whispering his name as the passion overtook her. David joined her after the second, but he didn't whisper her name, he shouted it, loud enough to make her tingle all over again.

Chapter Seventeen

"Explain to me how no one can get a job done that I hire them for?" Savage shouted over the whirl of the copter landing on his estate's helicopter pad. The paint job would fool anyone into believing the aircraft was authentic, but a night landing was his preferred method. This time it was just a precaution. Who would check that an emergency vehicle would hide anyone?

Soft. Americans are all soft.

Murphy took a seat across from him. He didn't wince, but the lines around his eyes whitened. He and Marcus had been attacked by special ops outside of Masters' home in Canada. Marcus was dead. Murphy had only gotten away by hiding in a barn six miles or more from the site. He'd been lucky Savage hadn't left his ass there.

The two additional men got in, and the doors slammed closed on the noise.

"Don't bother explaining. Sometimes the only way to do a job right is to do it yourself."

He nodded to the pilot, and seconds later they were airborne. They even had a patient—one of Potter's experiments who probably wouldn't make it past the first operation, let alone long enough to talk about what had been done to her.

"Jansen is set up for surgery tomorrow morning," Murphy said.

"Yes. Seven a.m., I believe. Quite early," Savage muttered. "Who is on the ground?"

"Two former Sentinels are in the area along with two Rangers, and"—Murphy rubbed his chin with his fingers—"Petrok and a squad of Delta Forces."

Savage nodded. *Petrok.* Or when he'd known her, Petrokski. She was high on his list of scores to settle. But first he would hand deliver a death sentence to Jansen for killing Martinez. Then, while the man took his last breath, he'd make certain he saw them carrying off his woman. Nothing got to a man like taking his dependents. Especially his wife.

"We focus on Jansen. Once he's in surgery we simply wait, and when everyone believes he is going to be fine, we make certain he isn't."

"And? If we see Petrok?"

Savage met Murphy's blue eyes. "We kill her and everyone else."

"Except Masters," Murphy clarified.

"Except Masters, and by the time Potter's done with her, she'll wish we had," Savage added, softly patting the woman strapped down on her gurney.

* * * *

"Princess, I think we can safely say you're going to feel this in the morning if we don't stop, not that there aren't a few hundred other things we could do..."

Paris groaned and let her legs fall open and off his sexy butt. He laughed and his penis slid free from her very, very happy body. He was right. She *was* going to feel this for weeks. She wasn't hurt, but when she squeezed her inner muscles, she could feel the impression of his thick, large cock where he'd been making her crazy for hours.

"I love it," she whispered. She peeked and found him hovering over her.

His grin said it all. He sighed, though, as if she'd spoiled all his fun. "Does this mean we're done? No anal, 'cause that might make an impression."

She was too weak to laugh, but did. "*You* are crazy."

"Hopeful, just making suggestions, planting seeds, you know, for when you're really horny."

"David, cuddle with me," she demanded, weakly thumping him on the shoulder.

He laughed and caught her hand. "First, let me get you some water, and see if I locked the door—"

"You locked the door, there's water there, come on," she murmured, and tried to tug him down. His arms were like solid steel.

"You're whining."

"I am. Why are you being so mean?"

He kissed her for an answer and tousled her hair after. "I'll be right back."

She curled on her side only to get the blankets thrown on her. They smelled brand new.

Has he come here often?

She smiled and stayed under and sure enough, David pulled them down and kissed her again. "How about a movie?"

"A movie? Now?" she asked.

"Sure, I have popcorn, too. It'll be fun."

"Are you nervous about tomorrow? And isn't it midnight? No eating after — "

"That's an ol' wives' tale, you can eat. Now, you're hungry, aren't you?"

She blushed. She was hungry and now that he was so energetic, she felt her strength coming back. "If we watch a movie, I might want dessert."

"Oh ho, is that so?" He tousled her hair again and laughed. "You recover and I'll go get some snacks. See about a movie. Nothing girly," he warned with a mock grimace.

"No? What about — ?"

"You decide, but be warned, if I hate it, I'm having sex with you while you watch it."

He said that so deadpan and walked away that she wasn't able to come up with an answer. The double whammy of his naked back and butt, along with the idea of him making love to her while she watched TV, was so completely stunning she simply stared after him until his chuckles grew too quiet to hear.

How does he know I even like popcorn?

She crawled around until she found the remote control for the huge TV, then straightened their covers and found most of the pillows. After that, she couldn't figure out the remote. The stupid thing was in English, but she had no idea how to make it work, and when she hit the on button, it did nothing. Instead of dealing with it, since she knew David could figure it out in seconds, she relaxed back on the very well-used bed and pushed the piles of blankets down around her and stared around the room.

Slowly it sank in that this was the first time since David had barreled back into her life that she'd been alone. *And now you're in his bedroom.* The private jet had been a blur. As promised, she'd slept, with him holding her, too. The shopping, engagement, then more grocery shopping, then here — all seemed unreal. At the same time, it'd seemed like weeks since he'd been back, not days.

His scent still lingered on her. *Probably along every inch, too.*

It'd been a whirlwind, but it had been like that since the first. She felt alive with him. Safe. Secure. More, she could tell him anything. Anything at all.

The bedroom was clean, and neat, a bit more stylish than she'd imagined he would have, but not girly at all. She sensed him in everything from the dark wooden furniture to the navy blue bedding. The pillows made her laugh, since he had around five or so, but since three of them didn't match the sheets, she thought he'd thrown them in here.

She glanced around, and couldn't remember if there were more bedrooms than this one, but she thought maybe there would have to be. The outside of the house had seemed big, so maybe it was a three-bedroom. What would he do now? He'd said he was done with the service.

Would she go back to teaching? She couldn't imagine not skating, and she couldn't picture David not finding a way for her to be able to skate. Already he'd told her there was a rink not that far from his house. He'd even suggested the skating would be good for his leg.

David. He simply took care of everything. It was startling, but sank in like one of his warm kisses. All her life, since she could remember, she'd been the one taking care of people.

Her uncle was safe. David had made sure of that when he'd come for her. He'd also set him up on a vacation, so he was probably more than fine as well.

She had a niggling worry that he'd paid for her uncle, but she'd ask him about that.

Tomorrow he'd be in surgery, and for some reason she was nervous. She knew why. Her dad had died during a 'routine' operation. She'd been a little girl, but old enough to know that he shouldn't have died. Plus, her mom had made certain she knew. Every time a man left her, her mom would drink until she'd cry and cry about her father deserting them. About every man deserting her.

David is different. He didn't desert me. Plus now I can take care of him.

"Hey, why the sad face, and why don't you have a show on?"

David not only had snacks, he had on a dark brown robe, which looked good on him, because what didn't? He carried a tray with drinks, popcorn, chips and a bowl of pineapple. She spotted two enormous sandwiches, too, and Skittles.

"When did you get Skittles?"

"I snuck them in at the grocery store. You like them."

"I do, huh?" She took a grape one and scooted over, handing him the remote when he positioned the tray to the side. On the bed. "Is that safe?"

He disrobed, taking her breath away, and got under the covers. Immediately he pulled her up close then took the remote. "It's safe, now what's the deal?"

"I couldn't figure it out and I knew you could." She wiggled closer and fixed the mess he'd made of the covers. "Why do you have so many pillows?"

He turned the TV on to illustrate her point, and immediately adjusted the volume and flicked through a few channels.

"Pillows?" he muttered, then glanced down and around. "Hell if I know. I threw them in here last time I was here, I think. After I did some cleaning. You don't like them?"

"There's five."

Attention back on the television, he said, "Ah, well, toss 'em down on the floor and you can use me."

She popped a Skittle in his mouth and smiled when he winced. "You don't like them?"

"Too sour, now why the sad face?" he asked, not looking away from the TV. "How about one of those sandwiches?"

"Which one? Ham?"

"Sure, ham." He flicked through a television guide. "Ah ha! Not *Iron Man,* but *Avengers,* that one with the Hulk, you know?"

"I like that, here, take a bite, Mr. Movie man."

He winked, got the channel set and took her and the sandwich. "Now, why the sad face?"

"Are you paying for my uncle's vacation in Florida?"

He'd taken a mouthful of food, so he choked a little, but, eyes watering, shook his head. "Hell no," he said around his enormous bite. "I let Uncle Sam do that."

"Is that the absolute truth?" He shook his head, more prepared this time. "Hand me the beer before you answer the real question."

"Just checking," she murmured, and handed him the beer, kissing his cheek when she did. "I was just worrying over you getting surgery. My dad died in a routine surgery. I don't like hospitals."

David chewed and swallowed with his mouth way too full. He took a big drink of the beer and wiped his wrist over his lips. "Is that so?"

"David."

"Princess, you could have told me this from the start. It kinda explains the marathon sex, but I hope you want a repeat of that, because that was a dream come true." He examined her face, then kissed her once, tasting like sweet beer mixed with sexy David.

"I'm not dying on a leg surgery. In fact, I've had more surgeries than you have pretty little white teeth. This thing" — he gestured with his beer to his leg — "is nothing more than one more, but to you, that's not the case. What are we going to do about that?"

"About that?" she asked and got a sandwich stuffed in her mouth. She bit down or the stubborn man would have kept it there, and chewed while he watched her with a big smile.

"You're so damn cute. So, yeah, you. I don't want you worried. There are drugs for that, you know."

"David, I am not taking drugs to not worry!" she said when she'd finished the mouthful.

"Good. I don't want you to. How's the sandwich?"

She stared at him and realized what he was doing. But the sandwich was good, and the movie was just starting. She leaned over and kissed him. "I love you. I don't want to lose you. I've never felt so free, and I don't want to go back to how unhappy I was, without you," she added, knowing her eyes were filling up, but the words had to be said. "I just might worry a bit, but once you're awake I'll be better, that's all."

"Paris, you are more than I ever dreamed, and this surgery and this screwed-up situation here" — he gestured to the room with a grimace — "isn't going to break us apart. I went out of my mind when you were gone. I don't want to go through that again, and I'm not putting you through that, either. Trust me."

He rubbed her arm and his warmth, along with his words, eased some of her worry. He was just too alive to not be.

"Okay, let's watch the movie, then. Is that pineapple for me?"

"Yeah." He chuckled. "Here, sit back, but watch the parts," he warned when he pulled her knee up his leg. She laughed and patted his covers over his hips. "Okay, okay, no patting, that's just insulting." He shocked her by biting her lightly on the top of her breast.

"David!"

"Okay, there," he murmured and pointed the remote at the lights. They dimmed and the TV's sound increased. "I soaked those in vodka," he added when she bit into the pineapple.

She swallowed the juice and vodka too fast and choked. He grumbled, but laughed when she glared at him until she could breathe properly again. "Why did you do that?"

He cuddled her closer at the beginning. "I thought it'd help you relax, now, shhh... The movie's starting."

The vodka might've helped, but it was David who really eased her worries. Or being in his arms.

She made it to the part where Iron Man got caught in the enormous plane's engines waiting for Captain America, but the rest of the movie was lost on her because there were some things that were much more fun than movie-watching in her life now. And besides, she rationalized, she wanted David tired enough that he stayed off his leg tomorrow after the surgery.

Chapter Eighteen

David caught Paris sitting down carefully at the kitchen table and his grin grew as he put the phone away. "Will called again. He likes to act like a mother hen, huh?"

"Are you really a bad patient?" she asked.

"No. Are you ok?" He parked his butt across from her.

She gave him a flat stare, or tried to. She was simply too cute to pass it off. Her eyes were sparkling anyway, and the longer he met her eyes, the more her face turned rosy.

"Because if you are, I was thinking we didn't—"

"David Jansen, stop teasing me," she grumbled and shifted in her seat.

"Seriously, are you…?" He paused, not sure how to ask if he'd done something wrong.

"I'm fine and thank you, I'm just a little tired, maybe a tiny bit bashed, but I like it," she added when he tensed.

Bashed. That did not sound good.

"And no—in case your next question was, can you see?—you can't."

Well, that's that. He couldn't just tip her over and peek under her dress. Besides, he assured himself, he'd showered with her, and when he'd gone down she'd been a little pinker than usual, but he knew intimately she was more than fine.

"True." He stood, drawing her up after him. "I got to see every inch of that pretty pussy this morning, so I'm guessing as long as you liked it, I liked it. But maybe next time we do the marathon, we hold off on the eighth or ninth round? My cock is rubbed raw."

She blinked, opened her mouth, shut it, then blinked again. "Are you teasing me?"

He reached down and adjusted his soldier. "Not really. Or we use some lube. They make this body butter. It's flavored—"

"David," she laughed, and covered his mouth with both hands, he guessed in case he tried to shout through only one. "Don't talk for a bit, okay?"

He nodded and kissed her fingers. He wasn't rubbed raw, in fact he had a tingling sensation all along his dick, a little reminder of how damn perfect and soft Paris was around his erection. He hoped it stayed there all day until he could be inside her again. In fact, she'd whispered just that when she'd thrilled the hell out of him by waking him up for more.

"Are we ready to go?" she asked.

Nodding wasn't going to work, so he pulled free and wrapped her arms around his neck. She was wearing a sundress and blue jean jacket today. The pendant was settled snugly between her breasts, right where he'd been most of the night. He licked his lips and got a hint of her flavor on his tongue.

"We're ready, I just have to lock up and show you where the spare key ring is in the truck. I also have your phone for you. You need to keep this with you," he added.

She blushed but took the phone. She was always leaving it lying around, so he had to wonder if that wasn't the reason she didn't carry a phone.

"I don't like phones. I don't carry a big enough purse for one."

"It's an iPhone, it's small and fits in your pocket. Leave it there. If we get separated, use it to call me."

"We're only getting separated when you're in surgery and then I can't call you, smarty-pants."

He cocked an eyebrow. "You can call me Smarty-Pants G.I. Joe anytime, princess." He loved it, in fact. Cracked him up. He might remember it when he was eighty.

She blew out a Skittles-scented breath and leaned into him more fully. "You know, we're going to be late."

"Yeah? I bet you a blow job we won't be."

She laughed and stepped out of his arms because he let her. She also handed him his crutch and patted his head. "Be good and maybe I'll feel sorry for you after the surgery."

"What? You mean you won't automatically?"

"Well, I will, but if you're good, I might let you think up something for me to do, to keep your mind off, you know, the pain."

He winked and kissed her once, too briefly. "I'm going to make you keep that promise, princess, and you already know what I'm going to want," he said.

She seemed more than okay with that. In fact, the smile he got seemed to say she was already thinking about new ways to make him insane with that mouth of hers.

Can I be this lucky? All I have to do is get surgery and I get this kind of treatment?

* * * *

Two hours later, David hid an amused smile every time Paris swung by his seat. He was tired of waiting, and if not for the crutch, he'd be the one pacing the room, but Paris was doing it for him.

She might have worn a hole in the floor, too. She'd met the doctor, interrogated him like a professional, then met Troy and had no patience for him. He knew it was because she worried for him, but the poor Ranger didn't know where to step with her. It had cracked David up until he'd finally pointed out she was scaring the man. She'd looked wild-eyed from him to Troy, then blushed and apologized, blaming him completely. He liked that, and fully accepted it, too. It was his fault. She'd lost her dad under the knife. It explained a lot.

He'd have to forgo the benefits of more surgery if she worried this much over him.

Troy was here, in the hospital, and from the nod he'd given David he was staying close. That could mean Will and Carson were just being cautious, or a whole lot more Troy didn't want to say in front of Paris.

He shoved the worry aside, and put his faith in God, and of course, the adorable woman worrying her pretty little head over him.

"So, what is taking so long? I'm not happy he won't let you come home after. Why should we stay here for the night, David? It doesn't make sense."

"Princess, it makes perfect sense. It's a quick surgery, but it's standard to stay the night."

"Not in Canada."

He held off the grin and nodded as if that was truly a good example of how wrong the doctor was. He'd pulled a lot of strings to get her in here with him, since it wasn't standard procedure, but neither was anything they were doing. Being ex-military did have its benefits at times.

"We get to go home, you know, when we want," she added in a huff, and walked over to tuck his blanket over his chest and smoothed it down a little, too. "Are you sure you want to stay here?"

"Hell no, but that door locks, so you can still make good on that promise, right?"

"David Jansen," she exclaimed, just like he knew she would.

He tugged her to sit on the bed and stroked her arm. She'd taken off her jacket and he could see her lacy pink bra straps, but she was so gorgeous he had trouble catching his breath around her long enough to suggest she put the jean jacket back on. She'd slipped on cowboy boots, and the combination with the sundress was stunning.

"You're worried. You shouldn't be. You're too beautiful to worry so much over a small surgery."

She blushed, but smiled at him sweetly, kissing him like he'd also known she would. "Why do my looks have anything to do with me worrying?"

"You'll get wrinkles."

He caught her by surprise if her spluttered laughter and collapse against his chest meant anything. He was pleased he could still get her. She was a quick learner, but he had a few more tricks up his sleeve.

A male intern popped in, then stopped at the door.

"It's okay, come in. She falls all over me all the time."

"David," she whispered, horrified now. "Is it time so soon?"

"You were just pacing and demanding to know why they were taking so long," he reminded her.

She bit her lip and nodded. "I have a bad feeling about this."

He caught her hand when she made to get up and stopped her that easily. All kidding aside, he'd learned to listen to her gut.

"You do?"

Wincing, she stroked his hand then ducked her head. "Maybe I'm just not used to taking care of you and it's worrying me. You take care of me."

His chest got all filled with silly crap over that. He didn't think about it that way, but he tried to make sure she was always happy and comfortable. Still, her instincts had been right before.

"I should have showed you how to use a gun," he muttered.

Her head came up at that and she scanned his face for how serious he was. "I know how to shoot a gun. My uncle taught me."

Something—and it wasn't relief—settled along his spine. His instincts rippled with unease, as if he'd walked into a sniper's scope. No one who survived combat didn't have instincts they knew better than to ignore. His were clearly worried over her, now more than ever.

"Look, I was half-kidding, princess. If anything isn't okay you call Troy, he'll forgive you. If he doesn't answer, you call Will. If he doesn't answer, you call Carson. He's listed in your phone. He's last, though, you got it?" There were men watching her anyway, but if she got scared, he wanted her to call someone and know she'd be safe.

She nodded at each name, made a face at his reference to Troy, then got all worried again at Carson's name. "Why is Carson last? Isn't he your commander?"

"Not any longer. I'm done with all of that. You're my mission now, and making us happy is yours."

"Funny, very funny," she muttered.

"I'm serious. Now, anything doesn't feel right to you, you call Will, okay?" he asked, eyeing the intern once before he settled his focus back on Paris' worried face.

"Okay." She squeezed his hand. Hers were cold and she trembled.

Hell, this is bad. But this is a surgery, simple stuff. It has to be bringing up losing her dad.

"I've had more than a few of these, remember," he told her, winking. "You've seen the scars, so it's fine. A knee is no big deal, and heck, this man is going to make sure I'm fine, aren't you?"

The guy nodded and stepped more fully in the room. "I'm James, Mr. Jansen. I'll be here to assist today. The surgery is quite simple, Ms. Masters. The doctor has him set for a three-hour window, but I've seen these done in an hour. I'll come get you myself as soon as he's out, and you can wait with him until he wakes up."

She nodded at that, but more people piled in the room. James moved over to inject his IV with something, probably to make him sleep. He said something along those lines, but David's focus was on Paris. She was white as a ghost, but smiled brightly at him. He wanted to reassure her again, but he could already feel the drug seeping into his muscles.

"I really am a bad patient," he admitted.

"You are?" she demanded, brushing his forehead with a hand. "I knew you would be. Demanding and cranky, probably, too."

"Yeah, a bit of both."

She rolled her eyes. "I don't believe you," she whispered. "Just wake up so we can talk about where we're going to live. I think Canada is much better for raising children, but I have this feeling you're going to argue."

He laughed, caught off guard. "Now you want to talk about where we're going to raise our kids? Woman, you have the worst timing, I swear."

"No, not the worst," she said, and leaned in to kiss him quickly. Still bent over, she smiled, filling his entire line of sight. "You do, remember? And you never did tell me why it makes it easier when you shave down there."

He choked on a laugh, but it was half-hearted. The drug was taking over, but that was okay, Paris had his hand and her pretty face filled his vision. He'd go down like that, any day, any time.

"Be here when I wake up."

"That's a promise," she whispered, or he thought she did.

* * * *

Paris looked up from her text to Sara to see the intern, James, pulling a hospital blue thing off his head. An older, gray-haired man walked next to him. David's doctor. She'd not met him yet, since he'd been flown in just to work on David.

"Ms. Masters, I'm Doctor Ford. It's nice to meet you."

He smiled and took her hand when she stood.

Her legs were wobbly with relief, but that was okay. As long as David was okay. She never wanted to see him grow limp like that again. Ever. A shadow moved along the hallway behind the doctor. *Troy. Has he been here the entire time?*

"He's done?"

"Yes, he's all taken care of. He should be up and walking on his leg by tonight. I'd like him to take it easy for a few days, small walks, but walking is good. Then he can start to take longer ones. No straining it for now, no crouching, or bending his knee too much at first, but by the end of the month he'll be as good as new."

"Oh my God, really?"

"Absolutely," he assured her. Two men in suits walked up and she caught her breath in surprise. They weren't the same ones from Wyoming, but they were the same breed.

"Ms. Masters, we're here to take Doctor Ford back to New York."

"Ah, yes. My, my, Mr. Jansen does merit a great deal, but so do all our heroes, correct?" Ford murmured to her. "Just try to help him take it slow, and he should be right as rain."

She nodded, too shocked by all the information to have it make sense yet. David was fine. That was all she could latch on to. The doctor walked off, a man on either side of him, leaving her with the intern, James.

"He's really okay?"

"The doctor said he was healthy as a horse. Come on, I'll take you to him," James added, and ushered her down a hallway. She didn't see a nurse's station, but that was okay. She would take care of David by herself. The entire hospital was quiet, and she'd only seen one other person while she waited. And Troy.

"Here you go, now he's going to be groggy, and since he was military, he might be a tad bit aggressive when he wakes up, disorientated at first," he advised, then opened a door. "But I'm sure you know how to handle him."

All she saw was David. He was pale and still on the hospital bed. The IVs and monitors and screens around him blinked and freaked her out badly enough her stomach hurt. His hand was warm, though, and the steady rise and fall of his chest was easy to see.

"You've lost someone?"

She turned partway to nod once. "My dad. I was young, but it made an impression," she whispered.

"He's healthy," he said with a laugh. "Heck, he's like a war machine, so don't worry on that score. I read his chart, he's gonna walk out of here tonight."

"We were told we have to stay the night."

He nodded. "That's true, but that doesn't always happen with men like your…uh."

"Fiancé," she supplied, smiling when she did. She'd gotten to say it first, and she had a feeling David would be very jealous of that.

"Ah, right. Anyway, if you need anything else I'm off to the side of the nurse's station. The nurses will be by in often to check on him. If he's not up and…well, getting around on his own in a few hours, call me."

"Okay, thank you."

"Yeah," James said, tipping his glasses up his nose. "Yeah, okay, well, I'm there if you need me."

She nodded and sat carefully on the bed next to David. All she needed was right here. *David, but awake.*

His leg was only wrapped with a bit of gauze and some padding, so she could clearly see the blood, and whatever the yellowish-orange gunk was that was seeping through. She ignored that and adjusted his covers, then felt his forehead. He was warm, but not too hot.

Suddenly she realized this was the first time, ever, she'd been awake and he wasn't. She knew he sometimes stayed awake when she slept, mostly because she could feel him rubbing her shoulders as she fell asleep, but this was her first time to be here, with him, when he wasn't awake.

For some reason, that made her smile and freak out at the same time.

David was a big personality. Asleep he was…still David, but it was as if he was frozen in time, inactive, or something. She smiled at the thought and got a tissue from the hospital table next to the bed and cleaned his face. He'd shaved just this morning, but already golden whiskers lined his jaw and chin. There was a slight crease above his nose, as if he was frowning even in his sleep. He also had fine lines around his eyes from laughing. *Probably at me so much.* She kissed them.

"You know, you are so interesting, even sleeping you fascinate me. I bet you know that, though," she whispered. She could just imagine him as an old man, like her uncle, fit, funny and full of himself. She laughed and curled up to rest her head on his shoulder, careful not to jostle him. "Maybe everything will be okay."

Chapter Nineteen

The sound of crashing glass and instruments hitting tiles hovered just out of David's reach. He knew something was wrong, but couldn't connect the sounds to meaning. He fought his way out of sleep, but got swept up in a memory from Afghanistan. He knew it was in the past, but the whirl of the blades dimmed the sounds he was trying to make sense of to the point that he thought he felt the sharp impact of metal to body he'd experienced on that mission.

"David!"

Paris. Her voice came in like that remembered bullet, quick, and with a snap jerked him upward, only to get tangled in something or someone. It wasn't Paris. He grabbed a man's arm and tossed him bodily over the bed. The move gained him enough space to clear his head of the last reside of sleep. He spotted Paris and the breath froze in his throat.

A man in a ski mask was dragging her toward the door. She fought to get free, kicking and sending broken glass everywhere. The man holding her had a hand over her mouth, but met David's eyes with a steadiness that promised she had seconds to live. The surety of it was there in his hard gaze. All the man had to do was wrap an arm around her neck and squeeze.

That isn't happening.

Another man edged toward him from where he'd thrown him to the floor. If not for Paris' yell David knew he'd never have been given this chance. *A dream can't be taken away like this.*

Save her.

He tore the IV out of his arm and barely dodged a knife from impacting with his chest. He twisted his body toward his opponent, caught his arms in a wrestler hold and wrapped the IV cord around his neck as quickly as he could. The bastard was a strong motherfucker, but David wasn't letting go. The drug from surgery weighed him down, making him slower, but the panic to reach Paris gave him what he needed.

With a crash they hit the floor. His leg shot agony up his spine, but he wrapped both legs around the guy's waist and tightened before he lost the advantage. If he reached his feet, David would be dead. At the thought, David strained harder to break the man's neck.

"Close your eyes, Paris!"

He didn't check that she did. For some reason he'd been given this chance, and he couldn't lose it. David tightened the IV tubing. It stretched to the point he worried it would snap. He wasn't chancing that. He strained harder. A crunch sounded and David shoved the dead weight off and dove for the knife that had landed on the floor.

The man with Paris dropped her and pulled a gun. Paris half crawled, half ran to his side, head down and clearly terrified, but alive. David shoved her to his left, near the wall and half behind him, but kept his focus on the gun, waiting for the bullet to hit his chest. The knife would do him no good, but for some reason the man hesitated. Then, loud and clear, two shots sounded in close repetition. Neither ripped through David, or more importantly, Paris.

The guy with his gun up and ready, grunted. Slowly, a red spot colored the black leather at his left shoulder, while another appeared at his stomach. In slow motion, he toppled face forward onto the tile.

Sonya appeared behind where he'd stood, Cody at her side, his firearm still up and ready.

Shouts sounded, and a second later, the intern from earlier showed up, breathless, behind them.

David shut them out and reached over to where a terrified Paris was sitting with her knees to her chest, eyes glazed. Her hands trembled so badly he had to ease her grip on her legs slowly. He was shocked to his soles to see his own hand shaking.

"Paris," he breathed, and as gently as he could he gathered her to him. She was shaking, and by her too wide gray eyes and pale face, clearly in shock.

"Get a doctor in here, now! No phone calls, no police, lock this wing down," Sonya ordered.

Cody walked off, but David heard him saying, "We made it, he's clear. Paris is fine as well, repeat, both are good. Two men down."

The words registered, but it was as if the Ranger stood a flight deck away from him instead of out in the hall. Paris filled every inch of his heart and mind.

"Paris, come here, give me my phone." He kept his voice lower for her, but no less direct. At the tone, she blinked and blinked again, seeming to register his face. Her eyes shimmered, but she nodded right when he would have said it again. He needed her to snap out of it. She kept nodding as she turned on her knees and pulled the phone out of her purse. He sat up taller, wincing as his leg shot a dose of agony up his spine.

"Get me off the floor," he growled to the intern.

Cody came back in, and both of them eased him to his feet. He nodded to the crutch, but Paris stopped them from handing it to him.

"No! Don't, please, don't, you just had surgery—"

"Princess, this kind of thing trumps surgery and doctor's orders," he began.

"No," she cried then drew in a ragged breath. "If you walk on it too soon, who will keep me safe?"

That tore his gut. *Who would keep her safe?* He thought she *was* safe. No one had thought she wouldn't be. They were in a hospital that had been locked down for them, with a doctor flown in for this surgery. This was supposed to be safe. Where could he take her that Savage couldn't find her?

"Jansen, she's right, this was a last-minute catch." Cody helped him down on the bed. He sat and immediately Paris was there.

"You need to get to one hundred percent, and walking on that isn't going to help," Sonya added.

David nearly tore into Sonya for the understatement.

Paris pressed into his good side, stroking his arm. He could feel her trembling. He put the gun on the bed and pulled her close.

"It's okay, Paris. You did good, and we'll be out of here real soon." Where, he didn't know, but if they had to move to Siberia, so be it.

She nodded and tightened her hand on his.

"How'd they get by you?" he demanded.

Cody winced and shook his head. "We only saw them from a camera on the stairs. They arrived with an air rescue, posing as family members to the patient on board. They had the right forms, and the patient was in critical condition. Still is, too."

David nodded as if the excuses were good enough. Savage was a mastermind at fitting in and getting by security, but he'd not only found where David lived, but where his surgery was being performed. He could have killed David on the table and taken Paris at any time.

"Did you secure the floor?" He could deal with missions gone wrong and how to clean up, but Paris, and her frightened gray eyes, he couldn't handle right now. He'd say the wrong thing, or do the wrong thing for certain, because all he wanted to do was rage at the world for bringing any of this close enough to touch her.

"The entire wing is secure," Sonya muttered, walking over and examining one of the two men. She kicked the one he'd taken care of over onto his back.

David grimaced and turned Paris' head away to rest on his shoulder.

"No one is here but patients and nurses. Even family members are limited right now," Cody growled. "So that tells us what? This bastard played us."

David nodded. "Get me the head of security," he said. "And I'll need something to drink, coffee, Red Bull would be better. Sonya, hit the hall while I get dressed. Paris, get my clothes and no worrying, I'll stay off it as long as I need to, but I need my pants on."

Sonya had the balls to laugh. "Men are like that. I once hit my mark because he was too busy trying to button his jeans."

"Sweetheart, I could have lived a long time without that information," Cody said, ushering Sonya, the intern and everyone outside his doorway away. The door shut and as soon as it did, David kissed Paris gently. She cried within seconds, silent tears that ripped him up, but he took it because he had caused them. His life was too dangerous. Maybe he wasn't the best thing for her. Not if he endangered her.

"Paris," he murmured, and pulled away to brush her cheeks off. More tears followed. "Maybe we should move you somewhere else until I can deal with—"

"Don't you dare!" She jerked out of his arms.

"That man almost killed you." He pointed to the dead man on the floor. "I can't let that happen. That means I have to go do some clean-up—"

She shoved his shoulder, stopping him that easily from getting off the bed because it startled the hell out of him how hard she'd pushed. *Damn, she is strong.*

Immediately she gasped and covered her mouth. "Oh, God, did I hurt you?"

He didn't answer soon enough for her, because she snapped her hands down on her hips and got right back on her scolding campaign.

"I am not leaving your side. I love you and you promised me forever, remember? That doesn't include leaving me every chance some mission, or someone needing to be *taken care of*, sneaks up on us, remember?"

Hell, this had to be hell. How had Tazz dealt with having Kristen near Duke? Or any of the men he knew that now had women they loved?

There were two dead men on the floor. His leg was bleeding steadily where he'd ripped the stitches in his struggle. Paris had a bruise on her jaw, and her tiny body trembled—with anger, sure, but the fear was there as well.

He'd do what he'd been trained to do — protect. Only now, he'd protect what was more valuable to him than any damn thing he'd ever been given. *Her heart.*

He took her by the hand and coaxed her back in his arms.

"You're right, I did," he said roughly, and kissed her right. She melted against him and wrapped her arms around his neck, tightly, as she had when he'd shown up at Duke's to get her out of that room.

Love was an odd thing. With Paris it had swelled up from the first with a tender feeling that had soon turned to possessiveness, then grief at her loss. Now, it was a steady, bright light that blossomed in his heart and soul. Someday, maybe, he'd tell her that, but right now, he wasn't letting her go or breaking his promises.

Before things got out of hand, he broke the kiss. She stared at him breathlessly, and must have seen what she wanted on his face because her slight frown turned to the smile he was never going to grow tired of.

"I love you, David Jansen. Now, I'll give you your pants."

"Damn," he muttered, and squeezed her ass with both hands. "I was kinda hoping you'd give me —"

"David Jansen!"

He laughed, feeling the terror of the moment slipping away. He had her, she was here, and if he had to move them to Siberia, he'd do it. First, he needed to get dressed, and he needed to call Carson.

"All right, but later, huh?" he teased, kissing her pink lips once more. He also rubbed his thumbs under her eyes to gently erase her tears then kissed her there, too. "No more tears."

"No more," she promised.

He let her go and watched her hunt through his bag for the sweatpants. She straightened and frowned at him. "What is this?"

A laugh burst free, followed by another, until he was holding his stomach.

She lifted a delicate eyebrow and tilted her head. "Was this for me?"

He laughed harder. "It sure the hell wasn't for another woman. You're about all I can handle, princess."

"Good," she huffed, and gave the little butt toy a curious glance. "Although, those things would probably be better for you, you know? Men have more nerves down there—"

"Not a chance," he growled, but grinned when she hid the toy and gave him a calculating look. "Now, help me get my pants on."

By the time they were done, he was sweating from the pain. Paris kept quiet, but he knew she knew. She'd rewrapped his leg with steady hands and hadn't commented on the mess he'd made of it except to say he needed to get the stitches redone. She also hadn't said a word about the two dead men.

"Let's get Sonya and her man back in here."

"She's the agent you told me about?" Paris asked quietly, tucking the collar of his shirt down.

"Yeah, she is." The Adidas sweatpants weren't made to be rolled up and were already sliding down his leg, adding a warmth to the already hot wound, but focused on Paris. "She's good at what she does. So is Cody. Let them back in and we clean this mess up, okay?"

"Okay, but no more talk of leaving me behind again," she stressed.

He nodded, not able to voice that promise. She noticed, he thought, but didn't stress the point.

He called Carson. The man picked up on the first ring.

"We have a situation."

"I know. Petrok called it in. Aren't you still supposed to be under?"

David checked the time. He was up early, but only by an hour. "I'm an hour ahead."

"Chung's drug?"

"I have no idea."

"You know the men?" Carson asked, moving back to what was important.

Paris opened the door and Cody came in first, followed by Sonya. David spotted three more of their men outside, all armed.

"Do we know these guys?" he asked.

Sonya crouched next to the man she'd shot. "He's a hired hit. He usually goes for less dangerous kills, though."

"We need to discuss where to move Paris," Carson said. Paris heard, since he'd put Carson on speaker. She glared at the phone.

"I'd say both need to go under. Deep," Cody said. "She needs protection and Jansen is her best bet."

"I agree. No separating," Sonya said. "He'd be of no use to us without her anyway, you should have caught that the last time he drank himself into oblivion."

Carson grumbled something about lovesick pups. Paris raised her eyebrows at the reference to him drinking too much.

He squeezed her hand. "What are your thoughts on Siberia?" David asked, only half teasing.

Cody laughed. "Paris, I'm Cody Johnson, and this is my soon-to-be wife, Sonya Petrok. We helped this guy find you when he forgot to ask your last name."

"Name? He didn't even get her number or what country she lived in," Sonya added.

"Thank you," Paris said quietly, blushing to her roots.

"Now that the introductions are out of the way, what about man number two?" David asked.

"Oh, that wasn't introductions, Jansen. I'll get her alone for those." Sonya laughed but walked over to the man David had killed and crouched over him. "Well, now, this is another ball game completely."

"What does that mean?" he demanded.

Cody settled his arms over his chest and gave him the calm down stare. David ignored him.

"This man is from a higher pay grade. You earned yourself a presidential kill, Jansen. Just what have you done?"

"Me? What the hell are you talking about?"

"This kind of killer isn't stupid, but he must have thought you were easy game. He works alone, too."

"Who is he?" Carson asked.

"He's just known as Mr. Smith," she muttered. "An assassin. But I'd heard he was dead," she added, nudging the man's face to the side and back.

David exchanged a glance with Cody.

"And?" Cody murmured, walking over to her side.

"And, he's used to take out heads of state, rulers, key players, so —"

"What's he doing here?" David asked when she stopped.

"That's a good question. There were rumors for a while that Smith was from the same unit as Savage, but that's never been confirmed."

"So Savage knows where I live. And my schedule?"

"It seems so," Carson supplied when Sonya merely stared at the man on the floor and Cody shifted uncomfortably. "Will's team has uncovered a spiderweb of intel, all on the Sentinels. Someone inside, I'm hoping Walters, but don't bet the farm on it, was drawing bank on our secrets."

David clenched his jaw at the implications. "And when was I going to be told—?"

"We just found out," Carson said. "You were in surgery, that's why Petrok is there heading the team."

David tightened his grip on Paris. This meant they would have to go deep undercover. New names, new looks, everything wiped clean. "So now we move out? Does Will have a local on Savage?"

Carson muttered, "Will—"

"Doesn't need one," Sonya said, and yanked something off the dead man's neck, then quickly shoved the guy's left shirt sleeve up to reveal a bluish-green tattoo. After that she grew so quiet he wanted to shake her. Almost appearing in a daze, she stood and turned to face them with an amazed expression.

"What is it?" Cody asked, and examined the pendant she'd taken from the man's neck. It was one of those Catholic saints, he thought.

"Petrok." David tightened his hand on Paris'. She was so quiet she worried him but Sonya slowly smiled, as if the game had just changed, and for once, for the better.

"*This* is Savage. New face, new suit, but too arrogant to leave it all behind," she murmured, then gave them all a grin he'd only seen her direct at Cody.

"Looks like we all just drew the get out of jail free card."

Chapter Twenty

Six weeks later

Paris settled closer to David on the park bench, worrying her shirtsleeve, but unable to sit still. Today David had been released from service. For real. He assured her it was a simple formality, but to her it meant a lot. She knew for him it did, too. Now all she wanted was to get him home to celebrate the right way. She'd settle for the hotel room he'd booked for them.

"Stop fidgeting."

"I always fidget when I'm...nervous," she murmured so Will wouldn't hear.

Will shot her a smile, no doubt hearing her anyway. "Nervous, huh?" he teased. "Jansen, you'd better get her home—"

"David. Not Jansen, David," she corrected, threading her fingers in between David's. They'd had a celebration lunch after the papers had been picked up, so she thought she was doing fairly well at behaving.

David hadn't been. He'd been teasing her under the table throughout the entire lunch.

"That's right. No more last names, Will. We're not in the service any longer," David said, giving her a bump with his shoulder.

Will shook his head, but she could tell he agreed.

He was going to New York, to work for some security company she couldn't understand. She thought it sounded as dangerous as what he'd been doing. David had agreed, but shrugged and said whatever floated Will's boat. She'd asked David what he'd do now, and he'd said taking care of her was enough for him. Of course he'd taken care of her right after he'd said it. Not that she'd complained. Right now would be a good time to take care of her all over again, but she still wasn't into public sex.

"So, you doing the security thing with Eagle?" David asked, shifting his leg.

It still ached sometimes, he said, but he could do everything—absolutely everything—he'd done before. She still tingled from the things he'd done after waking her up with his amazing mouth this morning.

"Yep. It's gonna be a new branch in New York. There's a ton of work to be done," he said.

Frowning, she glanced at David and caught him smiling at her. "That means desk work, if I'm guessing right," he said. "Will hates desk work. He'll be up to visit us in no time."

Will grunted. "Canada, huh? Pretty far from New York."

"Part of the time," she said, nudging David so he bent and kissed her.

"Then a bit of traveling when I can get her off the ice," David said, winking at her. She smiled. Their first trip was to Greece. He promised they were going from there to Rome, then on to conquer Great Britain, making love along the way.

She was more than okay with that promise.

"We've been in Vermont for weeks," she clarified. "You didn't stop by."

Will chuckled. "I didn't want to get shot."

"Shot?"

David shifted again, and pulled her to her feet when he stood. She zeroed in on him, and sure enough, he couldn't hold in his grin.

"David Jansen," she whispered, blushing. No doubt he'd threatened Will so he could keep her in bed, or wherever else he found to make love to her. He'd claimed it was good for his leg, and then had introduced her to his third leg. She still got a giggle over that. His third leg got a lot more attention than his other two.

"I might have threatened some bodily harm, but I didn't say anything about shooting you." He hugged her to him when he responded, making it clear he was more than ready to go if the bulge hitting her stomach meant anything.

"Oh, I think your exact words were, 'if you even think of interrupting us in Vermont, think twice unless you want your ass filled with lead.' We don't even use lead anymore for bullets," Will tacked on.

She laughed, and once she started, couldn't stop. She buried her head against David's chest and knew she was blushing even hotter. There wasn't a chance Will didn't realize David had a hard-on. She could hope he didn't, but knew better. Especially the way David had his hands up under her long jacket, squeezing her butt. It was so much like that first night with the two of them, she knew Will wasn't fooled for a minute.

"She gets like this," David offered.

"Yeah, you really crack her up, huh?" Will chuckled.

She pulled away and wiped her eyes. "He is a handful."

Both men laughed at that and she covered her face, realizing exactly why. He was more than a handful, though, so she couldn't take it back.

David pulled her hands free and kissed her cheek, then winked at her, making it even funnier. "You know it."

"Okay, you two, I'll see you tomorrow before we all leave, eh?" Will asked, already walking backward.

"Okay," she managed and smiled.

Will smiled back and saluted.

"Later, man," David called.

"Oh, David, I can't believe you threatened Will like that."

He focused back on her and squeezed her butt, grinding her against his erection. "What? It worked for your uncle, why not me?"

"You were never going to break my heart," she reminded him, tugging his blond hair just like he always did hers.

"No." He tugged hers. "I never will."

"Promise?"

Instead of answering that, he kissed her so well she was breathless, and more worried about getting him home to make love to him than what anyone else in the park would think of them. She snuck a hand down and stroked along his erection. He tightened his arms around her and growled.

"You're going to be ravished in the park if you don't slow down," he warned. "I know you're not into public sex either, princess."

"Oh, is that so? I think you're going to be the one ravished, David Jansen. For a very, very long time, too."

"Damn, now that's a promise I'm going to make you keep."

"Always," she whispered.

About the Author

Billi Jean has been writing since high school when she couldn't wait for Robert Jordon to write his *Wheel of Time* series faster. She writes from home in a little two hundred year old farm house in Western Massachusetts where she shares her space with her active children, an old dog and two lazy cats.

Billi Jean loves to hear from readers. You can find her contact information, website and author biography at http://www.totallybound.com.